CHANGED

By

K.A. Veatch

To Michael
Thank God for your unfailing patience and for sliced peppers.
I wouldn't want anyone else by my side on this journey through life.
Thank you for always believing in me.
I love you, heart and soul, forever.

And

To Dad and Mom
For teaching me to dream
I love you always!

Acknowledgements

I want to extend a heartfelt thank you to the many people who supported me while writing this novel:

Mike, Emma & AJ, I could not have done any of this without you. You are my greatest blessings. Thank you for giving me time to escape, for listening to me grumble, for putting up with my craziness, for your prayers and encouragement, and for being the best cheering section a girl could want. You are, and always will be, my inspiration. I love you all the numbers... and more.

Dad, I wish Mom was still with us so I could thank you both for inspiring in me a fantastical childhood imagination filled with pirates, trips to "Annie's mansion," and notes from Care Bears. Just think, if you hadn't screwed with my mind at an early age, I may not have turned out this way. I can never thank you enough for teaching me to dream—a gift that has not ceased—and giving me the courage to find my wings and fly, both literally and figuratively. I love you!

Pastor Robin and Pastor Scott, thank you for keeping me on the straight and narrow; for encouraging me; for helping to expand my knowledge and faith; for all the prayers; and most of all, for reminding me that God believes in me even more than you do. You guys are the best!

To my entire editing crew: Jan, Tim, Emily, Kara & Michelle. Thank you for polishing my work so it shines. I appreciate your faith in me and all the encouraging words. I couldn't have done it without you!

Thank you to Tom for, well, being Tom, and to Gayle for trying to keep him in line—I know how difficult that must be! You both are very special to our family!

Daron Otis—the man responsible for my cover design as well as all my promotional artwork—thank you for the long hours and putting up with me. Most of all, thank you for taking my vision and making it better than I could have dreamed!

Lisa Bergren, thank you for taking the time to generously counsel a newbie. I truly appreciate your insight and kind words.

Melinda Cote of 11-Eleven Publishing, you are the reason I was able to keep my sanity during the publishing process. Thank you for preparing my manuscript and for your patience while working with me. You took the most daunting task off my hands. I appreciate your guidance and professionalism.

Finally, I must thank all of my friends, family, and supporters who joined me on this journey. Your numbers are too great to list individually, but you all know you who are. The most important thing I've discovered is how blessed I am to be surrounded by wonderful people who inspire me every step of the way! Love you all and God Bless!

CHANGED

Listen, I tell you a mystery:
We will not all sleep, but we will be changed

1Corinthians 15:51 NIV

Would you trade your soul for a cure? For the ability to live forever?

I did and now my second chance is your final warning.

Where will you find hope in forever?

Do not be deceived—this is the beginning of the end.

This is my story.

Chapter One

I sat in the cramped exam room, feeling self-conscious in the flimsy hospital gown draped haphazardly around my body. Soft instrumental versions of popular music played overhead, yet the soothing melodies did nothing to calm my nerves. I hadn't been to a doctor in almost ten years— thankfully I was in good health until recently. The protective paper lining beneath me crinkled as I shifted my weight, nervously waiting on the doctor's return. A few chest x-rays and some blood work, what was taking him so long? Walking pneumonia, I was sure of it. Antibiotics, how hard were those to get?

After skimming both issues of the latest gossip magazine provided in this waiting room purgatory, I focused my attention on the speckled tile ceiling, counting dots on one of the water stained panels. I reached fifty-six when the distinct shuffle of paperwork on the other side of my door announced the doctor's re-entrance into my suspended, hopeful world.

"Miss Smith," Dr. Miller—the doctor who performed my initial exam—spoke as he ushered himself into the tiny cubicle and shut the door behind him. The doctor glanced from the chart to my face with a serious, yet seemingly staged expression on his face. "Maddy, I hate to tell you this..."

He stuttered and drew a deep breath while bowing his head and pinching the upper bridge of his nose with his thin fingers. Even this veiled attempt at sincerity felt awkward. Something wasn't right. I instinctively braced myself against the table. My stomach curled into an anxious ball while my emotions hovered somewhere above hysteria, suspended along with his sentence. I realized I was holding my breath.

"It's cancer...stage IV," he sighed, before looking up. "We need to run a few more tests, but I am certain it is ovarian, spread to your lungs. Visible tumors were present in your x-ray. I've seen this before. It's an insidious disease that often goes undiagnosed until in its final stages. If you were more attuned to your body, you might have noticed the subtle indications of the disease and we might have been able to catch it in time, but unfortunately there is really nothing we can do at this point. There is fluid around your lungs, the reason we first thought pneumonia. Traditional treatment is no longer feasible. Experimental therapies come with only a five percent chance of recovery—hardly worth trying. I predict you have only months to live. Do you have family? A husband? Boyfriend? Anyone who could care for you if you sought treatment?"

I could only shake my head. I had no one. The air in the room was thick—it felt heavier than before.

Sighing, the doctor said, "It is extremely difficult to fight this kind of battle on your own. You would be too sick to care for yourself. I don't mean to sound grim—and everyone must make their own decisions—but hospice may be the best option for you at this point. I realize this is a lot to take in. There are so many things you will have to consider. I need to step out and order a few more tests. I'll leave you alone to think things over and I'll be back in five minutes."

What?

He hastened from the room, leaving me alone to comprehend the gravity of my situation. The atmosphere within the small space grew unbearably hot as Dr. Miller disappeared, closing the door behind him—my purgatory suddenly transformed into hell.

It seemed cruel. Twenty-eight years old, finally getting my life on track. Sure, I had been feeling tired recently. A little stomach trouble. Then my cold wouldn't go away. Twenty-eight. Healthy. Just needing some antibiotics for a bug I couldn't kick.

I felt lightheaded. Glancing at the mirror looming across

from me, I saw the reflection of a girl I once knew, but now her ashen complexion cast a ghost-like glow against the auburn hair framing her face—a premonition of death itself. A clammy chill crept across my body.

What?

The word cancer hung there as if the doctor communicated the message via smoke signal. I turned the words over and over.

Cancer...spread...nothing we can do...hospice.

What?

I tried to feel the cancer taking over my body. I focused my thoughts inward, challenging my mind to sense the parasitic disease overpowering my organs in its fight for control.

Cancer?

As if the word opened Pandora's Box, I immediately felt weak, more sick. My mind fought against my will.

I was just a little ill, a little bit of trouble breathing. Cancer? Only months left? What?

My head spun. My pulse raced. My ears started ringing as a fuzzy, claustrophobic bubble squeezed my peripheral vision into a narrow grey tunnel.

Twenty-eight. Not even married. No family. Nothing.

I tumbled without moving. My heart thudded the lub-dub rhythm of a ticking clock, its frantic pounding overpowered the ringing in my head. No longer able to fight against the pressure crowding my vision into a smaller and smaller pinpoint of light, I let go, and traded my unexpected hell for a peaceful, numbing darkness.

Chapter Two

So, this is it. This is the story of my life. Twenty-eight. No family. One, maybe two good friends. Oh sure, Maddy, you survived for a reason. God has something special planned for your life. You are meant to make a difference.

Through all the heartbreak, abuse, and instability of my youth—bouncing from foster family to foster family—Ms. Shirley, my chubby case worker with the red, bulbous nose would reassure, "Madeline, everything that happens in life is only meant to strengthen you for God's purpose. I promise you are important."

Yeah, right. So, what did I accomplish in these twenty-eight years? I work for a small marketing firm in a go-nowhere job. I never married, never saved anyone from anything. I'm a mess, and now cancer is coming to take me away. What a crock! I am living—well, dying—proof that there is no God or greater plan.

I walked past the residential stretch of East Bay Street toward downtown Charleston, South Carolina, bouncing through the Kübler-Ross stages of grief. Some nurse—whose name I conveniently forgot—explained what I could expect to feel emotionally over the next few months, until...a lump lodged in my throat just thinking the words...the end.

Denial, anger, bargaining, depression and acceptance.

I wanted to tell the nurse—and this Kübler-Ross chick—to go to hell. Who were they to tell me how I would feel when *I* was the one with the terminal illness?

Stage two: anger.

Stupid psychologists and their touchy-feely crap. And what person in her right mind would ever accept the fact she was going to die?

If there was a God—and I had lost faith in Him years ago—He sure wasn't proving His case for existence in my book. How could a good and loving God let disease and suffering continue?

As the sun began its final descent behind buildings that lined the west side of the popular corridor, people emerged from their air-conditioned sanctuaries like desert snakes slithering from beneath rocks. These daytime hermits scattered into the fading light—relishing their deliverance from the smoldering heat of late spring that was now vanquished by a cool ocean breeze.

Historic structures, standing permanent, loomed over

the fragile lives of those traveling beneath their silhouetted skyline. Like me, people with hopes, dreams, and plans walked along these streets—miniscule organisms leaving little to no impact on these stone sentinels or the world they guarded. Now, many of those people were gone... nothing...just like I would be soon. Sure, a tombstone might mark someone's existence—but that too would eventually be forgotten in two or three generations, assuming that person actually had family that cared. I had no family. Anyone who might pretend to care would miss me for a few months, maybe a year, but then... I knew the reality. An unwanted orphan in life, I would be forgotten in death. The lump in my throat now felt like a boulder. The truth squeezed my heart, sending a shudder of emotion through my body.

As a child, I handled the loneliness and uncertainty of foster life with delicate grace, refusing to allow depression to filter into my heart. I knew I could not control my past, but I was determined to control my future. Yet the questions of my past—of who I was—plagued me, even as an adult.

Even at twenty-eight I longed to see my parents' faces reflected in my own. I wanted to know who they were, what they looked like, and most importantly, why they abandoned me. Every morning I studied my features—dark auburn hair, brown eyes, a small cleft in my chin, straight nose, freckles—but all I saw was a sad, lonely girl lost in this world. I had spent hours intensely memorizing every line, every detail, searching for similarities in every person

I met. I hoped I would find my parents, have the chance to ask why they left me. The only thing I wanted in life was an answer—I wanted to be whole. I wanted to know I had a place on this earth and that somehow, somewhere, my existence mattered to someone. I desperately wanted to know who I really was, but somewhere, deep down, I accepted the grim realization that I would always be guessing, always searching. Even as the sun set over Charleston, I sought a familiar trait in the face of every person I passed, but I knew—I knew there would never be any answers.

The sweet smell of climbing jasmine mixed with the ocean air filled each labored inhalation, soothing me with the familiarity of their intoxicating aroma. I felt more aware of everything in the past few days, all my senses intensified.

I will miss this.

Holding back tears, I observed my world through hazy eyes: the beauty of the architecture, the yellow-orange glow cast by flames of old gas-lit street lamps, hanging flower baskets spilling a kaleidoscope of color, turning and undulating in the breeze. My heart sank as I stood, trying to capture every detail of the moment.

I will miss this.

Skip to stage 4: depression.

Crowds of people flowed swiftly around me, spreading out in different directions, pushing time forward at a harried pace. Clean-cut men from the Air Force base, or perhaps the Citadel, rushed to one of the many bars or clubs. Young women—dressed in their Friday night finest —giggled and followed each other eagerly, eyeing every young man along their path. Couples rushed to dinner reservations, impatient to indulge in Low Country cuisine at one of the high-end restaurants nearby. Even couples enjoying a leisurely stroll or relaxed in horse drawn carriages sped forward in blurring cadence.

I suddenly hated all of them.

Back to anger.

How could everyone be so selfish? How could they not notice? Do they really want time to move faster? Couldn't they see? Hey, everyone, over here! Dead woman walking. Come, get a look at this life...it is worthless, nothing. I'd hate to burst your bubble, but there is no God. Isn't He supposed to give you hope for the future? Well, here's one woman with no future and no hope.

Of course I could rage inside my head all I wanted, but none of these people knew me nor could they discern my recent diagnosis. They just carried on with their lives the way I would if I had not been given a death sentence. Still, I wanted to scream at everyone to slow down. Stop moving forward. Couldn't they feel time disappearing? All I wanted was for the clock to freeze—for time to hang in space. I would give anything to stay right here, right now.

Get it together, Maddy. Breathe. You just need to make it through tonight—your last night in the land of the living.

I spent the past three days trying to come to grips with my situation. I decided I couldn't fight the cancer on my own and besides, mine wasn't a life worth saving anyway. I made arrangements to enter the local hospice care center, terminated the lease on my apartment and started packing my entire life into cardboard boxes acquired from the local grocer. Although I feared for the next morning when I would formally begin the process of dying, I felt more trepidation about the next few hours that were to be spent in the company of mere acquaintances whose interest in my situation would be unavoidable, thanks to my boss.

Though I felt more tired and weak than ever before in my life, so far no one was able to perceive the extent of my ailing condition, and I wanted to keep it that way. All I wanted was to keep my illness private—to die alone. I really couldn't handle the pitiful stares, regretful sighs, or otherwise sad remarks of people who were no more than mere acquaintances.

I knew people loved watching a train wreck. They loved to be reminded of the fragility of life, pass along some words of encouragement to the dying like, "Remember, everything happens for a reason," and then return home thanking their personal God that it wasn't them who would soon be six feet under. Of course, I knew most people didn't mean any harm by their reaction to someone else's terminal illness—I just didn't have the strength to deal with the thoughts and fears of others while I struggled to come to grips with my own.

As much as I wanted to keep my illness shrouded in secrecy, necessity determined that two people knew of my situation. First, I had to tell my boss, Steve Sharp, who insisted on a reason for my sudden resignation.

Mr. Sharp was a kind, caring, God-fearing man. The tall, sandy haired owner of Sharp Marketing was only ten years my senior, yet when he hired me, he took me under his wing acting, at times, more like a father figure than a boss. From that point, I continued to be a faithful, hardworking employee, even though the pay and benefits were not exactly what one would hope for.

Mr. Sharp turned white when I delivered the news. Steve, being a compassionate soul, insisted on throwing a going away party in my honor. I tried to decline, but he insisted, arguing that I would regret not having the chance to say good-bye. Knowing this was a battle I would not win, I agreed and the event was set for the next night, Friday. Although I consented to the party, I made Mr. Sharp swear that the real reason behind my departure would be kept secret.

After collecting his emotions, Mr. Sharp went out to announce my departure and subsequent bon voyage party to the rest of the office. A coworker, Bill, rented an upscale apartment downtown, complete with a rooftop deck featuring a view of Charleston Harbor. Always the entertainer, Bill immediately offered his place for the soirée. Bill's parties were infamous around the office, so it was assumed most, if not all, the company would be attending, despite the last minute notice—a fact that caused my stomach to turn little flips as I neared Bill's apartment.

I groaned at the thought of facing my coworkers and their inquisitive probing over the reason behind my departure. Fighting the urge to turn around and run, I gathered my schizophrenic moods and forced myself to continue walking, now only a block away.

Looking ahead, I was relieved to see my best friend, Jenn Franklin, waiting for me on the sidewalk outside Bill's apartment. Jenn was the only other person, besides my boss, aware of my death sentence. She agreed to accompany me to this party—backup support if I needed an excuse to leave.

Jenn is my polar opposite. She is tall, blonde, and blue-eyed. Always opting for anything that glitters, she likens herself to a human disco ball—constantly commanding the center of attention. I am happy to stay in the background, the result I assume, of trying to keep a low profile and survive in the foster care system of my youth. We met at a laundromat my first week in town. She was quick to point out my boring attire and I noticed her skintight, not-so-subtle wardrobe as we folded our respective loads. Somehow, despite our differences, Jenn and I hit it off.

Early on, Jenn decided to make me her project, to help me become the goddess she knew I could be under her expert direction.

"Maddy," she would tell me. "When you sparkle, you shine! If you shine, people notice, we *want* to be noticed." Much to her disappointment, though, I never mastered the art of accessorizing.

Now, six years after we met, her look of disapproval in my appearance—the same look I remember from our first meeting—was evident in the way she sized me up as I walked toward her on the street. Obviously, all these years later, she failed in her intentions.

Tonight, Jenn sported a tight leopard print skirt and a black blouse with a neckline plunging almost to her waist. I hoped she had taped that shirt to her skin, fearing a potential wardrobe malfunction in front of my boss and coworkers. Her accessories all sparkled—the human disco ball.

As I approached my prismatic friend, a sense of unease grew within my belly, gnawing its way into my courage. I hated parties, especially ones where I was the center of unwelcome attention. The desire to turn and run returned —I was pretty sure I could outrun Jenn in her three inch heels—but somehow I kept my forward momentum.

Standing beside my friend, a giggle rose in my chest as I fully appreciated her critical stare. Leaving my apartment I felt dressed up wearing black pants and a red satin v-neck tank, hair neatly tied up in a pony tail, but Jenn's grave expression made me realize I chose poorly, in her eyes at least. Jenn wielded a magic power over my conscious, being able to distract me from anything relevant and instead turn all focus to my fashion sense, or lack thereof. Generally, her frivolity annoyed me; tonight it was a welcome diversion.

Facing her disapproving stance I asked, "Um, are we going to a rave afterward that you haven't told me about?"

Jenn rolled her eyes.

"This *is* a party, you know?" she argued.

"Yes," I agreed. "An *office* party. My office party. Besides, shouldn't you leave *something* to the imagination?" I gave her a dramatic once over, trying to appear as critical as my friend.

Her wavy blonde hair danced around her shoulders as she shook her head. Jenn beamed, "I guess it is too late to fix you up now. I knew we should have met at your place first!"

I frowned, brought back to the reality of my situation. "Not much room, with everything boxed up."

Jenn bit her lip. Jenn was the closest thing I had to family, which unfortunately bestowed upon her the obligation of emergency contact, as well as the one who would be selling my stuff, arranging my funeral, and finalizing any other affairs before and after I was gone. Although she dressed the part of a wanton sex goddess, I knew she had the personality of a naïve, sweet, unassuming youth, and I hated burdening her with the business of death. I worried the responsibility of caring for me would force her to lose that childlike quality I loved so much. She accepted her position without hesitation, yet I could see the toll my terminal illness was taking on her after only three days. Things, I knew, were going to get a lot worse.

"I'm sorry," she stuttered. "I...I...I didn't mean..."

"Don't worry," I said, forcing a smile. "Tonight's a party, remember? Let's go have some fun, okay? Screw cancer!"

Her smile returned.

"Are you sure you're ready to do this?" she asked.

"Absolutely not, so let's go before I change my mind. Just don't stray too far from me, okay? If I start to feel weak or people start prodding too much, I'll need my wingman to get me out."

Her face became serious again.

"I really wish you would tell others about your illness," she said.

"Jenn, you know I don't want anyone fussing over me. I just want to be alone—die in peace and all that good stuff. Besides, you aren't the only one I've burdened. Mr. Sharp knows—thus the reason I am subjecting myself to this party with people who really don't care that I am leaving in the first place."

"I know," she said. "But what about Jake? I really think you should tell him."

I grimaced. My heart dropped in my chest, pulled by the heavy weight of regret.

"No, I can't tell Jake. He doesn't deserve to worry. He'll thank me, someday."

"I disagree." Jenn shook her head, her hair sweeping across her shoulders. "I think you feel *you don't deserve* to worry him."

"Well, I didn't ask what you think," I snapped. I immediately regretted it.

Jenn's face turned white, her bottom lip trembled.

"I'm sorry," I backpedaled. "I can't seem to control my emotions lately. I didn't mean to snap at you. I know you are just trying to help."

Jenn sighed. "It's okay. I totally understand."

"Thank you," I said, feeling despair wash over me. Jen smiled and wiped a single tear from beneath my eye. I took a deep breath and collected my emotions once again, "Okay, Let's go get this over with."

Jenn nodded as I turned on my heel and headed up the stairs.

Chapter Three

I was impressed with the number of people packed into Bill's spacious apartment. The entry opened into a large living space which had been cleared of furniture, while popular music pounded from a stereo system against the far wall. There was a small group of women I didn't recognize dancing awkwardly in the center of the room, looking around at the crowd, motioning for others to join them. Doors to the rooftop patio flanked the stereo. Through the doors I could see strings of white lights hanging from above, creating an artificial starlit glow for people enjoying the fresh air. Couples were gathered outside, chatting casually while taking refuge from the earsplitting music.

"Come on, let's go get something to drink," Jenn shouted at me, her voice barely carrying over the thudding bass line of the current hip hop song.

I followed her through the crowd toward the kitchen amazed how Bill and his wife could throw together such a successful party at the last minute. On second thought, judging by the number of individuals gathered that I didn't recognize, my event was most likely added to an existing venue. Either way, the party impressed me.

Jenn and I barely squeezed past a group crowding the entry when Bill popped up from the side, causing me to jump back startled. His wavy black hair was slicked with sweat from the heat of the crowded space.

"Hey, there's the girl of the hour! I was wondering when you were gonna show!" He too was shouting over the music.

"Yeah, thanks for throwing this little shindig in my honor," I yelled back. "I appreciate it!"

"Nah, it's nothing! Hey, I was going to ask, where are you going anyway?"

I winced. *Here it comes.* I knew people were going to bug me about this.

"Well," I began, unsure how to continue.

"Bill! Bill!" Another partygoer approached, flinging his arm around Bill's shoulder, steadying himself against his friend. The blonde, obviously intoxicated man took a moment to look Jenn up and down, then nodded with his own approval. I felt Jenn recoil beside me. Internally I mused at her naiveté—she forgets that she cannot always choose who notices her when she dresses in such a revealing manner. I immediately feared leaving her to fend for herself after I was gone.

Turning his attention back to Bill, the man slurred, "Dude! I need you on my team. Pool man! You've gotta help me! Come on, I need you man!" He glanced back at Jenn, winked and mouthed, "You are so hot."

"Please excuse me ladies, duty calls!" Bill said. "Make yourself at home. Drinks are in the kitchen. Dancing here in the living room, pool and darts are upstairs. Don't forget to check out the patio, the views are spectacular! Catch you later!"

With that, Bill disappeared through the crowd with the sleazy jerk. As disgusting as that guy seemed, I was eternally grateful he stole Bill away from the conversation, thus saving me from answering any questions.

"Wow. That was....something," Jenn said.

"Hey, you got noticed," I teased.

"Living the dream," Jenn laughed. "Come on, you look like you need a drink even more than I do."

We wandered through the masses, pushing our way toward the kitchen. A center island was the focal point of the large kitchen, offering bottles and tonics of every kind. People swarmed the space like bees in a hive, reaching and grabbing, pouring and toasting, before moving into the next room.

Amidst the chaos, I saw Jake Kavanaugh sitting at the far end of the makeshift bar—his motionless, sad posture in stark contrast to the activity surrounding him. With dark brown hair, light hazel eyes, square jaw line and naturally athletic build, no man that handsome should appear so despondent at a party—especially a party filled with eligible women trying to catch his eye from every corner of the room.

Jake was my co-worker, my friend, and well, the man I dreamed of marrying someday, although our relationship never ventured past the playful banter of friendly colleagues.

As we approached, I could see his tortured expression more clearly. I couldn't figure why he looked so glum. Jake looked up, frowning.

"Hey Jake," I said, trying to remain lighthearted.

"You're leaving?" he sulked. "And you didn't tell me?"

"I'm sorry," I choked, guilt wrapping me in a strangle hold.

"I mean, you know, it's not like you have to get it approved through me or anything," he retracted, concentrating on moving a shot glass between his hands, avoiding further eye contact. "I just thought, you know, we're friends and all. I thought you would at least give me a little notice."

"Jake, it's not like that, really," I said, trying, I think, to convince myself more than him. "This is a last minute thing. I didn't even tell Mr. Sharp until late yesterday. You were at that offsite meeting over the past two days, and I was out of the office today…"

"So what, did those guys from California snatch you up? I knew their head hunter was going after a few of us." His expression grew even more dismal when he mentioned California.

"Jake, I'm not going to California. I will still be..." I paused, trying to think of how to finish. "I will still be in the area."

"Oh," he said, glancing up to look me straight in the eye. "So, we will still see each other?"

"Sure, Jake. Of course," I lied.

My heart skipped with false hope. Jake's hazel eyes sparkled, his face radiating childlike joy against the backdrop of his dark hair. He smiled his sweet, dimpled smile that so often threw my heart into an erratic frenzy.

"Well, I will certainly miss seeing you in the office, but," he focused his gaze determinedly on me. "We will just have to make sure we see each other in more...social settings."

Jenn jabbed me in the rib cage with not-so-subtle grace. I would have jabbed her back if I wasn't spending every ounce of my energy trying to keep my pulse in check.

"By the way," Jake continued. "How are you feeling these days? I know you've been kind of sick lately. How did your doctor's visit go the other day?"

Cancer. The word screamed in my head even though I tried to block it out. *Cancer. Cancer. Cancer.* It taunted me.

"You know, doctors," I shrugged, trying to mask the increased anxiety in my voice, hoping my open answer would suffice.

Cancer. Death. The end. My mind raced. *Ha, you think you have a chance with him? You are dying. You won't have a happy ending.* Emptiness returned as fear grabbed control of my mind.

Shut up. Just shut up! I fought back.

"Maddy?" Jakes voice rose over the battle raging in my head. "Are you okay?"

I glanced at Jenn who stared at me with anxious concern. Obviously I wasn't pulling off healthy and carefree very well.

"Yeah, sorry. I just have a lot on my mind. Guess I got lost in thought for a minute."

"You look awful, like you saw a ghost. What were you thinking about?" Jake asked.

I laughed nervously, "Nothing, really. My mind just wandered, that's all."

I hoped my words sounded more convincing than they felt.

"Well, it looks like you could use a drink. Jenn?"

"I thought you would never ask!" Jenn reached forward, examining the bottles lined across the counter. "Maddy needs something strong tonight—shots maybe?"

"Oh," I shook my head. "I'm not really a shot person."

"Oh, come on," Jake encouraged. "Just one. What's your poison?"

"Jake," I said. "I really don't do shots."

Jenn laughed, "Tequila. She can shoot tequila." Then turning to me she added, "Remember Padre Island?"

Jake eyed me with curiosity. I blushed, turning to offer Jenn the most evil look I could muster.

"I'm not scared of you," she retorted, sticking out her tongue.

"Tequila it is, then," Jake said as he lined up three shot glasses.

"Lime?" I asked.

"Really? You need a lime? Come on, Maddy, that is so…weak," Jake teased.

"Sorry I'm not a tough guy like you," I fired back.

Jake smirked, "Yeah, I guess that would be kind of weird."

I blushed again as he lined up the shots, slices of lime beside them.

"A toast," he said as we all lifted our glasses. "To uncharted futures."

I was thankful my wince went unnoticed.

"Here! Here!" Jenn said, as we tossed back our glasses.

The immediate burn of the tequila faded to warmth after ingesting the lime. Jake smiled a crooked smile, pleased with my performance.

"Ready for another?" he pressed.

"Um, I think I should pace myself."

Jenn interjected, "Come on, Maddy, a second one won't *kill* you."

I glared at her, feeling the twinge of ire build as she so casually brought up my death. My irritation went unnoticed, though, as she turned to wink at Jake.

"Fine," I conceded, knowing I'd lost control over the situation—if I had any in the first place.

Jenn fancied herself a match maker, and even though I faced only months to live at best, I could see a spark of excitement in her eyes as she planned to bring me and Jake together under her supreme guidance. She was the last true romantic. In her mind nothing, not even death, could keep soul mates apart. Jenn could be a prison warden, walking a death row inmate to the electric chair, yet still try to convince him that she knew this fantastic woman he should meet, even in his final moments.

Jake poured another round which I drank with more vigor than the last. The alcohol provided an anesthetizing effect on my body and mind. I welcomed the calm.

"Jake!" Bill returned. Thankfully his drunken friend didn't accompany him.

"Hey Bill, great party," Jake said.

"Dude, you have to come meet these girls. They work with my wife and hey, you never know…"

Jake glanced at me, gauging my reaction which I tried to keep neutral despite the jealous monster sinking its teeth into my heart.

"That sounds great," Jake said. "But I'm kind of hanging here with Maddy and her friend. I don't want to be rude to the guest of honor."

"Aw, come on…Maddy won't mind, will you Maddy?" Bill's face pleaded for my permission.

Three sets of eyes fixed on me, waiting for my decision.

"Of course not," I offered, although my heart begged to keep Jake next to me. "Besides, I have to go mingle. I should probably thank Mr. Sharp for helping arrange this get-together in my honor."

"Excellent!" Bill said with genuine enthusiasm as he pulled Jake off his chair and led him toward the living room. He brought Jake straight to spot where the graceless, gyrating women danced.

Jake fired one pleading glance over his shoulder as he was dragged off to his new fate. I just smiled and looked away. Although jealousy commanded all emotion at the moment, I was happy to know that Jake would be okay— that he would eventually find someone, especially if Bill or Jenn got a hold of him.

"That was cold, sending him off to the wolves like that," Jenn laughed as she tossed back one more shot. "I mean, look at those women! So desperate for attention they are dancing in the middle of the room when no one else in the entire place is dancing. It's like 'Hey, look at me.'"

"Oh, *that's* the pot calling the kettle..."

"Yeah...yeah...yeah...blah...blah...blah," was Jenn's intelligent comeback. I couldn't help but laugh.

"Maybe they just like to dance," I offered. Jenn rolled her eyes.

I glanced toward the living room. The sight of Jake trying to dance along with the five women made me giggle. They flocked around him like vultures swarming their dinner. I'd never seen him more uncomfortable. He looked toward me and noticed me, noticing him.

"Come on Maddy!" he shouted over an annoying boy band song. "Get out here and dance with the rest of us!" The look on his face begged for help.

I couldn't hide my grin as I shook my head and pointed toward where Mr. Sharp and his wife were standing near the exit to the rooftop terrace. Jake smiled back, but it was an awkward smile. Impatient, one of the women forcefully danced herself into our line of sight, shoving one of her companions out of the way as she vied for Jake's full attention. I was worried that Jake—being gorgeous and the only man dancing—would soon start a riot. These women seemed more competitive than World Cup Soccer fans.

"Hey, would you mind if I found the rest room?" Jenn added. "I know you don't want to be left alone."

"Don't worry," I said. "I think I'm getting along okay. I am just going to head over and talk with Mr. Sharp and his wife. Meet you on the patio?"

"I'll be quick, I promise"

"Take your time. I'm fine, really. See you in a bit."

I watched Jenn tactfully avoid another encounter with the sleazy jerk on her way to the restroom, and feeling like she was safe and not in need of immediate rescue herself, I left the kitchen and proceeded to where Mr. Sharp and his wife were standing.

I made one careful glance out of the corner of my eye toward Jake as I passed through the kitchen. He continued struggling to free himself from the gaggle of overly eligible women fighting for his attention. I couldn't help but feel sorry for those women, though, as they were at a disadvantage. Jake's striking good looks and witty charm gave him the ability to choose any woman in the room. I knew his standards were immeasurably high. In the three years we'd known each other, not one woman captured his heart—at least not that he'd talked about with me.

I edged toward Mr. Sharp and his wife, Vanessa.

Vanessa was a strong Christian woman whose well manicured appearance was far too classy for this kind of party. I wondered what she thought observing the scene playing out around her.

Upon seeing my approach, Mr. Sharp smiled the smile of a concerned father. He motioned in my direction and Vanessa, turning to meet my gaze, also looked at me with a warm, albeit sympathetic expression. I glanced around trying to determine if anyone else noticed their heartbroken demeanor as I approached.

Crap, I thought. *This is exactly what I wanted to avoid. Sympathy. Sorrow. Please don't draw attention to the situation. Please?*

Chapter Four

"Good evening Mr. Sharp, Mrs. Sharp," I said politely. "Thanks again for organizing this with Bill. It really is nice of you to throw me a going-away party."

"Of course. How could I not? You are one of the best employees I've ever had the pleasure of working with. You've been with this company almost as long as it's been in existence. I think of you..." Mr. Sharp stuttered. "You are like my own daughter."

His eyes moistened, but thankfully he quickly regrouped.

"How are you feeling tonight, dear?" Vanessa asked, lines creasing the corners of her soft brown eyes that seemed to match the exact color of her classically bobbed hair.

A worried look crossed Mr. Sharp's face. "I hope you don't mind. I had to tell Vanessa. I can't handle these things on my own, you know?"

"It's okay," I lied. "I am feeling alright, thank you for asking."

"Well, if you need anything, sweetie, we are just around the corner," Mrs. Sharp said. Then in a hushed voice that almost disappeared into the background noise she added, "Steve tells me you are checking into hospice tomorrow. Oh sweetheart, it just...well...it just breaks my heart."

I forced a smile. "It's okay, Mrs. Sharp. I am trying to stay positive about this."

I hated being the one to comfort others about my death. It didn't seem fair, but what else could I do? This was the exact reason I wanted to be alone.

"Please, just call me Vanessa," she said. "And please, if you need anything, don't hesitate to ask. Steve and I are praying for a miracle."

"Thank you, I appreciate that."

I didn't have the heart to tell her that I knew there were no such things as miracles. I knew there was no God. If He existed, He certainly gave up on me a long time ago.

Suddenly, the music cut off. I realized Mr. Sharp gave some unseen signal. He cleared his throat, drawing attention to our corner of the room.

Oh no.

"May I have everyone's attention for just a second,

please?"

As the crowded quieted, Mr. Sharp began, "Madeline…Maddy…has been an invaluable part of our team for almost seven years now. I still remember the I first time this beautiful young girl came in, fresh out of college, looking for a job. All I could think was that this cute girl is going to be trouble—I wouldn't be able to get the men to do any real work!"

The crowd laughed. I felt myself turning red.

"Maddy, I know there are circumstances beyond my control taking you away from Sharp Marketing, but please know, if you ever want to return in the future, you will always have a place here with us."

I knew Mr. and Mrs. Sharp held out hope for a miracle. I appreciated the gesture, but I also knew that day would never come.

I once again looked toward Jake. He watched me, smiling.

"So, let's all raise our glasses in a toast to Maddy! The future is never set in stone. I pray that the path God is leading you on will be filled with miracles and wonder. To Maddy!"

The entire room repeated, "To Maddy!"

There was a half second of silence that was almost instantaneously filled with pounding music and noisy conversation.

"Thank you," I said to Mr. and Mrs. Sharp.

"Of course," Mr. Sharp embraced me, then keeping his hands firmly placed upon my shoulders, he looked me in the eye. "I meant every word I said. Don't give up hope. We are praying for you to be healed."

"Thank you again," was the only thing I could say. "Please excuse me. I think I need some fresh air."

Still flushed, the heat of the room seemed unbearable. I edged my way to the doors that lead to the patio outside.

Wiggling my way through a crowd that hovered near the door, I looked toward Jake again, unable to hide my grin as he returned to playing defense against the heavily stacked, estrogen filled, dangerously competitive team that was once again closing in around him. His eyes met mine, causing a little jump in my heart. I giggled as I proceeded out the door.

The fresh air felt wonderful. I inhaled a long, deep breath trying to clear my head. Unfortunately, my lungs weighed heavy in my chest, anchors pulling my ailing body down. My mind returned to thoughts of impending death.

The scent of jasmine still wafted through the night. White lights dangling from above were also wrapped around topiaries that lined the terrace wall. Couples occupied the two small café tables perched in the far corners, each couple entranced with their own partner's conversation.

Despite my depression, I couldn't help but feel the atmosphere take on a romantic, magical glow. I envisioned Cinderella and Prince Charming from the dreams of my youth dancing on a patio similar to this, spinning and twirling, falling in love. My heart ached with the realization that I wanted that picture for myself, even now.

I stepped toward the terrace wall, looking out across the night. The sun set earlier, but the horizon still clung to its light blue hue as darkness encroached from above. I sighed.

Disappointed pleas coming from inside drew my attention back toward the crowded apartment. I turned to see Jake dancing his way through the patio door, one of the girls in his arms. I grimaced as I watched them float across the floor together, just as I pictured Cinderella and Prince Charming moments earlier. My heart broke watching them.

As if reading my mind, I watched Jake spin the girl out of his grasp, and in one swift move, he turned and swooped me up in his arms. I craned my neck to watch the poor thing twirl about three feet before stopping short, realizing she had been replaced. If looks could kill, I was certain I would be a smoldering pile of ash at that very moment.

"Um, I'm pretty sure your partner wants to kill me," I said, trying to avoid her scowl.

Jake grinned, once again hypnotizing me with his dimpled smile.

"She's just jealous that I might be interested in someone other than her. I think she will get over it," he said. "I'm sure she will find another guy around here."

"Really? Who?" I asked, forgetting the last part, instead focusing on who might have gained his interest. I wanted Jake to be happy, yet deep down I couldn't bear the thought of him with someone else.

"Who is she going to find to drool over her?" he shot back.

"No," I said, warm heat filling my cheeks. "I meant who do you find interesting... other than her?"

I suddenly felt open, vulnerable, realizing my worried prying alluded to the actual motive behind my question. Ignoring the question, Jake just held me closer, swaying to the music. I became concerned when he looked at me with a gloomy expression.

"You know, that was pretty cruel of you, not coming over to rescue me. Those women were animals!"

Grateful for the change of subject I jeered, "You look like you can hold you own. I wasn't too worried."

"Didn't it concern you at *all* that those women only wanted me for my body? I feel so dirty...so used," he teased.

"Ah, yes. I forget how often women treat men like pieces of meat. I see your point now. Next time, I will step in before it gets out of hand."

"That's more like it," he said as he dipped me backward, beaming with childish delight.

After he returned me to my feet, I stepped back, starting to move away as the end of the song flowed into a slower melody. Jake's hand reached out and pulled me back. His arm wrapped around my lower back, tighter than before, his other hand clasped mine as he pulled me near.

"Just one more," he whispered. "I'm not ready to leave. Please don't send me back to those piranhas."

I felt the flush deepen across my cheeks. I hid my face in his shoulder, hoping he wouldn't feel my heart rocketing through my chest. He took that as a sign to draw me even closer.

Head spinning, heart racing, stomach feeling like it was in free fall—I couldn't be entirely certain I hadn't died and was now having an out of body experience.

I felt the heat from his arm as it tightened around my waist. I noticed his chest, muscle hardened, yet soft and warm, burning against me. Without realizing how it was happening, our foreheads met. Next, our noses came together, bringing our lips dangerously close to each other. I could feel the sweet humidity of his breath against my mouth.

Wake up! Wake up Maddy! You can't do this! You have to stop! It will break his heart.

But I don't want to stop! I've been waiting for this moment for three years! I love him. I can't stop. This is what I want.

Maddy, you have to stop. You are being selfish.

I was so close to him. Everything I had always wanted suddenly seemed within reach. I pulled my head back, looking into his eyes. I refused to believe that he could possibly be feeling the same way. There was no way he could actually love me too. He returned my gaze, assessing my reaction. I tried to make myself leave. Before I had time to think, my head rested against his again. I was breathing his breath, my mind whirling in a dizzy blur. I took back what I thought earlier, about wanting time to freeze there on East Bay Street. If time was going to halt, this was the moment I wanted to suspend for eternity.

Stop it, Maddy! Just stop!

You're not the boss of me! Why can't you let me be happy?

My conscious screamed louder.

Happy? What about Jake's happiness? Do you think he will be happy watching you die? He will feel trapped into the responsibility of caring for you. Isn't it bad enough Jenn has to plan your funeral? You can't do this to him.

A sudden vision of my deathbed flashed across my mind—Jake sitting there beside me, wishing he was somewhere else. Wishing he hadn't made his move the night before I went into hospice to die. He would resent me. He wouldn't remember me as pretty, or admirable. Instead, he would see me as a skeletal shadow of how I look tonight. He will be haunted by my final days. He would carry a feeling of guilt about leading on a poor, dying woman, then realizing how trapped he was, wishing he could leave the situation. I couldn't do that to him.

This time, I looked up and pulled myself further, although not completely from his grasp. Again, he looked at me expectantly.

"I can't do this," I whispered. "I'm sorry, I have to go."

He froze, his stare searching my eyes for a reason I couldn't vocalize.

"Don't," he said. "Just don't go yet. We can move slower. I mean, it's been three years, what's a little longer?"

A laughing whimper escaped my lips. How could I answer him? Time? Slower? Time was the one thing I didn't have. I wished with all my heart it was that easy.

"I have to go," I whispered again, this time pulling free from his reach, exiting toward the open doors leading into the apartment.

I noticed Jenn, standing near the doorway watching, a perplexed look on her face. Without a word, I passed her by, trying to leave gracefully but realizing sobs rocked my body so that anyone watching would notice my anguish. I pushed through the mob, racing to escape. But it wasn't the party I was escaping. It wasn't even Jake. I wanted to escape life...it was escaping me after all.

Tears blinded my vision as I reached the front door. I didn't know if Jake or Jenn pursued me. I didn't know if anyone noticed my departure. I didn't care if I had caused a scene inside.

I hoped the night air would clear my mind, or at least calm my nerves, but it did neither. The air felt heavy and thick. I braced myself against a lamp post, unable to control my sobs. I gasped for oxygen, realizing my fluid trapped lungs were not helping the situation.

"Do you think this is funny?" I looked up and yelled to a God I didn't believe in. "Do you enjoy watching me suffer? Has this been your grand plan the whole time? What? Huh? You don't want to answer me? Answer me!"

Something inside me snapped. I was hysterical, past the point of caring who saw my raging lunacy.

"So, twenty-eight years of struggle," I screamed at the sky. "Twenty-eight years of dreams! You bring me this close—this close! Now, you are going to kill me? Do you enjoy giving people cancer and watching them lose everything? Their hopes? Their dreams? What the hell kind of God are you? Loving? Ha! You are just a big bully! Screw you!"

"Maddy?" Jake's voice came from behind. I turned to see Jenn, and half the other party attendees standing with him, watching my tirade, mouths agape. Mr. Sharp stood among the crowd, looking distraught, but at this point I had lost the ability to care if I had offended him or his faith in God.

I regained a small amount of composure and straightened my stance.

"I have to go," I stated matter-of-factly, wet streaks running down my cheeks.

"Maddy, wait..." Jake started.

"Jake, just leave me alone. Please," I drew a jagged breath. "Just leave me alone."

I turned and walked down the once beautiful street. Now, all I saw was a dark, hopeless road to nowhere. I couldn't tell if Jenn followed after me. I didn't turn around. I walked the five long blocks back to my apartment and went straight inside, slamming the door behind me.

I examined my apartment; the place I called home for the last seven years. I looked around at my belongings, boxed and ready to be sold or donated. The numbing effect of the tequila had worn off, emotions overwhelming me to a point that I couldn't tell what I was feeling. I seemed to experience every emotion at once. I crumpled on the floor, lost in the mire of every dark, unhappy place my mind unearthed. Sometime during the night, my tears stopped flowing. Sometime during the night I allowed myself to slip into a bleak, restless sleep.

Chapter Five

I woke in the morning, but couldn't find any sense of relief usually brought by the light of day. Despair from the previous night clung to my heart and grew with each labored inhalation. My breathing this morning was far worse than in the weeks leading up to my diagnosis.

I reviewed my appearance in the mirror—face puffy and red from crying, eyes a sunken, dull shade of brown, hair disheveled atop my head. It wasn't worth trying to hide the toll the last night had taken on my appearance. Who did I need to make myself beautiful for anyway? I was going to the place I would die today. My journey this morning would lead me to the gates of a hospice center in Mount Pleasant, across the Cooper River. I was certain that no one I'd meet would care how I looked, so unkempt and indifferent I would leave the beauty of this world and begin my transition into the next.

I paused for a moment to wonder what, if anything, lay beyond this reality. I shivered thinking about a possible nothingness where I, my friends, everything ceased to exist. It hardly seemed fair that I would be forced to live this life of struggle and heartbreak and never receive answers or learn the meaning of life. But I guess, in the end if I ceased to exist, I wouldn't know the difference anyway.

I threw on a pair of sweats and looked one last time around my home, trying to determine what, if anything, I had left to pack in my small suitcase. I gazed upon furniture, paintings, electronic equipment. Everything that used to define success—my success—now seemed irrelevant, left behind to give meaning to another person's existence. Suddenly, my life felt empty. What did I truly offer this world that said Madeline Smith was here?

I startled at the knock on my door, precisely at seven in the morning. I knew it was Jenn arriving to drive me across town, yet my heart pounded an unsteady rhythm as a vision of the Grim Reaper flashed within my mind. Although I outgrew the anxiety of monsters, ghosts, and demons lurking in the shadows long ago—of course I knew humans with the same capacity for evil still roamed the earth—I couldn't force my feet to move.

Another impatient thud hit with a bit more force than before. My pulse raced as I pictured a scythed skeleton grinning, waiting for the door to open.

Again, a louder, more persistent knock.

I forced myself to move toward the door just as a fourth knock—actually several loud bangs—rapped against the solid frame. Mentally fighting against this irrational sense of terror, I drew a deep breath and turned the knob.

Jenn stood there, fear creasing the corners of her eyes, her mouth turned downward. It was a look that added years to her beautiful face.

"Geez, Maddy," she said. "You scared me. I thought..." Her voice trailed off as she looked down, kicking at a dried leaf on my stoop.

I hated that my stupid reaction caused Jenn grief, but I couldn't bring myself to apologize. Unable to look her in the eye, I picked up my small overnight bag and stepped into the foyer. Locking the door behind me, I silently turned and handed her my keys. I kept my eyes focused on my feet as I let them carry me down the hall and into the stairwell that lead to the street. Jenn followed noiselessly. If she wanted to say anything—to ask if I was okay or to confront me about my behavior from the night before—she didn't. She allowed the moment to flow as naturally and cautiously hushed as a funeral procession.

I reached Jenn's green Honda Civic, threw my bag into the trunk and let myself into the passenger side. The driver's door opened and she sat down beside me. Our silence continued as she started the engine and pulled into traffic. I sat speechless, staring out my window. I watched as we passed streets beginning to swell with people who were opening stores, getting their morning coffee, jogging—all starting their day oblivious to my pain, oblivious to anything outside their own personal, happy, little bubbles. I retreated further into despondency.

My heart weighed heavy, squeezed by some unseen force that shaped it into an unrecognizable blob that could no longer feel anything but pain. My stomach curled into a tight ball. I felt pressure and exhaustion draining my life from within. I wanted to close my eyes and make everything disappear having no desire to see anything, hear anything, feel anything. I withdrew into the shell of my body, trying to ignore the physical and emotional pain of my disease as it wrapped around me, strangling all it touched with its twisted, miserable fingers. In the past, depression came with the hope of better days. Today, my days were limited, offering no hope for a future. I no longer cared for this life or any of its inhabitants. Everything and everyone now only existed as shadows around me.

Crossing the Ravenel Bridge, I gazed out across the harbor. The bridge, the city that lay behind me, ships, palm trees, dolphins making their appearance above the wake, Fort Sumter, Patriots Point—I watched it all pass by the thin glass knowing I would never again look upon the beauty of a world I so often ignored while I rushed around, concentrating on the trivial events of daily life.

My throat tightened and closed, my head ached as I forced my tears inside. I knew I should try to make my last moments alone with Jenn meaningful—filled with polite conversation and remembrances of happy times passed— but I no longer had the ability for small talk. It seemed insignificant, so instead, we traveled in silence.

The trip took us across Charleston Harbor through the south part of Mt. Pleasant, merging onto the highway heading west toward Daniel Island. Minutes later we exited the highway and pulled onto a tree lined street. A sign for the hospice center greeted us as we turned into the forested drive. I was surprised at the center's peaceful and relaxed appearance. Having made my arrangements through my doctor's office, I expected a dark, gloomy structure complete with cobwebs, caskets and a hearse waiting at the door. I couldn't say why I thought the way I did, but it seemed fitting in my mind—my vision of a death house. I was taken aback by the facility's cottage-like feel. From the exterior, it looked like a quaint southern inn nestled in the woods.

As we traveled along the private road, I noticed the building was painted a cheery yellow. A wall of windows lined a large courtyard—two courtyards, actually, that sat nestled between three wings of the E-shaped building. Several intimate seating areas, a screened-in porch and elegant trees provided a serene locale for the ill and their family members to gather outdoors. A large oak tree with winding branches gracefully arcing in every direction stood as a centerpiece just beyond the beautiful courtyards.

As Jenn pulled up to the entrance, a woman stood on the steps, smiling at our approach, obviously expecting our arrival. I figured Jenn called before we left to inform the staff we were on our way. The woman was dressed in casual attire, but she bore an official looking nametag and stethoscope that set her apart from a patient or visitor. She looked to be in her mid-thirties, with shoulder length dark brown hair and a pleasant smile. I felt a rush of relief at the sight of this woman realizing I had been expecting my caretakers to be dark shrouded individuals with black circles beneath their eyes and pale, lifeless expressions—the kind of people I imagined would be drawn to death. If she did moonlight as a vampire or Hitchcock character, she did nothing to reveal that side of her nature here.

Jenn parked in the entrance's circular drive, cutting the engine and hopping out first as I cautiously opened my door. I was suddenly apprehensive about leaving the safety of the car. Jenn was already rounding my side of the car, so instead of making her worry and wait like I did at the apartment, I quickly propelled myself out of my seat, stumbling as I rushed. Jenn reached me in time to catch my arm, looking disappointed that I did not wait for her.

"I wish you would let me help, at least a little," she mumbled.

I kept silent. I couldn't think of anything to say that would make her feel better. And why should I? I was too far lost in my own anguish to help her with deal with her feelings of grief.

The pleasant woman on the steps smiled at me, although I could not force one in return.

"Welcome. You must be Maddy," she said. "I'm Nancy Simon, the daytime charge nurse. I know this is difficult, but I assure you our staff is here to make things as comfortable as possible. I will be assisting you with the admittance process, answering any of your questions and helping to get you settled in your room. Please, follow me inside to my office where we will perform an initial exam and go over your care plan. Will you need a wheel chair or any assistance?"

I tried to swallow, but my throat felt dry, tight. "No, thank you," I managed.

"Is it okay if I come too?" Jenn asked.

I shrugged.

Nancy smiled her warm smile, "Friends and family are always welcome. We do everything possible to respect our patients' wishes. Don't worry about moving your car; I will let the staff know you are with me inside."

Jenn retrieved my bag from the trunk then proceeded up the stairs behind Nancy. I reconsidered my need for a wheel chair. Paralyzed, I couldn't compel my feet to move. My reality melted into a surreal mirage. This was it. Once I entered, I was never leaving—alive anyway. Like a woman walking to the gallows, fear, despair, and deep sadness choked my soul.

Noticing that I wasn't following, Jenn stopped at the top of the steps then returned to my side.

"It will be okay," she said taking my hand. "I'll be here with you."

Emotions swirled like a tornado inside my soul. Things weren't going to be okay. I didn't want her to stay with me - and watch me fall apart, watch me die. Yet now, taking Jenn's hand as she helped me navigate the short set of stairs, I was grateful for her friendship.

Hand in hand, Jenn and I stepped through the door of the place where I would die.

Chapter Six

I expected the smell of disinfectant combined with a stale, lingering stench of illness and death that one often encounters within hospital walls. The aroma of lavender confused my prejudiced mind. We passed a greeting station just beyond the building's main entrance where two seemingly pleasant and upbeat female volunteers sat ready to help visitors. They smiled gracious, caring smiles in our direction as we passed. I chuckled internally at the juxtaposition of what should be a gloomy place, smelling of lavender and containing within its walls only smiling, happy faces. Perhaps I had been transported to a Stepford Wives cult, and soon I too would be immortalized in cheerful, robotic fashion.

Entertaining my otherwise distraught mind with these

nonsensical thoughts, we passed the animated robots and walked into a common area that offered several couches and chairs grouped together in sections throughout the space. A row of floor-to-ceiling windows graced the outside wall, allowing one to feel as if within the courtyard space beyond. The room currently sat empty, save one guest. I looked at the lovely woman, probably in her forties, as she leaned close to the glass fortification conversing in a hushed manner on her cell phone. Her eyes, swollen and red, were shadowed with dark circles— evidence of very little sleep. She glanced toward me, sensing my stare, but no programmed smile crossed her face. Her expression, which appeared lovely from a distance, displayed the heartbreaking pain of someone in the throes of losing a loved one.

As we passed, the grieving woman turned her gaze to look back beyond the glass fortification, returning to her private conversation. I pictured Jenn, months or maybe even weeks from now, wearing the same expression—lines and wrinkles contorting her youthful, vibrant face. It wasn't fair to put my friend through such pain. I wanted her to go on living—be happy. It would be best for her to forget about me and move on and I would tell her that. I decided that after today she shouldn't visit again. I would not put her through any more heartache and worry. I would die alone, for her sake.

Sure, maybe my decision would upset Jenn. She would fight me at first, demanding to stay by my side, but I would hold Nancy to her statement that nurses will respect the wishes of the dying, and if I wanted to die alone, there would be nothing Jenn could do. I was certain she would thank me later.

I seemed to be leaving a path of destruction in my wake. My thoughts drifted to Jake—the way he took me in his arms, the tightness of his grasp, the almost kiss and how I could still feel his breath as his mouth lingered dangerously close to mine. I hated the way I left things the night before—no answers, just the knowledge that I was dying.

I swore Jenn to secrecy about my illness as well as the place where I chose to live out my final days. Now, more than ever, I hoped she kept her promise. Maybe hurt Jake too, but that hurt would be short lived. I was convinced a clean break was the best option—it was the only option, really. This way he wouldn't be burdened. He wouldn't feel as though he had some stupid chivalrous responsibility to a dying girl. He would move on, meet someone and live a long, happy life with her. I still struggled to believe he might love me the way I loved him. As the memory of last night's events grew fuzzy in the light of morning, I became convinced that the tequila must have played tricks on my mind.

Lost in thought, I hadn't realized we entered Nancy's office until she offered me a seat. Like the rest of the building, this room was pleasant enough. Instead of a desk, a round table sat in the middle of the office surrounded by five chairs. Bookshelves housing several editions of medical dictionaries and reference books, as well as a small selection of romantic fiction lined the walls. I assumed romantic escapism helped Nancy get through her day—a distraction from the depressing atmosphere surrounding constant death. A large window produced enough light that indoor illumination was not necessary, but Nancy switched on the florescent tube lighting nonetheless, finally giving the room that hospital-like glow I had been expecting.

"Jenn, you are welcome to take a seat also," Nancy said as she motioned to another chair beside me at the circular table.

Nancy proceeded to a phone that hung on a wall next to the door. "Yes, please tell Dr. Moody we are ready for him. Thank you."

Returning to the table, Nancy said, "The doctor will do an initial exam to determine what level of care you need to start. We, of course, will modify things as the end draws near."

I was startled by the frankness in which she spoke of my death, but I also appreciated that she didn't feel the need to pussyfoot around the subject.

"I know this sounds crazy," I said, feeling a bit self-conscious. "But, what is it like? I mean, the end...well, if you know, that is." The thought had been lingering in the background since I received the news of my terminal illness. I don't know why I asked when I did, but Nancy didn't see surprised by the question.

Jenn shifted in her chair. I wondered if she regretted her decision to join me.

Nancy sat down next to me, leaning forward to

grasp my hands between hers.

"I know death is frightening, but from what I have seen working in hospice for ten years, is that although there may be some differences in the way people pass, there are also many things that they have in common, and for the majority, passing is a calm, peaceful experience."

I was trying to imagine a peaceful transition, but honestly the thought of dying terrified me.

Jenn spoke. "What will happen to Maddy?"

Nancy kept her focus on my face while addressing the question.

"Well, although I can't predict with certainty what you will experience, I can tell you what generally happens to terminally ill patients. First, they grow weak and tired. They want to sleep a lot and their appetite decreases. If a patient experiences pain, we medicate him or her to keep the pain under control. As the end draws near, the patient won't eat, won't drink. The body just begins to shut down. We, of course, do everything possible to help relieve any pain until the very end. Most patients slip into a coma sometime in the weeks or days leading up to their death and most pass peacefully in their sleep. Maddy, rest assured that our staff of nurses, doctors, and chaplains is here to assist you and your loved ones with whatever needs may arise."

"Oh, I don't need a chaplain. I don't believe in God," I said, but suddenly wanted to take my statement back. Lack of faith was probably frowned upon in a place like this.

Nancy just smiled, "Don't worry, we don't push religion

here. Staff members respect the faith and beliefs of every patient. I just wanted to let you know there are services available, should the need arise."

I blushed, still worried that my atheistic beliefs somehow blacklisted me in the land of the living dead. Fortunately, my internal debate was distracted by a rap on the door and the entrance of the doctor.

Dr. Moody was a stocky, partially balding man with a round, pleasing face that possessed the same comforting expression I suspected was intentionally worn by everyone working in this facility.

"Hello, Madeline, my name is Jim Moody. I know you have been through a lot in the past few days, so I will try and keep this short and sweet. I just need to perform a quick exam and a blood draw. After that, you will be able to get settled in your private room. Before I begin, do you have any questions for me?"

I shrugged.

Introducing himself to Jenn, he said, "Hello, I'm Jim."

"Jenn," she said in return, shaking his hand. "I'm a friend of Maddy's."

"Nice to meet you, Jenn," the doctor continued. "Maddy is very fortunate to have a friend who can stay by her side through this."

I could tell his regard for Jenn was sincere and Jenn seemed pleased that someone noticed her efforts. I was glad that someone could provide reassurance that her sacrifices for a friend were appreciated.

"Okay, let's have a quick listen," Dr. Moody donned

his stethoscope and began the examination. After a few minutes, he stepped back and gazed into my eyes. "Well, your lungs definitely sound wet, evidence of the fluid surrounding and filling them. How is your breathing?"

"I feel like I can't catch my breath, especially these past few days—like someone is giving me a giant bear hug. Does that make sense?"

He smiled. "It certainly does. Unfortunately, I believe that feeling of tightness will only get worse. Plus, you may start to experience a nagging cough as fluid fills your lungs."

I noticed the color drain from Jenn's face as the reality of this news sunk in. Somehow, this news didn't shock or frighten me...yet.

"I don't want to scare you, but I feel it is in the best interest of our patients that they know the truth, so when the time comes, there is no shock. I promise we will do everything in our power to keep your pain to a minimum. Please don't be afraid of asking us for help."

"How much time..." I allowed my voice to drift off.

"I'm not certain," Dr. Moody said. "But based on experience, I would place you at six months, maybe sooner. I'm sorry."

I stared at the doctor, feeling he must be talking to someone else. I felt numb. Nothing seemed real. I barely noticed the lab tech enter to draw my blood. I looked up as he took my arm. Nancy excused herself to go check on my room, smiling on her way out the door.

As the exam finished, the doctor and his tech excused

themselves from the room, leaving me alone with Jenn. Our silence was an uneasy quiet. I stared at my feet, unable to make eye contact with my apprehensive friend.

Six months. Maybe sooner. I considered how that thought should scare me, yet it didn't. Maybe late at night it would hit me and I would find myself lost in panic. For now, I just wanted to be through with the whole miserable dying thing and rid of the smiling faces that continued to pop up around me—as if a smile would fix everything.

Nancy re-entered the room and declared that my suite was ready. As we followed her down another narrow hallway, brightened again by full-length windows over-looking the courtyard, I peered into the rooms of other patients around me. Although many of the doors lining the hall were closed, there were a few that remained open. Beyond their thresholds I witnessed people—or more appropriately, the shadow of people—lying motionless, alone, waiting for the hand of death to relieve them from their suffering. I shuddered realizing that I was next. I too would be alone, waiting.

My room, just past a nurses' station at the far end of the building, was the last room in the hall, next to a separate entrance for family and friends of patients who occupied this wing of the center. My room had one window with a partial view of the courtyard and the parking lot beyond. A bench was fixed on the wall below the window, a bookshelf flanking its left side and cabinet on the right. A TV sat atop the bookshelf and occupying the center of the room was a hospital grade bed. The room contained a private bathroom complete with red emergency pull cords. Strangely, I saw no medical equipment in the room. No IV stands. No oxygen units. By all appearances, this could have been a room in a boarding house, not a place for a sick and dying person.

"This is your room, Maddy. A few features for you to know about. Extra blankets and pillows are here," Nancy said, motioning toward the tall cabinet to the right of the window. "You have a private bath for yourself and your guests. And, if we need any medical equipment like oxygen or suctioning devices, those are found here."

Nancy went to where a painting hung over the bed, sliding it up toward the ceiling she revealed the equipment I thought didn't exist.

"Of course, these are only to make you more comfortable if needed, we don't use them on a regular basis. I'll let you get settled and return in a bit to see if you need anything." Motioning to a button on a remote control next to the bed Nancy added, "In the meantime, here is the nurse call button. Don't hesitate to ask for help."

Nancy left the room and I plopped down on the bed, exhausted from even the little morning activity. As I surveyed my new residence, Jenn sat beside me, leaning her head against my shoulder. I gave her a sideways hug, continuing to avoid eye contact.

"Do you need anything?" she asked.

"No, I don't think so," I replied.

Another long silence lingered, interrupted only by the lively chatter of the hospice staff at the nurses' station outside my door.

"Maddy," Jenn broke, shifting uneasily beside me. "I have a confession to make."

In the hallway, I heard a familiar voice that I didn't want to believe I recognized.

"I'm here to see Madeline Smith," a man's voice said. It was a voice that hung on my every thought. The voice I woke up each morning hoping to hear. Unfortunately, the sweet timbre of his words now echoed like the screeching of a train sliding off its tracks. I both loved and despised that voice as it reverberated through the disparaging chamber of my mind.

"What did you do?" I fumed in a hushed voice, the articulate beats of anger striking with more ferocity than any piercing scream.

"You don't know how upset he was last night, Maddy." Jenn's words flew from her lips so rapidly I struggled to catch them all. "Jake was beside himself with worry. He wanted to go after you. I had to tell him. He had the right to know. He loves you. He wanted to come this morning and escort you here, but I convinced him to wait until you were settled. Of course, he could have waited a bit longer."

Jenn sighed. I glanced up in time to catch her roll her eyes.

"No," I growled.

"Maddy..."

"No!" I wanted to scream. I wanted to stomp out of the room in hissy fit fashion. Of course, there was nowhere for me to run, except perhaps the bathroom, which didn't seem very dignified.

"You had no right," my brow furrowed. "You promised."

"Maddy, you are being irrational. He loves you…"

"Get out. Just leave me alone." I turned my back on my friend.

"Maddy…"

"Get out!" I interrupted before Jenn could say anything more. Turning again to stare her down I spoke through gritted teeth, "Get out and don't come back. Some friend you are!"

My words were shards of glass, piercing Jenn's good heart with their fury. I could see moisture fill her eyes. She contorted her face to keep from falling apart, but I knew the damage was done. Part of me wanted to apologize, wanted to beg forgiveness. Unfortunately, a greater part of me was livid and decided to ignore my friend's pain. I turned to stare out the window onto the tree lined courtyard beyond.

"Maddy," an unfamiliar voice came from the door. "You have a visitor…a Mr. Jake Kavanaugh."

"I don't want any visitors," I declared. "In fact, my friend was just leaving."

Another strained silence filled the small living space.

"Are you sure?" the polite nurse questioned.

"Yes, positive. I want to be alone."

Without a fight, Jenn rose and moved toward the door. I didn't bother looking up to say good-bye.

"I'm sorry," she whispered.

Nearby, I heard Jenn's muffled weeping as the nurse

delivered the news to Jake. My eyes watered, but I refused to allow my conscience gain the upper-hand. I lay upon my bed, facing the window, staring out at the world I once knew—a world of hope. I tried to drown the familiar voices from my head as they spoke outside my door. Frustrated, I lay down and hid beneath crisp hospital linen, marring its starched-white sterility with my street clothes and shoes. The more I tried to distract myself from those horribly beautiful voices, the more they echoed in my ear, so I placed the pillow over my head. I struggled to hide from the encroaching madness threatening to steal my sanity.

I squeezed my eyes shut, determined to make everyone and everything disappear, I continued to hear Jake's voice resonate in the hall. "Tell Maddy that I'm not giving up. Tell her that I am going to come every day to be with her. Tell her she can turn me away a thousand times, but I will still return. Maddy, I love you. Do you hear me? I love you!"

He shouted so I was certain everyone in the facility could hear.

"I'm not giving up. I am going to be with you until the end and I'll keep on loving you after that. You are so stubborn, but I'm persistent. I'm not giving up. I'm not giving up!"

I choked and pressed the pillow tighter to my ear. I couldn't let him see me die. I didn't want to hurt anyone else the way I hurt Jenn. How could he possibly want to watch me waste away?

Bundled in my cotton cocoon, I hid from the world. Jake

and Jenn eventually left, deciding that I wouldn't change
my mind. Nurses performed their rounds. Orderlies placed
lunch and dinner on the table next to my bed, and later
returned to retrieve the untouched trays. I remained
hidden, sometimes allowing myself to peer out the window
toward the fading light. Tomorrow would be another day. I
should be thankful for the time that remained, but instead I
waited for my lungs to fill with liquid, causing me to
drown inside my own body. As night closed in, a nurse
came and asked if I needed anything to help me sleep. I
nodded and moments later she returned with a small pill
and a glass of water. I took the pill without question, and as
its drowsing affect crawled across my body, I allowed
myself the solace of sleep, wishing that in the morning I
would not wake.

Chapter Seven

Morning came as I feared, and several mornings after. Each day I woke hoping death would claim my failing body during the night—painlessly stealing me into its empty void—but each day I saw the sun shining, watched the nurses come and go, and heard that same dreaded, sweet voice proclaim itself outside my room. Arriving once each morning and again in the evening, Jake was true to his word; he would persist until the end.

"Please inform Madeline," he used my formal name, "that I am here to visit."

Soon after, one pleasant nurse or another would enter my room announcing what I already knew and true to my word, I would send her away to offer polite refusal to the man who seemed to love me more than I deserved.

Days blended as I kept myself in a shell of emotional numbness, staring distantly through the window out at the world beyond. I longed for distraction, but nothing held my attention. Television possessed no entertainment value. Soap operas, talk shows, even the news irritated me in ways I still cannot communicate. Situation comedies and their brainless plot twists seemed inconsequential and utterly dense, making my wish for death's quick arrival more intense.

Fevers spiked throughout the day, swinging me between shivering chills and scorching heat, but at least they were controlled with over-the-counter medication. More frequently I found myself incapacitated by coughing attacks—the slow build up of fluid in my weakening lungs. My sides ached. Physical pain in my extremities increased. At first, discomfort presented as pins and needles, but as I labored for every breath, cells would burn for want of oxygen. Fortunately, I could clear my lungs after several agonizing minutes, but I knew this was only a precursor to the time when cancer would win its fight.

Muscles that were atrophied from my self-imposed bedridden state and lack of appetite now limited my unassisted travels to the bathroom and the window seat, although I rarely ventured either place for long.

This morning, three weeks after my admittance into the Hospice Care Center of Charleston, my wet coughing once again woke me from a numbing trance, back to the stinging reality of impending death. It was this morning, after

Jake's routine dismissal, that a new nurse—a chipper girl, with curly, shoulder-length blonde hair, a pointed nose, and sparkling eyes that remained yet undisturbed from the daily routine of death—came bouncing into my room. Although every employee wore the same sincere, yet somehow robotic smile, she was the first to display any genuine enthusiasm for what little life remained inside these walls. It made me want to hit her.

"I'm Sabrina," she said, placing in my hand a small cup filled with three pills and another cup of water. "Rough morning?"

I swallowed the medicine dutifully.

"Well," she continued. "I still think we can make the most of this day! Now, what I am about to do is probably going to anger you, but if you just wait until you see..."

"Too late," I rebuked, choking on my last pill. "I'm already pissed. Now, unless you are going to give me an overdose of this medication and save me from my suffering, go away and sell Jesus to some other poor, dying sap."

"No, I'm not here to kill you or bring you to Jesus," she was still beaming.

I hated her.

"This is something altogether diff..."

"Get to the point or go away," I cut her off, refusing to look in her direction. Sabrina had been in my room for approximately thirty seconds and had made it to the top of my fecal roster. I silently debated whether a jury would have time to convict me of murder when I was this close to death. Heck, I probably wouldn't survive until arraignment. My chances looked pretty good.

She drew a deep breath.

"Okay, it's about that man who comes to see you."

"Get out!" I fought to expel the words through sputtered coughs, "Who are you to even…"

This time she cut me off, "Look, I said you would be upset, but you need to know what I am about to show you. Now, like it or not, you are coming with me. Do you need a wheelchair, or can you walk?"

The gumption displayed by my perky caretaker was impressive, but I was feeling especially cantankerous. I was ready to make her little, intruding life as difficult as possible.

"You can get me a wheelchair, if you think it will matter, but I'm telling you, I'm not going."

I wondered at what point I'd became such a severe, mean person. I didn't especially like this dying version of me, but then again, what part of dying was there to like? I knew I was difficult, but I was past worrying what others thought of me or my personality. Besides, even if I did care what others thought—a fact I didn't want to admit—I would be out of their lives soon enough. Everyone continued with their lives, forgetting the brief moments in which I occupied their existence.

Sabrina floated out of the room while I pondered what on Earth could possibly be so important that she felt inclined to remove me from the sanctity of my death chamber and force me back into a world I'd already left behind. Before I could formulate any solid answers, she returned, wheelchair in tow.

She helped me into the chair. I made it notably difficult by turning limp as a rag doll, but despite her petite stature, she was amazingly strong and got me situated with remarkably little effort.

Grumbling my protest in an unintelligible voice, we wheeled past the threshold of my door and into the hallway. I stared down at my feet sitting atop metal supports, watching the tiled floor flow swiftly beneath them. Feeling every eye upon us as we moved past the nurses' station, I refused to look up and meet anyone's gaze. I didn't want to acknowledge the condemnation of my behavior that I was certain to find in their expressions.

I glanced around in my peripheral vision as we moved down another hallway, trying to think back to the day I arrived—trying to determine where my transport was taking me—but nothing seemed familiar. As always, doors to other patients' rooms remained closed, preventing me from observing others who waited outside Heaven's gates. But then again, that was probably for the best—I didn't want to admit that anyone else could be as tormented by their situation as I. It was empowering to feel like I was the only one who knew suffering. This depressing indignation was my stronghold, my comfort, the only thing that remained in my control.

We rounded another corner and proceeded through a door marked Chapel/Quiet Worship.

Heat flushed my cheeks as infuriation tore an emotional

hole in my chest. Who did this woman think she was? She insisted that she wasn't pushing Jesus or salvation and now she had me sitting outside a chapel!

Before laying into her and making her wish she hadn't come to work today, I took a moment to look around. Intricate and beautiful artwork surrounded the walls. A grouping of angelic faced women—one looking directly at me—seemed to float from the mural, comforting and bringing tidings of peace and tranquility. There was a valley—shadowy figures passing through. A man knelt in a meadow, praying. The images were vague, yet descriptive at the same moment. My anger briefly passed as I marveled at the artist's multifarious work.

Although I lacked faith of any kind, I did have a basic understanding of the Christian Bible, thanks to a year I spent living with one particular foster family that insisted on reading Biblical passages to the foster kids in their care. I remember that family as kind and generous—a rarity in foster life—but despite their desire to save my soul, I never took to Christianity. Despite the Bible's teachings, I struggled to believe in a God who was good, yet continued to allow bad things to happen in this world. I knew firsthand of pain and suffering caused by evil—some of which I experienced during my tumultuous years growing up as an unwanted, castaway child. As I mentioned before, the fear of ghosts and goblins seemed silly compared to the true source of terror—evil that lurked within human hearts. I didn't need some religion to warn me about sin and evil spirits. I had seen plenty of demons in human form. I had yet to see any angels.

Looking up at the sweet nurse who delivered me to this chapel, I remembered why I was here. My ire boiled. Before I had the opportunity to unleash hell's fury, my fuming was cut short as Sabrina quietly knelt beside my chair and, pointing toward the back of the room, whispered, "Over there."

Struck with morbid curiosity, I abandoned plans of retaliation and turned to look toward the far corner of the room. There, upon the last pew in a row of five, was a clump of blankets and a pillow, along with an overnight bag stuffed beneath the bench. It took me a moment to notice someone lay wrapped in the blankets, emitting a muffled, rhythmic snore.

Jake.

He had camped out, waiting to see if I would allow his visit. I was speechless at the sight.

Satisfied, Sabrina wheeled me back outside the chapel door and into the common area. The vision of Jake, sleeping cramped into the tiny pew made me regret denying him this morning's visit. He must have been exhausted balancing work and attempting to visit every day. I assumed he was too tired to drive anywhere, seeking refuge in the quiet chapel where he would not be disturbed. I couldn't remember what day of the week it was. Could it be Saturday? I was certain Jake would be at work if it was a weekday, but what if he took time off? Did he exhaust himself to the point of missing work? Lost in thought, I didn't notice Sabrina stop and park my chair in the common area. She proceeded to sit beside me.

"I thought you should know," she started. I could only nod, thankful she was pushy enough to show me.

"I know this is a difficult time for you, and although I've never met you before, I know this cold personality is not the person you once were. I know how angry, scared, frustrated, sad...well...I know how it all feels. If you will allow me to tell you a bit about myself?" She hesitated, waiting on my approval. Again I nodded.

"When I was a teenager, I was diagnosed with Leukemia. My chances didn't look good. I can't say I felt exactly the way you do, but I bet my reaction was fairly similar. I was mean to everyone. I wanted everyone to understand that they couldn't possibly know how I felt. Although I was only sixteen, I was nasty enough to make one nurse cry. I felt so out of control. It seemed like every decision was made for me and the only way I had any real influence was by getting angry and making people upset. It helped me to feel like I still had some power over something, although I will admit that it wasn't really the best way of influencing the world around me. I just figured that, when it all boiled down, it made no difference how I behaved. No one could tell if I was going to live, so chances were that I wouldn't be around to suffer the consequences of my actions. I just assumed that nothing I did really mattered."

I saw myself reflected in her story. I saw past my catatonic farce and realized I was like that same, scared sixteen-year-old yearning for any bit of control, even if it came at the expense of my sweet, lovely, wonderful friends.

"Thankfully," she continued, "the chemo worked and I had an opportunity to make amends. The ability for people to forgive never ceases to amaze me. I became a nurse hoping to share my experiences with you and others like you. I'm not trying to celebrate my recovery. I know I was blessed. My mother attributed my healing to the prayers and support of the many friends and family she recruited in my honor, but as promised, I'm not here to push Jesus on you. I just thought you should know that your actions do still have an effect on others and there are people, like your friend, who aren't giving up on you and probably won't until you pass. You need to make the choice, though, about how you want to be remembered. You can still control that part when you feel like you can't control anything else. I would hate to see you waste something that could be really amazing—something you might regret missing at the end—because you are frustrated and scared. People still want to be a part of your life; they feel invested in this process too. They want to help and by denying them that opportunity, you are denying them the ability to feel as if they have contributed to your life. You are fortunate to have somebody who cares. I have seen many die alone."

We both sat in silence as I continued staring out the windows, contemplating her words. She was right. I was stubborn and difficult, not the person I once was. I had tried to convince myself that my new attitude was what others needed to move on, but in reality, I never looked at it from Jenn or Jake's point of view. I realized that the idea of dying alone was something I needed—or thought I needed.

"Was he too exhausted to drive home this morning?" I asked, finally breaking our silence.

Sabrina sighed.

"Sweetie," she said, sadness creeping into her tone. "He has slept here day and night since you were admitted. What, about three and a half weeks now? He only leaves a few hours every other day to go home to shower and change clothes. We tried offering him one of our family rooms, but he said he preferred the chapel...that his prayers might be more readily heard from there."

"Every day?" I asked, whirling to look into Sabrina's sweet face. "What about his job? He can't possibly have that much time off."

"I don't know," she shrugged, her hands folded in her lap. "Maybe he took his three months of federal unpaid leave. That would be my guess anyway."

We sat again without speaking.

Three and a half weeks? Unpaid leave of absence? Could he afford that? Could he possibly care that much about me? Perhaps Mr. Sharp was kind enough to give him a few extra days of paid time off, but how long did Jake plan his vigil? My time, although short, may still keep me in this world a few months more. What was he thinking? What was I thinking?

My eyes opened. I suddenly wanted to see him. Part of me wanted to chastise his crazy behavior, but then again, who was the crazy one here? I wondered if he could forgive my stubbornness.

I knew life was slipping from me. I realized I could

not die without letting those I loved know that I truly did care about them. I thought I was helping everyone—helping them to move on. Sabrina showed me the grim reality that my actions weren't letting anyone move on, myself included. My friends needed me as much I needed them. My head began to spin. Could I repair what was already damaged?

Strength washed from my body and it must have shown because without asking, Sabrina rose from her seat and pushed me back to my room.

I asked to sit on the window bench, not ready to retreat back into my bed, although I was tired enough to sleep. I was afraid of falling asleep. I was afraid that death would finally come and I would not wake—the very thing I prayed to happen so many nights prior. I didn't want to lose my opportunity to make things right with Jake and Jenn.

Time pressed in, sand draining more rapidly from the hour glass. I could hear the thudding beat of my heart booming within my chest.

"Do you need anything?" Sabrina asked.

I drew a staggered breath.

"Not right now. Just..." I stammered, trying to steady myself against the flood of emotion overtaking the numb fortress that protected me over the past few weeks. "...Please, just let Jake know when he wakes that I want to see him."

"Of course. If you need anything, I am right outside your door."

I watched as Sabrina floated from the room. When she was gone, I returned my attention to the unsteady ticking of my heart—a clock, winding down to its final stroke.

I drew a deep breath, as an emotional deluge flooded in, threatening to overtake my soul. I permitted fear to block everything and everyone from my heart for so long it seemed ironic that now, as my life faded, I recognized how many amazing opportunities I allowed to pass me by. I yearned to be free of the chains I wrapped around my soul, to make everything right with the people I loved, but I wasn't sure how to begin. Lost and afraid, I finally did what many people do when they feel the walls crumbling around them: I prayed to a God I abandoned long ago—a God I thought had abandoned me. I spent years refusing to believe in His existence, but now, as the shadows of my life flickered before me, I cried to Him.

"Please God," I whispered. "Please, if you are there, I need you. I can't do this. I'm terrified. Please God, save me!"

Agonizing pain tore inside my chest. Although manifested physically, my heart recognized the sorrowful grief of a soul, long lost, begging for salvation. Again, I drew a breath, ready to release emotions jailed for weeks... perhaps even years. I was ready to let God in. Emotions surged. I inhaled—my spirit breaking and longing to be rebuilt—when suddenly my throat caught. A gurgling sound struggled to escape the blocked entrance of my lungs.

Dumbstruck, I gagged and again tried to draw air. I

emitted a strangled cry as fluid prevented my lungs from expanding.

Panic.

I tried to cough. I gagged. I jumped to my feet, fumbling for help, unable to speak or cry out. I groped the space around me in horror, searching for something... anything. Deep down I knew my furious clawing would prove ineffective. Somewhere my subconscious begged me to conserve energy—find the nurses' call button—but I was already at the mercy of my hysteria. My flailing body spun in a circle. Each attempt at breath failed.

Change.

My mind blurred, the world grew fuzzy. I realized I was no longer thrashing around my room. At first my body felt as though on fire, but now I sensed only the remnants of a dull flame...a memory of sensation radiating within. My cheek lay against the cold tile floor, although I could not recall how I came to rest there.

I no longer struggled. The lingering embers burned out as I relaxed into a new, breathless self. Could this be the end? I thought of Jake and Jenn. Surprisingly, I found happiness in that thought.

Peace.

Something in me let go. It was not complicated or terrifying. It was safe, ordinary, instinctive.

Dying wasn't as bad as I had imagined.

Chapter Eight

Letting go was easy, natural. There was no fear. I unchained the bothers and annoyances carried in my human life—those burdens replaced by a sense of freedom and peace. My world changed around me. Vaguely aware I still lay on the hospice center floor, I saw no walls, no furniture. Form disintegrated from my space, replaced with light, brighter light than if I stared into the sun. As my soul's tether frayed—a balloon set to release—I perceived I was not alone. A figure. A man, maybe? Yes, at my side, there was someone...

I didn't notice the strong arms that lifted me from the floor. I didn't hear the flurry of activity as nurses rushed in. I didn't feel slight hands forcefully open my jaw and insert a suction tube drawing out mucous and fluid from within.

...Yes, a man. He was next to me. A sound. Something... something caught me, tugged on me, anchored me. I wanted to let go. Why could I not let go? I looked at the figure, his form fading...

Commotion.

An alien sucking sound reverberated inside my head. My body convulsed as my lungs filled with air. No, I didn't want to return. Everything hurt.

Pain.

My eyes flew open—a comparatively dull light illuminated my clouded vision. Sabrina stood over me, a mask hiding half her face, eyes blazing with determination and concern. What was she doing?

The sucking noise faded. I gagged as Sabrina removed a tube from the depths of my burning raw throat. The pins and needles sensation pricked across my entire body as my nerves wakened and normal breath returned. Sabrina placed a mask over my face, pelting my mouth and nose with cool air. I watched her carefully, dazed, trying to comprehend what was happening. Something pulled at my memory. Something important. What was it?

Sabrina looked across my body to the other side of the bed.

"She's okay," she said. "Her O$_2$ sats are back up. We caught her in time."

Something tickled the fringes of my mind. What was I trying to remember?

"She's okay," Sabrina said again.

I turned my head to see Jake, standing next to the bed. He was still the same, sweet man I loved, although he looked a bit more disheveled than I remembered. The whites of his eyes burned red as he held back fearful tears that threatened to erupt. He didn't notice me—he concentrated on Sabrina's reassuring words, appearing unconvinced. I took the opportunity to study him in greater detail. Jake looked tired. His usual neatly pressed wardrobe was replaced by old sweat pants and a faded t-shirt. His face was unshaven. Any onlooker might mistake this person beside me for some homeless man. He looked desperate and defeated.

Despite his unsightly outward appearance, I discovered that I found him attractive even when he no longer looked the part of the urban businessman. I realized that if our roles were reversed, I would want to be at his side. I wouldn't care what he looked like or how his body would change and fade. I loved the man inside, and I suspected watching him now, that he loved me with the same commitment.

Jake glanced down and met my gaze with his glistening red eyes.

"I'll give you two some time alone," Sabrina spoke as she stored medical equipment above my head on the wall.

"I'll be back in a few minutes to check on her. Will you be alright?"

Jake nodded, keeping his eyes locked tight on mine.

"Okay, then," she said. "Here is the nurse call button, just

80

in case."

Sabrina stretched the remote behind my head, laying it next to Jake. She moved away from the side of the bed. Still staring into Jake's eyes, I heard the door to my room close behind her.

"Maddy, are you alright?" Jake managed to whisper, still fighting back his tears.

I nodded. My throat was raw. I wasn't sure if I could speak.

"I just had to," his throat caught. He obviously fought to control his emotions. "I'm sorry. I just had to make sure you were okay. I'll leave you alone now."

He choked. Jake moved around the bed toward the door, tears streaming down his face.

"Wait," I pleaded in a hoarse voice that was muffled beneath the oxygen mask. My tender throat would not allow me to cry out.

He didn't hear me. I watch him hurry across the room.

I tore the mask off my face. "Wait!" my voice faltered.

He still couldn't hear me.

"Wait!" I bellowed, but my ears perceived only a gruff whisper.

Jake walked out my door. Maybe he didn't hear me.

Or maybe he doesn't really love you the way you imagine.

I tried to push the negative voice from my mind. I didn't want to let it destroy my resolve yet it continued to toy with my thoughts. I wondered if maybe the sight of me—a shadow of my former self—forced Jake to face the reality of my situation. Perhaps his leaving was for the best.

Jake was already in the hall, unable to hear my pleadings for his return. This time, though, I refused to allow my defeatist thoughts to subdue my action. I would not allow death to take me until I could make things right with Jake. I looked around. How could I get his attention?

The call button.

I pressed the nurses' call button, once, twice, a third time. I wasn't sure if it rang each time I pressed it, but I was determined. My repeated attempts to page the nurse's station simultaneously prevented the nurse from answering my call.

"Maddy!" Sabrina came to the door exasperated. "I can't pick up your call if you don't take your finger off the button."

"Jake, wait!" My voice strained as I pointed out the door.

Sabrina smiled then called down the hall, "Hey, Jake. You're wanted in here."

Then, giggling, she crossed the room and leaned down beside me. "I'm probably in trouble for getting involved. We aren't really supposed to revive patients…so if anyone asks, do me a favor and say that you asked to be suctioned for comfort, okay?"

I smiled and nodded. Her secret was safe with me.

Giggling again, she left the room as Jake staggered in. He looked weary, pensive.

He pulled the lounge chair next to the bed, then sat, eyes level with mine. We looked at each other for several minutes. I broke the silence.

"Jake," I said, still forcing my vocal cords to produce

sound. "I'm so sorry, I've been a real jerk. Please, please forgive me?"

Jake chuckled. Although he had regained control of his emotions, tears continued to seep from the corners of his eyes.

"You haven't been a jerk," he consoled.

"Ugh, don't lie to the dying girl. I don't need you to be *nice* to me. I know what I've been."

"Okay," Jake smiled while he shook his head. "I'll agree you were *kind of* a jerk—but I get it. I do. If you want to hear I forgive you, well, then sure, I forgive you...although there is really nothing to forgive. If it was me, I'd probably act the same way."

"Yeah, well, it's still no excuse."

My throat hurt. It felt like I was swallowing rocks.

"Hey, as much as I love hearing your voice, give it a rest for a second, okay? I can tell it hurts. Let me say a few things. Just listen," Jake said.

I started to protest but Jake gave me a stern "go ahead and try it" look, so I let him proceed.

"Okay, here goes," he started. "I know you don't believe me when I say I love you, but I do. Remember the first week we worked together? Remember when I asked you out for drinks that Friday night after work?"

He waited for me to nod in confirmation before continuing.

"I liked you from the minute we met. All I could think was 'This is such a cute girl. She's smart, quick witted, funny...how did I get so lucky?' At the bar, while we sat there talking about work, life...you know, everything...I realized I could really fall for you. When it was time to leave, I knew I didn't want that night to end. I was ready to ask you out the next night, but I hesitated, worried you may not feel the same way. I feared our working relationship would suffer. What if my advances made things uncomfortable the next week? What if you insisted we couldn't work together? I figured I would rather see you every day just as friends than speak up and ruin any chance at being near you. I was miserable, but at least I got to see you every morning."

I smiled, astonished how that night was the same night I fell for him too. Funny how two people could be in the same place at the same moment, yet convince themselves they were worlds apart.

"As much as I wanted to pursue you, I told myself it wasn't the right thing for me, you, or the company. Three years I spent sitting beside you, loving you. I tortured myself planning our future together, but I couldn't figure out how to expose my feelings without ruining the friendship we built; fearing all the while that you would find someone else before I could get my act together. At first I was excited when I heard you were leaving— realizing it would be my chance to make my feelings known. Then I panicked because I imagined you moving to California..." he stifled a laughing sob. "Lord, how I wish you were moving to California instead..."

Jake's voice trailed off as he slumped over, laying his head on the bed beside my chest. I stroked his hair as his emotions broke. Jake kept his face buried in the mattress.

"Honest to God, Maddy, if I could take those three years back, if I could go back to that Friday night at the bar..."

I let him cry, working through his sorrow and grief. I was glad Sabrina opened my eyes and gave me this opportunity to be there for him before it was too late.

"Maddy," he breathed, still hiding his face in the mattress. "We might have been married by now. Maybe a couple of kids. If I was with you, we could have caught this disease before it took over. I should have seen it. I could have saved you."

"This isn't your fault," I said, my heart breaking. I couldn't believe he would blame himself. "This isn't anybody's fault. We can't change the past, Jake. I love you too. Just stay here with me. Be here until..."

"I don't want to *just* be here with you," he replied.

Jake picked his head up, the matted sheet had creased lines across his tear streaked face.

"Jake, this isn't your fault. There is nothing more anyone can do."

"There is something I can do," Jake said.

I looked into his eyes, confused. What could he possibly do? He fumbled for something below my line of sight. My mind raced trying to determine the meaning behind his words.

There, in front of me, Jake held up a small, sparkling object.

"Maddy," he said, taking my hand, his light eyes staring directly into mine. "I've screwed this up for three years. I have known from the start there couldn't possibly be any other woman that I would ever want to be with. I'm sorry *I've* been a jerk for so long. Madeline Smith, I love you. Three years, three weeks, three hours—I promise to be at your side every second of the time we have left together. Just say you will be my wife. Marry me, Maddy? Please, will you marry me?"

Chapter Nine

"Oh my goodness!" Jenn shrieked into the phone, piercing my ear drum through the receiver. "I have to be maid of honor ready by tomorrow afternoon? There is so much to do! When did this happen? Tell me all about it! No wait, I'll come over!" Her voice raced with enthusiastic joy.

"Slow down Jenn!" I smiled, knowing my request that she be the maid of honor in our wedding immediately absolved our strained relationship.

Of course I said yes to Jake's proposal. How could I refuse his glowing, expectant eyes? Part of me still wanted to protect him—spare him from the loss he would soon experience. I wanted to argue a million different points about why I wasn't a good choice for him, but in the moment, as I stared in astonishment at the large solitaire diamond he held before me, as I gazed into his loving, sweet face, I could only whisper the word "yes," barely audible to my own ears.

Deep down, I felt a pang of selfishness for agreeing to the marriage. The proverbial devil on my shoulder who had said yes fought against the angel, who tried to discourage my own happiness at the expense of others. I knew the dream of children, dogs and white picket fences was beyond attainable, but in these final days, if I could be Jake's wife, I decided that alone would be enough—for me at least.

Jake, sitting on the window seat, hung up his cell phone after talking to his parents, announcing his good news. I wondered what they thought of their only son marrying a woman who would be dead in a matter of months.

I insisted that our marriage not be legal, in the governmental sense of the word. I knew that if we were truly married, I was sure to leave Jake with large medical bills and an unpaid balance on my student loan. I expected the sale of what little I had would pay off a portion of my expenses, knowing the rest could be written off as my solitary status would allow no avenue for banks and state agencies to collect any funds. With a husband, I realized they could go after Jake for the money. Jake reluctantly agreed, deciding that as long as we were married in the presence of God, that would be enough for him. I tried to argue that we didn't really need to be married—that our love was enough without any sort of legitimate blessing, governmental or otherwise—but Jake refused such thought. So, selfishly I allowed him to marry a dying woman. I felt guilty, but when he looked at me like he'd just won the lottery, how could I possibly say no?

"Maddy?"

I was pulled back from my thoughts, realizing Jenn was still on the phone.

"Maddy, are you there?"

"What? Oh, Yeah, sorry Jenn."

"Oh, well don't scare me like that," she said. "As I was saying, what colors are you choosing for the wedding? I look really great in blue."

"Jenn," I sighed. "This is just a small ceremony in the hospice center's chapel tomorrow night. I haven't even thought about colors. Wear what you want I guess."

"Okay, okay," Jenn sounded disappointed. "Well, anyway, can I come do your hair? What are you going to wear?"

"I am probably just going to wear a hospital gown."

"Never!" Jenn's somber attitude changed to alarm. "I won't let that happen. I let you be a fashion misfit every day of your life, but this time I'm stepping in. Think of this as a fashion intervention. I *will not* allow you to get married in a hospital gown, do you hear me? I am going to buy you a dress tonight."

I couldn't argue with the indignant tone in her voice.

"Fine, whatever," I tried to sound nonchalant, but I was happy she wanted to help.

90

"What size are you now?" Jenn asked.

"That's a good question," I said. "I really don't know. I suspect I've lost a lot of weight."

"Okay, then I am going to find a dress and I'll bring it to you in a size six, four, two, and zero. One of those should fit and I will return the rest."

"I'm not sure you can get wedding gowns in all those sizes without special ordering."

"Are you kidding? I'm disappointed. You forget how resourceful your friend is, especially when it comes to shopping! It's prom season. I am going downtown and I know I can find something in white—or at least white-ish— in the junior department. Just leave it all to me. I will come by this evening."

"Just one request: please keep it classy. I'm not sixteen, remember?"

"Maddy, when have you ever known me to pick out trashy clothes? Don't answer that. I promise I won't disappoint. I've got a lot to do! I will see you in a few hours," Jenn's giddiness made me smile.

"See you soon," I replied.

"Oh, and Maddy?" Jenn said.

"Yes?"

"Thanks for calling. I've missed you."

"Sure," I replied, feeling a twinge of guilt over my behavior from the past few weeks, "And Jenn?"

"Yes?"

"I'm sorry. I really have been a jerk."

"Don't even worry about it. I'd probably act the same

way."

"Why does everybody keep saying that?" I demanded. "Quit being so nice! I don't deserve it."

"You're crazy," Jenn said. "I love you."

"I love you too."

I hung up the phone and looked over at Jake, who was watching me, grinning his incredible dimpled grin, making my heart race and my head spin without even trying. I still had a difficult time grasping the fact that he wanted to marry me.

"What did your parents say?" I questioned, not sure I wanted an answer. "Did they talk any sense into you? You certainly wouldn't listen to me!"

"My parents are very happy, although they don't think they can get a ticket out here until the day after tomorrow. They are excited to finally meet the woman I have talked about for three years."

"Did you tell them I am dying?"

Jake flinched, "Yes, they know."

I looked down at my fingers, focused on twisting the top sheet of my bed into different spiraled patterns. I couldn't think how to break the uncomfortable silence that filled the space after that last question.

"Maddy," Jake finally spoke as I continued creating cotton origami, "I don't know why, but I still have hope. I can't believe this is the end. I guess maybe it is just my wishful thinking, but something inside tells me there will be a miracle. I know it sounds silly and I almost lost faith myself today when ..."

He choked on his words, pausing to regroup.

"Maddy, this isn't the end. Call it a gut feeling, but I can still see us living together, having kids. I still see it. I've been praying for a miracle. I still have faith in a miracle."

I wanted to tell Jake he was nuts. I didn't want him holding out false hope, but the gleam in his infallible, light eyes prevented me from setting him straight. I knew I was dying. My number was up. If my episode today didn't prove it, the wet cough that continued to irritate my raw throat provided a constant reminder that my moments were limited. Despite the signs, I couldn't bring myself to crush Jake's faith. Besides, I was no expert on the subject of faith and hope. Maybe he had some connection with God I was missing. Maybe he could inspire a miracle. I wasn't going to hold my breath, though.

Once again silence hovered in the space between us. I wasn't sure what he wanted me to say. His eyes searched mine, looking, I suppose, for some sort of confirmation that I believed as strongly as he did, that there was still a chance. I could not, though, provide that kind of reassurance.

Sabrina popped her head in and called from the door, "Just checking...how are you feeling?"

Thankful for the distraction, I called out, "Fine," but as I did, fluid caught my inhalation, setting off a coughing spell. Jake pounced from the window seat, racing to my side. I waved him off knowing it would pass, for now. After about thirty seconds I cleared my lungs sufficiently so that my coughing ceased and my breathing steadied.

"Good girl," Sabrina encouraged, standing at the ready beside my bed.

"Thanks, it comes and goes," I responded with a harsh, gurgled voice.

Jake looked apprehensive, but smiled when he heard me speak.

"Really, I'm okay," I told him, my voice scratchy from the flaring pain in my throat. He seemed convinced.

"So," Sabrina regained our attention. "The chapel is set for tomorrow night, and I hope you don't mind, but we nurses wanted to do something, so we all chipped in and ordered you a cake. I hope that's alright?"

Her smile was infectious. This woman, who upon first meeting I wanted to destroy based solely on her sweet disposition, made me realize how cranky I really must have been.

"Thank you so much," I returned her smile. "You really don't have to do that."

"Yes we do," she said. "This is the first wedding we have ever hosted here! It is so exciting! We want to do this for you both."

"Thank you," Jake smiled.

Then, flashing a determined look toward Jake, she added, "Maddy, Jake and I were talking earlier, and it seems that you don't have a living will, power of attorney, or last will for that matter."

"I guess not," I said, watching as an unspoken conversation seemed to take place between Sabrina and Jake.

Turning toward me, she continued, "Well, I just thought it might be a good idea to get such paperwork in order, you know, so Jake has permission to care for you and has the appointed rights of a husband, even though you insist this marriage won't be real in the legal sense. We have such documents available here."

She was right. If I was going to allow Jake to be my husband in the eyes of God, but deny him any legal rights to make decisions about my care when I became too incapacitated to do anything myself, it wouldn't be fair.

I saw the concern in Jakes eyes, waiting for my decision. "I think that sounds reasonable," I shrugged. "Can you get the documents ready?"

"Absolutely. I'll have them ready before I'm off shift this evening! I asked for tomorrow afternoon off so I can help prepare for your wedding, but I'll still be your nurse in the morning. I hope you don't mind."

My approving smile lit Sabrina's joyful expression even brighter.

"Okay, back to the grind," she replied. "I will be off shift in a few hours, so I'll get moving and help prepare those documents for you."

"Thanks," I called out as she skipped toward the door.

"Dum, Dum Da Dum," she sung the wedding march, turning to smile as she left the room.

"She's sweet," Jake said.

"Yes she is. Should I be worried about the competition?"

"Did I ask *her* to marry me?"

Jake came and sat beside me on the bed, gently tucking

a lock of hair behind my ear.

"Maybe you should," I countered. "I mean, at the very least she's probably showered in the last three days, and she doesn't look like warmed over death...literally."

Jake grimaced, "You could lose all your hair, all your teeth, not shower for weeks and I wouldn't care. I love *you*, Madeline Smith."

"Ha! You say that now. Trust me, after a week of no showering, you wouldn't come within ten feet of me," I teased.

"That sounds like a challenge," Jake countered as we relaxed into our old, flirtatious banter.

"I suppose that just because I love you, and tomorrow *is* my wedding day, I will shower tonight. You will just have to wait to see how badly I can stink until after we're married. But..." I hesitated, trying to determine how to continue, "Maybe you don't really know what you want. Do you really know me well enough to want to marry me? I mean, we're friends and all, but do you realize we've never even kissed?"

I instantly regretted asking such a stupidly obvious question. My heart pounded sending blood rushing. I was embarrassed that I exposed my insecurity. Of course he knew we had never kissed.

Jake's dimples reemerged. "If I remember correctly, it wasn't from a lack of effort on my part. *Somebody* fled the ball early and it wasn't even midnight! How's a guy supposed to work around that?"

Blushing heat filled my cheeks — at least it was helping

my coloring.

"Were you trying to kiss me?" I asked, trying unsuccessfully to feign innocence.

Jake leaned closer, eyes locked on mine, our faces only inches apart.

"I'm willing to prove it right here, right now."

His mouth lingering dangerously close to my own, Jake watched me intently. I stared into his expressive hazel eyes as he placed his hand gently aside my head. I hoped he couldn't hear the unsteady rhythm of my heart.

"I haven't brushed my teeth today," I panicked, turning my head aside. I was immediately disappointed in myself as I pushed him gently away.

Jake erupted with laughter and sitting up said, "Darn it Maddy, if I didn't know any better I would think you were trying to *avoid* kissing me!"

Completely flushed with humiliation now, I said, "I promise, I really do want to kiss you, it's just..." I tried to think of how to finish, "...it's just, this is not how I want our first kiss to be, me laying here in a hospital bed, unkempt and un-showered. I want it to be...romantic."

Saying those words I realized how unrealistic those expectations were. How romantic could a hospice center be?

"Hmmm," Jake thought carefully. "You're right. This isn't very romantic." He looked around, assessing our surroundings. "I promise you, Maddy, tomorrow will be the most romantic day of your life. Who says a wedding takes months to plan? Just wait..." he trailed off.

Suddenly, Jake leapt from the bed, startling me enough to stop my fluttering heart momentarily, before returning it to the rapid, pounding cadence of moments before.

There was a spark of energy and determination in his expression as he gazed down at me, "Will you be okay if I leave for a few hours?"

His enthusiasm was overshadowed by a glimmer of doubt as he spoke, a flash of concern flickered in his eyes. I wondered how he could be so certain a miracle would occur, yet so worried about leaving me for a few hours.

"I'll be fine, trust me," I assured him, although I couldn't believe anything I said would dispel his angst, "Where are you going?"

"First off, you've convinced me that *I* need to shower, or *you* may have second thoughts about marrying *me*," he winked, distracting me once again with his devastatingly handsome smile. "And I have some things I need to do before Sabrina goes off shift, stop being so nosy. I'll be back soon. Is it okay if I sleep here tonight?"

"Aren't you going to tell your *fiancé* what you're up to?"

"Nope."

I tried my best to pout, but his goofy, devious smile forced the corners of my mouth upward.

"Well fine, be that way," I protested, still trying not to smile. "Maybe you should just stay at your place tonight."

He looked stricken. "What? I'm sorry, I didn't mean…"

I smirked, knowing that I gained the upper hand. "You aren't supposed to see the bride after midnight on her wedding day until she walks down the aisle. It's tradition and bad luck if you don't obey!" I teased, hoping he would stay despite my lame argument.

Relaxing Jake countered, "Good point but, I think we can make an exception in our case. Nothing about this wedding is traditional, and as for the bad luck..."

"Right," I interrupted, wanting to steer the conversation away from my depressing circumstances. "I just thought I should point out the facts, or superstitions, or whatever you want to call them. I want you to stay tonight. On the couch, I mean...not...you know..."

"Of course not!" Jake said. "Just what kind of man do you think I am? All you women are just trying to use me for my body!" He winked though his face flushed in embarrassment.

"*All...*" I rolled my eyes, realizing his statement was truer that jest.

He stared for a long moment, focused ardently on me.

"What?" I finally asked, feeling self conscious.

"Nothing, I'm just thinking."

"Don't hurt yourself."

"Ha, ha."

In a more serious tone I asked, "What are you thinking?"

"You'll find out tomorrow."

"What are you up to?"

His eyes sparkled as he spoke, "Okay, I'll only be a few hours, and this doesn't count."

Leaning forward he kissed me on top of my head, then grinning, he walked toward the door. Just before exiting, he called, "Get some rest, soon-to-be Mrs. Kavanaugh! I'll be back!"

Chapter Ten

Forty-five minutes after Jake left, Jenn danced through my door carrying a large bundle of white garments.

"We're in luck!" she mused. "I hit the jackpot of white prom dresses at the first store! White must be in vogue this season! These are my favorite three and I have two more in the car. Come on, get your behind out of bed and let's try them on!" Taking a moment to look around the room, she added, "Where's Jake?"

"I don't know," I shrugged.

Jenn's disapproving frown demanded further explanation.

"Well," I met her expectant stare. "He mentioned he had some errands to run and left kind of mysteriously, like he's up to something. He wouldn't tell me anything. He only said he'd be back in a few hours."

Appeased by my response Jenn teased, "He just proposed and you've already lost track of him? I thought you were supposed to be the old ball and chain! Oh, that reminds me, let me see that rock!"

I held out my left hand so Jenn could appraise the ring now adorning its third finger.

Jenn gave a low whistle. "Wow, that's a big diamond," she said.

I realized I hadn't stopped to admire the ring Jake offered with his proposal. I studied the band that dwarfed the slim finger it rested upon. A large emerald cut diamond, at least one karat, sat on a gold band. The precisely cut diamond glinted little specks of colored light as I rotated my hand back and forth. The beauty of it took my breath away. It was the exact ring I would choose if given the option.

Jenn forced a crooked grin, "I didn't realize he picked the biggest diamond of the bunch."

"You *knew* about this?" I gasped.

"Well, um, we might have gone shopping a couple weeks ago," she said, unrepentant. "I borrowed one of the rings you wanted me to sell so they could size this one correctly. I hope it fits."

"Yes," I sighed. "It fits perfectly."

I looked disparagingly at the diamond.

"What's wrong? Don't you like it?"

"I love it."

Jenn's brow furrowed, her eyes focused on my expression, "What is it then?"

"It's just, well, I've been such a complete (and pardon my French)...ass...to you both, yet you loved me anyway. How could you even put up with me? I feel so ashamed of myself."

Jenn placed the mound of dresses on the room's lone reclining chair, then sat on the edge of the bed, laying herself against me in a gentle embrace.

"Hey, give us a little credit; we knew that wasn't the real Maddy. I kept thinking how difficult this must be for you. How unfair it seemed and how, if I was struggling to come to grips, well, it must be twice as disconcerting for you! We both understood that you had to deal with your feeling and that before..." she trailed off. "Well, we knew you, the real you, would be back."

"I still don't know how he could possibly want to marry me. Is he only doing this because I'm dying?" The question felt unappreciative, but I knew I could ask Jenn anything and she would answer me honestly.

Jenn rolled her eyes, "Maddy, that guy loves you and I know he would marry you whether you were dying or not. Trust me on this."

"Yes, but I *am* dying, so maybe that swayed his decision. I just don't want to see him setting himself up to get hurt. I mean, I'm not going to be around much longer and there will be bills to pay..." I hesitated, trying to come up with more reasons why this marriage would not be advantageous. I felt torn between the idea that Jake must be forcing himself to marry me in an act of chivalry and the fact that he may just love me the same way I loved him. Part of me, the bigger part, selfishly wanted to be Jake's wife despite the circumstances. Yet another part kept screaming inside my head that this would end up hurting him more in the end. I knew I couldn't argue with Jake, not that it would change his resolve, but I needed to voice my concerns to Jenn. Maybe she could talk some sense into him.

"Okay, so the fact that you're dying might have inspired him to act a bit quicker—let's face it, the guy waited three years to expose his feelings, he's not a fast burner—but I sincerely believe, with all my heart, on a Bible if you want me swear to on it, that he would have proposed at some point. You two were meant to be together. Aren't you best friends at work? Don't you hang out together all the time during the day?"

"Well, yes, but that's work..."

"Hello? Maddy? Where do you spend the majority of your day?"

"Work." I conceded.

"And if he is your best friend for, say, eighty percent of your waking hours—and I'm willing to guess one hundred percent of your dreams—then why does it matter where you two got to know each other? *You* love him enough to marry him after *only* working together for three years, right?"

"True." I didn't like that my self-deprecating theory was being blown out of the water.

"So *why* is it so difficult for you to imagine that he feels the same way about you? You *are* worth it, Maddy. Believe it or not, you are worth it."

I felt my eyes moisten. I sighed once more, staring at the ring, the symbol of Jake's never ending love for me. Reluctantly I decided to be content with whatever time I had left to spend with him, crazy as it seemed or not.

"Okay, before I start crying, can we please try on these dresses?" I muttered, wiping the moisture from my eyes.

"Yay!" Jenn cooed, leaping from my side, gathering the mound of dresses into her arms.

I sat up slowly and slid myself to the edge of the bed. As I stood, my legs buckled. I began to fall, but I quickly threw the weight of my body back toward the bed. Clinging to the hospital bedrail, I waited, annoyed with my lack of strength as Jenn dropped the dresses on the floor and rushed to my side.

"Sorry," I apologized as she helped me to my feet.

"For what?"

"I guess I'm just a little weaker than I realized."

"Oh, Yeah, that's something you need to apologize for," Jenn mocked, once again rolling her eyes in an overly exaggerated motion.

She helped me to the bathroom, propping me against the sink. I reached out to brace my hand on the metal chair rail that lined the wall beside it.

"Will you be okay for a sec while I get the dresses?"

"Yes, I'm fine."

I looked at my reflection in the mirror for the first time

in weeks. Until now I avoided seeing myself, trying to escape the grim reality that my body was quickly deteriorating. My ashen skin intensified the dark circles shadowing the space below my sunken eyes. My disheveled hair stood in knotted clumps around my head. I laughed internally at Jake's resolve to marry a deathly clown. Glancing down, I was shocked by the appearance of my thin frame; I realized how quickly I was fading. Bones protruded beneath my skin, visible through the hospital gown that attempted to cover me. I grimaced, realizing that I would not be a beautiful, blushing bride. Instead, I would be the pale vision of death—a ghostly figure floating down the aisle with transparent skin holding up a white gown that matched my complexion—that is, if I could even walk by tomorrow.

Jenn skipped back into the room and noticed my glum demeanor. "Now what?"

"Nothing," I lied. "Just wondering what I am going to do with this hair…"

Hanging the dresses on the shower curtain bar behind us, Jenn turned and briefly picked at a knotted wad of my hair. "That will depend entirely on which dress you choose!" She obviously thought my hair was not beyond repair at this point. "Here, try this one first," she offered up the first gown. "I won't tell you which is my favorite, but…this is my favorite!"

Jenn could always make me smile. We closed the bathroom door, not so much for privacy but for use of the full length mirror that hung behind it. With help from Jenn,

I slipped into the strapless gown, detailed with sequins and lace, marked size four.

"Oh, this will not do," she said as she zipped up the back.

The dress hung loosely, forcing me to hold it in place so it wouldn't slip down my torso. My skin looked completely washed out next to the bright white coloring of the dress.

"Seriously? I figured I wouldn't be a size six anymore, but smaller than a four?"

"Hmm," Jenn deliberated. "Now that I see this one on you, I don't like it. Let's try the next."

"Okay."

I didn't need to unzip, the dress slid right off my skeletal frame. Jenn held up the next selection. It was also strapless, formfitting, with a crossing pattern in the front and frilly ruffles starting just below the hip.

"Um, I don't think that's my style," I said without even trying it on.

Jenn looked at the dress, then nodded in agreement, "I took a chance on this one, but I think you will like the next one even better. I'll be right back."

A few seconds later she returned with the third gown. I stepped into this dress noticing the tag read size zero. I winced. Looking at my sickly body, I realized how many models intentionally made themselves ill to become a size zero. I shuddered over our culture's misplaced sense of beauty. I wondered what young girls would think if they saw how a size zero truly looked, when not gracing the photographically enhanced cover of a magazine.

Ignoring the ghastly person in the mirror, I slipped my

arms through the dress's spaghetti straps and Jenn zipped it up the back. We both looked up and smiled—it was perfect.

Instead of gleaming white, the dress's ivory color reduced the severity of my pale skin, making me look like a porcelain doll from the early nineteenth century. Above its empire waistline, soft chiffon gathered along the bosom, then cascaded long and flowing to the floor. Below my chest, a two inch band of small, silver beads adorned the fitted bodice, swirling in an intricate scroll-like pattern

Jenn whistled, "I think we have a winner."

I started to agree, but my throat caught. I fell forward, grasping for the guard rail on the wall, trying to keep from gagging on the wet mucus lodged within my trachea. Bracing my body against the sink, I labored to expel the junk that blocked my airway. Finally, able to breathe again I glanced into the basin shocked to see it stained with streaks of red. Blood. The salty metallic taste lingered in my mouth.

"Get this dress off of me!" I stammered.

Jenn didn't move. I knew she was terrified, but I needed her to grasp the urgency of my request.

"Now, Jenn, get the dress off!"

I continued clutching the counter, hanging my head low inside the sink. As crazy as it sounds, I was afraid of splattering blood across the dress, worried Jenn may not be able to return it if I stained it red. I watched as random trails of blood trickled toward the sink drain.

"I think we should call the nurse." Jenn started for the

red call cord hanging next to the toilet.

"Wait," I begged through gagging breaths. "Get me out of this dress first. I don't want to ruin it."

"You are coughing up blood and you're worried about the dress? Maddy I..."

"Jenn, don't fight with me! Just get the dress off!"

My frustrated bark set off another round of wet coughing. After what seemed like an eternity I spat more blood. I once again caught my breath.

"I'm sorry," I apologized to Jenn, hoping she wouldn't freak out.

"Has this happened before?" Jenn asked, ignoring my apology.

"No," I admitted. Staring her down in the mirror I added, "But we can worry about that in a minute. Now get the dress off of me or you won't be able to return it."

Jenn hesitated, a flash of uncertainty crossed her face, but finally compliant she unzipped the dress and helped me back into my hospital gown.

Another spasm rocked my body and I crumpled against the counter, heaving unsteady breaths, trying desperately to force the sludge from my lungs.

Jenn pulled the cord. I heard the voice of a nurse come over the speaker, "Yes? What can I..."

"She's coughing up blood! I need some help in here!" Jenn's pitch was high and panicked.

I managed to free a large clot just as Sabrina and her aide rushed into the bathroom. My airway finally cleared, the aide stayed behind as Sabrina helped me to my bed. I felt guilty leaving a disgusting mess behind.

"Please," I said, catching my breath as we hobbled across the room, Sabrina bearing most of my weight. "I'll clean up, just give me a second to recover."

Sabrina's voice spoke with sweet compassion, "Oh sweetie, don't worry. We deal with this every day. It is our job. Do you need any oxygen?"

"No, I think it's passed."

Sabrina swiftly picked me up and laid me on the bed, then stuck a thermometer into my mouth.

Jenn stood against the far wall, clinging to the ivory garment like a security blanket. I tried to smile, reassuring her that I was okay, but before the thermometer beeped its finish, I was hacking up more blood. This time, Sabrina reached above my head, withdrawing the suction tube from its place on the wall. Despite my mental protest, I allowed her to force the tube down my burning throat and free the large amount of blood choking my airway.

"I think I'll page the doctor," she said. "I think we need to update your medications after this new development."

I nodded and she left the room. The nurse's aide appeared from the bathroom smiling her gentle, strategically placed smile and said, "All cleaned up. Let me know if you need anything else."

"I'm so embarrassed," I muttered.

Jenn trembled in the corner, using the wall to steady herself as she spoke, "Embarrassed? Seriously? Maddy... I..."

I looked at Jenn, her eyes brimming with tears as she

stifled a sob. She clung to the dress like a child, holding it for security as the grim reality of my death sank in. There was nothing I could say. It was time to face the fact that my end was near.

Chapter Eleven

The next few hours were a blur of activity as doctors, nurses, and specialists traipsed through my room offering advice, updated care plans, and extremely potent medication for my comfort. My coughing spells continued, although the amount of blood lessened after I expelled the first several clots.

Jenn sat entranced, ignoring the commotion, staring at the painting above my bed that now not-so-secretly housed emergency medical equipment. The last doctor to enter my room gave me a strong dose of morphine. I didn't need to wait for the drug to kick in.

Jenn and I hadn't spoken. Periodically we glanced at each other, uncomfortable with the silence that now consumed our visit. The clock read six thirty when I heard Jake's voice in the hall. I knew Sabrina was giving him the latest update.

I wished the morphine, and whatever else they gave me, would knock me out completely. I desperately wanted to be asleep so I wouldn't have to face his concern. He wished for a miracle. I knew this news was sure to crush him.

Jake appeared in the doorway, eyes creased with worry.

I offered a goofy, intoxicated smile. "Hey you," I slurred.

Jake's dimples appeared as he smiled back, but his eyes remained cautious. "I see the drugs are kicking in."

"Yeah, I'm kind of sleepy."

Jake came and sat beside me on the bed. "Listen, before you head off to dream land, I need you to sign a few papers, you know, just in case."

"What papers?"

Sabrina entered the room with two aides. "Hey Maddy." She stood above me looking down, trying to draw my attention back from my fuzzy morphine-laden world. "Remember earlier…we talked about a living will and power of attorney for Jake?"

"Oh Yeah," my voice sounded silly, carefree.

"Okay," she continued. "I understand this probably isn't the best time to do this, but I brought witnesses and you can say no to anything I go over with you, okay?"

"Where do I sign?" my voice slurred.

"I don't know if she has the capacity to do this right now," Jake's voice came from the other side of the bed. I tried to turn my head in his direction, but the ceiling started spinning.

"This might be your last chance. Maddy may never again have the capacity..." Jenn's voice came from across the room.

"But what if someone challenges its legality," Jake's voice volleyed back. This tennis match of an argument was driving me insane,

"I am capable of making a decision here," I challenged, shouting to the ceiling which, for the moment, had stopped spinning.

"Of course you are," Sabrina's voice was steady, strong,

I turned my head back toward her voice, "Where do I sign?"

Sabrina held up several papers in her hands, "I'll go over each form with you so you know what you are signing."

"No need," I said. "Just hand me a pen and show me where. I trust all of you."

"Maddy, I really think..." Jake began.

"I trust you," I interrupted.

Sabrina flipped pages and I signed each line. Jake signed them too.

"Last one," Sabrina said as she laid the paper in front of me. I noticed her expectant glance toward Jake. Something about her look struck me as funny and I giggled. I didn't turn to see if Jake's reaction held any meaning, because truly, I don't think I could decipher the letters of my own name at this point. The morphine had me on the edge of reality.

I glanced at the paper through dreamy eyes. It looked different than the others, familiar somehow, but none of the jumbled words made sense.

"Sign here," Sabrina pointed to a line. I tried to make out what the paper said, but everything blurred together.

I shrugged, or at least I think I did. Unable process the mystery words on the page, I scribbled what hopefully looked like my signature across the line. Sabrina handed the document over to Jake, whose hand I heard sign the document, then it returned to Sabrina.

Jenn walked cautiously over to stand next to Sabrina. "How are you feeling?" she asked.

"Oh good," I replied, "It's all good."

Jenn smiled—I think—amused by my intoxication. I smiled back.

"We better to do this quick, before she fades," Jenn said as my mind floated.

"What are we doing?" I sang. My musical whimsy triggered another giggle.

"Just call it a rehearsal for tomorrow," Jenn replied.

"Rehearsal?" I found this extremely funny and erupted with hysterical laughing. "Re-hear-sal. Re-*hear*-sal." I repeated. "That's a funny word. Re-hear-*sal.*"

"This isn't going to work," Jenn sounded annoyed, a fact that continued to amuse me.

"Let's just try," I heard Jake's voice. "Maddy said earlier that she is all about tradition." I perceived a hint of sarcasm in his voice, but it seemed less important than my newfound favorite word.

The only words I remember were, "Will...Jake... husband...death?" Jenn's voice sounded like it came from across the room, growing more distant with each articulation.

"Um hmm," I mumbled in approval, slipping into a dream where Jake was my husband and we were living in a little cottage by a lake.

I didn't hear the rest of what she said. I smiled in my dreamy world. Everyone sounded happy, and so was I— somewhere in the recesses of my mind.

Jake moved beside me on the bed. I felt him kiss my forehead, "Well, get some rest now. You have a big day tomorrow."

"You can still back out," I tried to make my words coherent, but they sounded jumbled even in my own ears. Turning toward him I said, "Tell Jenn to return the dress. I tried to not get blood on it. It's too pretty."

I heard Jenn choke back a sob.

"I'm not backing out," Jake said.

"Fine," I said, retreating further into my drug induced haze, "I love you, you know?"

"I love you too," Jake whispered and gently kissed my cheek.

"Tell Jenn I love her too, and I am so sorry for scaring her," I garbled.

*****

I woke to the sound of muffled snoring coming from the recliner beside me. I knew it was Jake; he had spent the night like I asked. Though the room was dark, I could see his tall frame scrunched into the little chair. I felt a twinge of guilt about his sleeping arrangement, but was glad to see that he could somehow sleep despite his surroundings. I supposed the recliner was more comfortable than the hard wooden pew he had slept on over the past few weeks. I couldn't tell how long I had been asleep and wondered if I should call for a nurse to administer more drugs. I sputtered a few coughs, trying to contain them inside my chest, not wanting to wake Jake.

Turning my body to search for the nurse's call button, I noticed a figure looming in my open doorway. The shadowy outline of a man filled the frame, his appearance masked by the backlight emanating from the hallway. I assumed he was the guest of another patient, curiously peeking in on one of the neighbors. My room sat adjacent the nurses' station and the back entrance to the facility, so it wasn't odd to see someone glance through my open door now and again. It was odd, though, for someone to stand motionless, so brazenly inquisitive about another patient.

As my eyes adjusted I could make out his face, his eyes staring directly into mine. Most people, when caught intruding, would turn and walk away. This man continued to gaze directly at, almost through me. I made a quick glance toward Jake—still snoring quietly in his chair—wondering if the nurses were away from their station. My heart raced as I marveled at what this man could possibly want. How he could be so bold standing there, unconcerned that at any moment a nurse could return and catch his nosy intrusion?

My eyes returned to the man's face. His features were attractive, yet hard. Foreign, yet familiar. Dark, yet filled with light. As I tried to piece together the stranger's identity and what he could possibly want, a feeling of calm washed over me. I took a full, deep breath of air as my lungs instantly cleared of obstruction.

I must be dreaming, I thought. *The drugs are still in my system.*

The man smiled as if reading my thoughts, still focused intently on me. I was no longer concerned about his intentions, instead we stared, both curious about the other. My whole body relaxed. I didn't feel ill. I realized the calming waves that lapped over me felt familiar. Something about the stranger pulled me, called to me. I wanted to follow him, but he raised his hands, motioning for me to stay. Still hypnotized, it did not seem odd that he knew what I was thinking.

From the corner Jake muttered, releasing me from my trance. I quickly looked toward him again, worried that if he woke, he would alarm the stranger in my doorway causing him to flee. I didn't want to lose this feeling of peace. But Jake slept, the quiet, steady rhythm of his snore returned.

I glanced back at the door, but the man was gone. I had looked at Jake for less than two seconds, there was no way the stranger could have completely disappeared from view.

I should have seen movement in my peripheral vision. I glanced all around. He was gone, but the feeling of peace remained. I took another deep breath, reveling in the fullness of air that filled my lungs.

A nurse walked into the room and approached my bed.

"How are you feeling?" she whispered, noticing that I was awake. "I've just come to take your vitals and give you more morphine."

"That man in the hall, who was he?" I asked.

The nurse looked confused. "What man? I didn't see anybody."

I shrugged, "He must be visiting another patient. Maybe he left through the exit before you returned to the nurses' station."

The nurse touched my forehead then said, "Sweetie, I haven't left the nurses' station in over an hour, and we lock this exit after eleven. No one is allowed in or out. Morphine does crazy things to the mind...probably just a hallucination. Did he look familiar? Like someone you know?"

"No, I've never seen him before. Just a hallucination, I guess," I sighed.

I thought certain I saw a man, but the hallucination theory made sense—especially since this man seemed to read my thoughts. Still, the peaceful feeling that overcame me while in his presence lingered.

The nurse nodded as she pushed more morphine into my mouth through a tiny syringe. I grimaced at the awful taste. At once the drug's artificial calming effect replaced the surreal peacefulness of before. I wished she could take it back out of my system as its heavy, disorienting fog fell over my consciousness.

Maybe I was just hallucinating. I considered the nurse's suggestion as my thoughts retreated back into the shadows of my mind.

******

I woke, yet my eyes remained closed. I was afraid to open them and see what today, my wedding day, would deliver. A memory of a dream lingered, but I could not remember its details or importance. Whispered voices conversed behind me on the other side of the room. I lay still, straining to hear.

"I heard she slept well last night." I recognized Sabrina's voice.

"Yes," Jake whispered. "I don't know what to do. There was so much blood. I knew this would be difficult, but..."

I heard him choke. I opened my eyes and noticed darkness still hung over the world beyond my window.

"I'm so sorry," Sabrina consoled. "I will be honest; things are going to get strange at this point. She's not long for this world. People this close start to act in a way that we consider to be odd, but..."

She trailed off.

"What do you mean?" Jake asked after a few moments of silence.

"Well," Sabrina answered, hesitation in her voice. "The

night nurse told me she saw someone in the doorway last night."

"What? This door?" Jake startled. "Who?"

My mind flickered to an image of the man at my door.

"There was no one there," Sabrina said.

"Was it the drugs?"

"Could have been, but these types of visions are not uncommon. Many people approaching death begin to see things that we do not."

"Like, hallucinations?"

"Possibly, but personally I think it is more than that. I think as we grow closer to death we start transitioning to the other side. I have witnessed some people nearing death say they see light, angels, family who have already passed. They have a way of traveling back and forth between this world and the next."

I certainly didn't believe in ghostly visitations, but the peace I felt while observing my unexpected guest seemed too surreal for anything from this world.

"So, she saw an apparition?" Jake asked.

"I don't know," Sabrina replied. "But she saw *something*. The fact that she is coughing up blood and seeing things outside our view makes me feel she is growing close."

"So, what does that mean? How will it happen? How much time do I have left with her?"

"I can't tell you with any certainty how much time is left, although the dying can control their passing more than we give them credit. Maddy will get sicker. She will start to cough up more blood. Soon, she will no longer eat or drink and will slip into a coma. At some point she will decide it is her time. It will be peaceful."

Jake's stifled cry broke my heart. I wanted to stay with him—grow old with him—but some dreams would never be reality.

Jake sobbed for several minutes before he gathered himself together.

"Will you be okay? I have to make a quick check on my other patients," Sabrina said.

I assumed Jake nodded because she immediately said, "Call if you need me."

I listened as Jake returned to the recliner and fought against his emotions. I wanted to tell him I was awake, to hold him, yet I knew he needed to be alone. He needed time to grieve.

As I lay watching the darkness of night outside my window give way to the breaking dawn, a voice repeated in my head, *There has to be something more. There just has to be.*

This was not how I imagined waking on my wedding day.

Chapter Twelve

I waited to speak until I heard Jake's cries subside...until his grieving ran its course. I rolled over and smiled, trying to appear like I'd just awakened, pretending to be unaware of the conversation he and Sabrina shared earlier.

"Hey," I mumbled as daylight filled the room.

"Good morning gorgeous," Jake smiled back. "How are you feeling today?" he asked, coming to sit beside me on my bed.

"Okay," I answered, drawing a deep breath, thankful that whatever relieved my coughing the night before seemed to have continued into this morning. "How are you?"

"I'm fantastic. Today is the day I get to marry the woman I love," Jake's smile broadened, yet behind his smile he looked defeated. His words did not produce the enthusiastic tone they meant to convey.

"Still time…" I offered, but stopped short seeing distress contort Jake's otherwise happy face.

"I heard you had some pretty interesting dreams last night," Jake redirected our conversation.

"I guess. I can't really remember much," I lied.

"Yeah, they have you on some pretty strong meds, huh?"

A laughing sigh burst from my throat, "I think I'm going to ask Sabrina to not administer any drugs today."

"Maddy, if you need…"

"I'll be fine for one day," I argued. "I don't want to be a zombie at my own wedding. Do you really want to marry the Bride of Frankenstein?"

"Was the Bride of Frankenstein a zombie?" Jake chuckled, tucking a lock of hair behind my ear.

"You know what I mean!"

Jake relaxed, "Okay, I guess I can understand, but if you start to feel ill and need…"

"I promise I will take my medication if I truly need it."

He seemed appeased. "I have to run a few errands this morning." Frowning he added, "I don't want to leave your side, though."

He searched my expression, looking for any sign that I wanted him to stay.

"I'll be fine for a few hours, promise," I replied.

"Yeah, you said that last night," Jake argued.

"I will be fine. Will you please trust me?"

Jake looked uncertain, but he shrugged. "Okay. Besides,

Jenn is coming in a bit to start your makeover. I'm hoping to be back before the fun ends."

He grinned knowing I dreaded allowing Jenn full reign over my appearance.

"On second thought, please stay!" I pleaded. "Keep her from making me look like a disco ball...or *worse*."

"What could be worse than a disco ball?" Jake tousled my hair.

I stuck out my tongue.

Jake added, "As much as I would love to protect you from Jenn's sinister devices, I've already been informed that once she arrives I'm kicked out until I meet you at the altar."

"Fine!" I pouted. "Well, in case you can't recognize me, I will be the one in white."

"I'll keep that in mind," Jake smiled. Hesitating, he added, "You're sure you'll be okay?"

"Do you think Jenn will let you stay if I say no?"

"Probably not."

"Just get out of here and go make yourself pretty for me," I teased.

"You will have the nurse call me if you start to feel ill?" Jake procrastinated.

"Go!" I ordered.

"The nagging starts already!"

"You'd better believe it! Wow, maybe I have a natural talent for being a wife. Now get out of here!"

Jake kissed my cheek and left.

Minutes ticked by in the stillness of the morning. I

listened as hospice workers busied themselves in the hallway. Outside, clanking trays announced my breakfast delivery before it came through my door. When it arrived, I forced myself to eat, trying to gain strength for the big day's events. The most I could force down was one quarter of a bagel with cream cheese and a small piece of banana. Food no longer appealed to me. Everything was tasteless. The act of chewing drained every ounce of energy from my body. Swallowing no longer seemed a natural reflex— eating had become a chore. I was starting to understand why someone would accept death...welcome it, actually.

I had yet to see Sabrina this morning. I figured she was busy with other patients, but I wanted to ask her about my hallucination. I didn't want to bring it up around Jake, knowing it would upset him, but I knew Sabrina would provide me with straightforward answers. Somewhere, deep inside, I needed confirmation that I wasn't going completely insane.

A man's voice came from the hallway. I probably would not have noticed it except for the fact that I heard him speak my name, "Madeline Smith," and a nurse's voice direct him toward my room. I didn't recognize the man's voice. I thought I'd met all the doctors and nurses at this facility. It wasn't Jake, or Mr. Sharp, the only two men I knew who would visit, and I hadn't seen the latter since that fateful going away party.

I watched the man approach the nurses' station outside my door.

"We're here to see Madeline Smith," the voice echoed

through the small corridor.

We? More than one? I didn't understand why my heart pounded, but suddenly my body's flight response took over. Too weak to move, I felt vulnerable. Instinct warned me of some danger that I needed to escape.

I recognized Sabrina's voice say, "Hi. May I help you?"

"Yes, I'm Doctor Dennis Anderson, and this is my research assistant Dr. Samantha Blakemore. We need to see a patient of yours, a Miss Madeline Smith. We think she may qualify for an experimental treatment we've been working on."

"If she agrees to be our test subject," another voice, this one female, chimed in.

"Of course," Doctor Anderson said. "If she agrees."

Experimental treatment? What did that mean?

"What agency are you from?" Sabrina's voice carried authority, un-intimidated by the doctor's pushy nature.

"We work for Senator Clay Morris. He is the funding behind our research. Samantha, please show her the paperwork."

There was a rustle of papers, followed by Sabrina's voice, "Right this way please doctors."

I watched as three figures filled my doorway. First Sabrina entered, coming to stand directly beside my bed. She was followed by the two doctors, the female lugging a large suitcase on wheels behind her. The man, who I assumed was Dr. Anderson, was tall, in his mid forties, with graying hair that he kept closely cut against his receding hairline. His face showed signs of exhaustion, wrinkles highlighting frown, rather than laugh lines, and his eye brows seemed permanently drawn together in the act of deep concentration. His eyes were a soft shade of brown, but nothing in their expression reflected any softness of heart. My fear response seemed warranted in his presence.

Doctor Anderson's companion, Doctor Blakemore, stood about four inches shorter than Anderson's tall frame. Her brown, shoulder length hair framed her pretty, oval face that was adorned with a pointed nose, expressive green eyes and a smile that balanced against Dr. Anderson's stern and hardened appearance. As they entered the room, I could deduce that she was the Yin to his Yang. She compensated for his clunky, determined steps with an elegant, yet at the same time awkward glide. It was difficult to imagine what cosmic forces drew these individuals together as research partners, but whatever fate brought them together, it seemed to work in their favor.

My heart slowed, somehow comforted by Dr. Blakemore's appearance—probably the precise reason for her presence.

"If you will excuse us please, nurse," Dr. Anderson glared at Sabrina.

Sabrina's eyes focused on me. The same sense of worry that was eating around the edges of my sanity flashed across her face. "Are you okay?"

"Yes, sure. No problem," I answered, hoping she didn't notice my voice waver.

Sabrina held her stare a moment longer, then shrugging,

turned for the door. "You know where the call button is if you need me."

Dr. Anderson followed Sabrina, closing the door behind her. Alone with the two doctors, my heart restarted its fearful flurry inside my chest.

Leaving the suitcase by the door, Dr. Blakemore walked over and lugged the cumbersome recliner closer to my bedside. She sat down beside me as Dr. Anderson stood impatiently at the foot of my bed.

I felt Dr. Blakemore take my right hand in hers as she began to speak, "Hi Madeline, my name is Dr. Samantha Blakemore, but you can call me Sam. This is Dr. Dennis Anderson."

I didn't take my eyes off Dr. Anderson. He seemed annoyed that Sam was doing all the talking, yet he never said a word. Turning to face the other doctor, I saw a gentleness in her eyes that calmed my racing heart.

"Hello," I said. My feeble voice sounded weaker with each passing hour. "Are you with hospice?"

Dr. Anderson let out an exasperated cough but Sam continued, ignoring him. "No, we are not from hospice. We are from a research lab working on regenerative medicine. Specifically, cancer related regenerative medicine."

"Regenerative medicine?" I asked.

"Yes," Sam continued. "For years we have been studying cell-based therapies to help the body fight disease and repair damaged tissues. Since the early nineties, institutions like ours have been trying to use stem cells to help in the fight against certain genetic and chronic diseases."

I nodded, recalling bits and pieces of this controversial research reported in the news.

"Funded by a grant from Senator Morris of Alabama, we studied cell modification. We knew that immortal stem cells could morph into other types of cells through a process called differentiation. For awhile now we've used stem cells to replace damaged cells in the body, but then we considered the possibility of using stem cells to replace every cell in our bodies. Or, I guess a better way of saying it—we've researched the ability to change every cell in our body back into its fetal stem cell form."

Dumbstruck, I stared blankly at the sweet doctor.

Dr. Blakemore drew a deep breath. "Well, in the course of our research, we think we've not only discovered a cure for cancer on this cellular level, but we stumbled upon something that will alter the lives of humankind for eternity. Six genetic mutations and everything in our world will change forever."

"A cure for cancer?" My soul swelled with hope. Did I dare believe there could be a chance for me?

"This is where we run into a bit of a snag," she sighed, looking very serious for the first time since she entered my room. "You see, we have only tested on mice and rabbits. The gravity of what we've discovered makes this research very...sensitive. Senator Morris doesn't want our discovery to go public until we are one hundred percent certain that our hypothesis will work on a human. He is worried that if this information is released, it would create mass hysteria. People would loot and riot just to get their hands on our serum, even before its safety is confirmed. But without releasing information and receiving FDA approval for human trials we won't be able to prove our hypothesis. It is kind of a catch twenty-two."

"I don't understand," I interjected. "Experimental cures for cancer are announced all the time. What makes this one so sensitive?"

"It isn't just a cure for cancer," Dr. Anderson spoke, drawing my attention to the foot of my bed. "We believe six genetic mutations will heal our bodies on every level. Nothing, not even death, can harm us any longer. These mutations will make everyone immortal."

Chapter Thirteen

"Immortal?" I wondered how much morphine the nurse administered the night before. Sabrina was right; things were starting to get strange the closer I got to death.

Dr. Anderson stated, "We think that as long as an individual receives this genetic treatment within one hour, on average, after death—before the body's major tissues begin to break down—or well before death occurs as a preventative measure, this serum will unlock the cell's potential to repair itself. We believe, if the individual has already received treatment, catastrophic damage can occur to the body and that individual's cells will heal themselves, returning back to normal, like nothing ever happened." He gauged my reaction closely.

I turned to face Dr. Blakemore again, who was also watching me. "So, there is no way someone could die?" I asked.

"We believe that will be true," Sam answered. "Short of complete cellular disintegration, that is. The problem we face, though, is that although we can heal our injured test specimens in a lab, and their cells show all signs of a complete transfer to an immortal, stem cell state, we can't reproduce a postmortem return to immortality in these animals. Once euthanized, they remain dead."

"I'm confused. You say you've found the key to immortality, but it hasn't worked? Then how can you make such a claim? And where do I fit into all of this?"

"Genetically, humans and animals are close enough in structure for research purposes—some estimates bridge the genetic gap between us and other species within one to five percent, but that percentage varies. Ultimately, one tiny difference can affect the outcome of any study," Sam responded. "Technically, based upon our research and computer simulation, our genetic therapy should work on humans. I can't quite understand what separates us from animals in this case, but I'm sure, in time, we will discover the answer. But I feel this is something the world needs now, not fifty years from now, which is why we need a human test subject to prove our theory."

"And I would be that test subject." I wasn't certain I liked the idea of becoming a human guinea pig. "What about monkeys?"

Dr. Anderson scrunched his face in disgust, "We don't

have the funding. Besides, what monkeys make up for in genetic similarities, they lack in hygiene."

Sam rolled her eyes at the doctor's disdain for primates then added, "We've been looking everywhere for the perfect patient. We needed someone...like you."

"But, why me?"

"You're basically dead," Dr. Anderson cut in. "You are alone, no one will miss you and if this doesn't work, our research will remain safely unknown until we work out the kinks."

Although true, Dr. Anderson's words sucked the air from my lungs.

"You have to forgive my associate," Sam threw a stern look in the other doctor's direction, which he ignored. "Dr. Anderson is so used to working with lab animals he forgets the human element of emotion at times." Returning her attention toward me, she added, "I know this is a difficult decision to spring on you, but I'm afraid I can't give you much time to think it over. We have to leave this morning if you choose to participate. I apologize for the abrupt notice, but we have one other qualified candidate across the country we must reach if you choose not to participate. If something goes wrong, we may not be able to reach him in time. I fear he is a bit closer to the end than you. You must understand that I don't want to wait another two years for someone with your...unique set of circumstances to become available."

I twisted the ring on my left hand that remained

conveniently hidden beneath my bed sheets. Its weight anchored my hand against my heart, reminding me there was one person who would miss me. But this was my only chance. Certainly Jake would understand my sudden departure once he knew the truth.

"I'll do it," I said, ignoring the nagging inner voice that warned me how my decision would hurt Jake...denying him a chance to say goodbye, especially on our wedding day.

"Excellent," Dr. Anderson moved toward the door. "I'll get the nurse to start working on your discharge papers. Dr. Blakemore, have Madeline sign our liability release paperwork and administer the treatment."

"Already?" I stammered, already second-guessing my decision. Dr. Anderson was out the door barking orders at the nurses.

"Don't worry," Sam comforted. "It really should be painless. The mice and rabbits never complained."

"Oh, yes, that's comforting," I mused as she rose from her chair and proceeded to the large suitcase she'd parked in the corner of the room.

With Dr. Anderson absent from the room, and Sam's back turned to me, I slid the engagement ring off my finger and hid it under my pillow. My heart broke imagining Jake's face when he found it, but I had to concentrate on the greater good. In a month or two, when he saw my face, full of life and happiness, he would forget this moment and we would have a real wedding, the wedding of our dreams.

I intentionally avoided the thought that this experiment

might fail and I may never see Jake again.

"Alrighty then," Sam returned to my bedside with a tray of medical supplies. "First I need to start your IV."

In a matter of moments she donned a pair of gloves, swabbed the top of my hand, and inserted a needle and tubing.

"Geez, you were quick," I commented.

"You'd be surprised how large human veins look compared to mice."

"Again, not really comforting," I said.

"I like you. You've got a sense of humor. I think we are going to get along," Sam smiled. "Now, I am going to administer the translated genes into your body through a viral vector, which is essentially a carrier. These little viruses will attach to existing cells, altering the cellular DNA structure. The mutation will affect every cell in your body, turning each cell, in essence, into a stem cell. Affected cancer cells, along with any other damaged or abnormal tissue will be repaired or destroyed and replaced with healthy, immortal genes. During fetal development, your cells sense where they belong and what their function is. Of course, like stem cells, your new cells will maintain their correct function, so you won't grow a nose where your belly button is or something like that."

"Of course, this has only worked with mice," I added.

"And rabbits," Sam chuckled. "So, I have to warn you there is a chance you might end up a little furry."

The astonished look on my face made her burst with laughter, "I'm only joking! And here I gave you credit for having a sense of humor!"

"Sorry," I said.

"No need. I can be a bit cheeky at times," she winked.

"I'm glad. I honestly don't think I would have considered participating in your experiment if Dr. Anderson was the one presenting the case."

"Oh, Dennis is a good man, just a bit out of touch with anything...human." Sam attached a saline bag to the port on my IV.

Sabrina popped her head in my door. "Maddy, I'm sorry to interrupt, but can I talk to you for a second?"

Sam rolled her eyes so only I could see. Like her associate, she obviously didn't hold nurses in very high regard.

"Is that okay?" I asked Sam.

"Sure, I need a minute to get your treatment ready. Nurse, do you have a space that I can use to prepare?"

"Of course, Doctor," Sabrina replied. "Just around the corner—the second door on your left."

Smiling, Sam offered a polite thank you, then zipped her suitcase and wheeled it out the door.

Sabrina approached my bed cautiously.

"Maddy," her soft voice was barely audible. "What are you doing? You can't leave this morning. Whatever treatment these doctors are offering, I'm sure it can wait another day."

"No, Sabrina, it can't," I said in the same hushed manner.

"What about Jake? You're just going to leave him today just before your..."

"I know what today is," I interrupted, not wanting anyone to overhear. "Please Sabrina, please understand. This is my only chance. Sam, I mean, Dr. Blakemore, thinks they've found a cure. *A cure*, Sabrina. Imagine how happy Jake will be when he realizes I am alive."

"But I think Jake should have a say in this too," she countered.

"Sabrina, I appreciate what you are trying to do, but this is for the best. Jake is not my husband yet, and these doctors wouldn't accept me as a test subject if he was. They want me because I am unattached, alone. If I don't go with them, I will die. Maybe not today, but I will be dead soon and that will break Jake's heart more than if I leave now and have the chance to return to him. Please, *please* tell him I didn't mean to hurt him, but at least this way we have a chance. I know you can understand that."

Sabrina bit her lip. Deep concern lined her youthful eyes. She looked like she wanted to say something more, but she only nodded.

"Thank you," I said, my voice barely a whisper.

Again, she nodded and started for the door.

"I'll be back in a moment with your discharge papers." Then turning back toward me she added, "I'll miss you. Promise you will keep me informed on how you're doing. I'll be praying for you the entire time, and I'd better be invited to the wedding when you return."

I winced when the words escaped her lips, but she said, "Don't worry, no one's outside the door. I'll go retrieve the doctor from the break room and tell her you're ready to leave."

"Thank you for everything. I mean it," I said.

Sabrina smiled and left the room. Stillness filled the small space I'd come to call home. I recalled my hallucinated visitor from the night before—trying to conjure his image and the accompanying sense of peace. I forced thoughts to the back of my mind about leaving Jake at the altar. I wondered if Jake would wait for me. I wondered if I would survive. What if I died? Loneliness and fear swept over me in waves.

Chapter Fourteen

With my paperwork signed and good-byes said to Sabrina and the few other staff members I knew, I waited impatiently for Sam and Dr. Anderson to return. The digital clock beside my bed read ten thirty in the morning. I wondered how long Jake had been gone—I didn't notice the clock when he left. My stomach coiled in knots as I realized he could return at any moment. Jenn would be here soon too, wedding dress in hand. I grew restless, uneasy. I had to leave before they got back. In fact, I knew I needed a decent head start. I couldn't have Jake ruin my one chance at life, especially when it meant a real life with him.

My heart picked up its cadence as suffocating pressure

crept across my chest. Anxious to leave, I listened for any sign of Jake or Jenn's arrival. I jumped when the door opened, relieved to see only Sam occupying the threshold.

"Dr. Anderson is getting things set up in our little hospital transport out front. Are you ready?" she asked, bouncing into the room holding a large syringe filled with yellowish liquid. "Last chance to back out."

"No, not backing out, but I'm certainly glad that's going through my IV," I said.

"Ha ha! I could never be *that* sadistic."

Sam hooked the syringe top into the catheter port on my line. "Well, maybe I could be a little," she reconsidered, laughing. "Here we go!"

I watched as she slowly pushed the gelatinous fluid through the syringe and into my body. The burden of Jake's reappearance and the discovery of our engagement disappeared as the fluid flowed into my bloodstream. I breathed a sigh of relief. There was no turning back. Soon, though, panic returned. What if the doctors needed to run tests...maybe this isn't the only part of the treatment. If Jake returned, I could still be rejected as a patient. A clammy chill swept across my body.

"You will feel very cold at first. After a few minutes that will change and you will suddenly feel extremely hot, a byproduct of the heat released during the cellular change."

The injection emptied—its contents coursing through my veins—Sam produced a smaller syringe and plugged it into the catheter. "Just a saline flush," she assured. "To guarantee you receive the entire dosage."

When she finished flushing my line, she walked back to the hallway and returned with a wheel chair, bringing it to my bedside. "Is there anything you would like me to pack for you?" Sam asked, glancing around the room.

An alarm went off in my head, *Time to leave. You have to leave now.*

"Just grab the small suitcase behind that door," I said, pointing to the closet. "I don't have anything else. I really think we should get moving."

Without questioning my anxious tone, Sam grabbed the small bag then hurried to help me into the chair. My body convulsed. Uncontrollable chills shuddered through my body.

Grabbing a few blankets and putting them across my wasted frame, Sam said, "Don't worry, this is all natural. The cold will soon pass."

"M...m...m...mi...mice," I stuttered.

"Mice and rabbits," Sam smiled. "It happens the same way for both. I promise you will be okay in a few minutes."

She grabbed my small overnight bag and set it across my lap. We wheeled out into the hallway which, thankfully, was abandoned at the moment.

Setting off through corridors toward the front entrance of the building, my body shook more violently than before. A nurse emerged from another doorway—as she observed me, concern twisted her pretty face.

"She's fine," Sam assured the young woman. "I'm a doctor. It's part of her treatment."

The nurse only nodded, but kept her eyes fixated

on my face as we passed. We turned another corner, transiting the open common area and the greeter's station, which today occupied two different, yet similarly smiling robots. No one said a word as we hurried by.

The front exit's glass, double sliding doors provided a clear view of my transport vehicle. An unmarked white, boxy van that resembled an ambulance waited, backed to the stairs, its doors open wide displaying a lone gurney and standard medical equipment lining its walls. Dr. Anderson sat inside adjusting knobs and dials.

Almost to the door, a voice came over the greeter's station panel, "Is Maddy still up there?" I recognized Sabrina, but my heart stopped when I heard another voice across the speaker, "Maddy? Maddy!"

Jake had returned. Oh God, no.

"N...n...no" I said through chattering teeth. Looking up at Sam I begged, "Please....you ha...have t...t...to hurry. G...g...get me in the v...van, now!"

"Maddy!" his voice carried from two halls over.

Without question, Sam rushed me out the door and, with the swift grace of an Olympic shot put thrower, launched my bag into the van, just missing Dr. Anderson, but getting his attention nonetheless.

As suddenly as they came, my chills turned to fevered waves, lapping first at my toes then washing across my entire body. The pain from the heat swept over me and at first I didn't notice Sam picking me out of the chair and carrying me down the stairs.

"Don't hurt yourself!" I managed to say.

"You're light as a feather, trust me, I'm fine."

She threw me into Dr. Anderson's arms. He laid me on the gurney as Sam jumped in behind and closed the transport's doors.

"Time to move, Corson!" Sam shouted to the front. The engine started at the sound of her request.

I sat up as the vehicle pulled from the away from the building, watching our departure through two small windows, one on each of the ambulance's back doors. Dr. Anderson worked feverishly at something behind me, while Sam plopped down on a bench next to my gurney. The driver bounced his way over a curb.

"Dude, Corson, take it easy up there. Just drive like a normal person!" Sam said. Then to me she added, "Whatever *that* means to him." She rolled her eyes again.

I smiled, looking back out through the windows. The waves of heat slowly died into dull embers. I hoped the worst of my treatment had passed.

The ambulance traveled a few yards, almost to the end of the main parking lot, when the front doors of the hospice building slid open. I saw Jake, closely followed by Jenn and Sabrina. Jake was screaming something at the van as he chased after us, his face twisted in pain. I glanced over at Sam who also watched the commotion—I'm sure wondering if she'd made a mistake in her choice of test subject. But it was done, I was changed. I made my choice.

Jake stopped his pursuit as we turned the corner toward the forested exit. Realizing he wouldn't catch our vehicle on foot, I saw him kick the ground in frustration, then turn and run around the building toward the back lot where he parked.

"He's going for his truck," I said astonished, forgetting my audience.

"You gave her the treatment?" Dr. Anderson's voice said from behind.

"Yes, doctor. A little over five minutes ago," Sam replied.

"How are you feeling?" Dr. Anderson's asked, placing one hand on my shoulder.

I felt drained. Cringing at the thought of Jake chasing down our vehicle, I looked over at Sam, who gauged my reaction.

"I'm okay," I said, uncertain as to what answer Dr. Anderson expected.

"Heat flashes passed yet?" he asked.

"Actually," I thought for a moment, "yes. I feel...fine."

For the first time in weeks I didn't feel sick. Weak, yes, but not sick.

"Good," he said.

I watched Sam's eyes grow wide as I felt Dr. Anderson's grip on my shoulder move to my forehead, forcing my head backward.

"My God! What are you doing?" she screeched.

I heard gurgling before I felt pain.

"We need to know if it really works. This is the quickest way to find out," his voice was indifferent, distant. A loud buzzing filled my ears, drowning out the world around me.

My hands instinctively came to my throat. When I

pulled them away, in my fading vision I saw blood, lots of blood. My last thought was of Jake. Although I wasn't sure there was a God, I said a short prayer just before my world went black.

Chapter Fifteen

Bright, blinding light, yet I could see. Colors in varied hues, unknown within human experience, indescribable even with the greatest imagination, swirled around me. Voices exploded from every direction singing chords and layered harmonies in tones and tongues absolutely foreign to my ears, yet more beautiful than the most intricate symphonic masterpiece. Joy. My heart contained more joy, peace and overwhelming love than I'd experienced at any time during my short, earthly life.

All this began to fade as I opened my eyes to a dimly lit room.

"Heaven," I mumbled, merely wanting cling to the memory of what I had seen; to return to the beauty and joy.

"Heaven?" A familiar voice came from beside me. "I'd peg this place as more of a sterile, boring purgatory than Heaven, but whatever floats your boat."

I turned to see Sam writing feverishly on a clipboard as she observed the hospital-type monitors overhead. I realized the beeping pattern matched the beating rhythm of my pulse as it pounded in my ear.

"I knew it would work," she said, drawing her attention away from the monitor and down toward me.

As my eyes adjusted, I realized I was lying in a traditional hospital room complete with boring beige walls, bedside curtain hanging from the ceiling, a plethora of medical equipment and cheesy, hotel quality artwork adorning the walls. Daylight filtered through the room's solitary window. My surroundings became brighter than moments before, but not because more light entered the space; my eyes were adjusting to the dimmer reality of our human world.

"How do you feel?" Sam regained my attention.

Still in a daze, I touched the leads attached to my chest, trying to recall where I was. Why was I in the hospital? I didn't feel sick.

Sick. Cancer. I had cancer.

I looked at my arms, no longer atrophied. I lifted the sheet and glanced at the rest of my body which, days before, was a skeletal outline of my former self, but now looked healthy and toned. My mind returned to the last moments I could remember. My hands. The blood.

My arms flew up, hands grabbing at my neck. Nothing

met their frantic search. No blood, no bandages, not even the bump of a scar.

Sam's face twisted in disgrace. "I'm so sorry about that, Maddy. You have to believe I had no idea Dennis was going to do that."

I only nodded.

"Can you forgive me?"

"Yes, of course," I sputtered. I couldn't be angry. I didn't hold Sam responsible for the actions of a mad scientist. I was, after all, alive. "How long have I been out?"

Sam winked and raised her hands with dramatic flair, "On the third day she rose again!"

"Three days?" I asked.

"Yep. You were completely dead on day one...no heart beat, nothing. But on day two everything started to return to normal, you healed, your scars disappeared, and now, here you are!"

"Here I am," I said, a feeling of defeat, rather than joy tugged at my soul.

"What's wrong? Don't you feel any better?" Sam asked. I'd taken the wind out of her sails with my melancholy tone.

I sat up on the edge of my bed. Physically, I felt amazing. I drew a deep breath into my lungs. Nothing obstructed. I stretched, twisted, moved. Nothing ached, no sore muscles.

Sam watched me, jotting down her observations on the clipboard. "So," she pressed. "How do you feel?"

"Amazing," I shrugged.

I felt healthy enough to run a marathon if she asked. My heart, though, ached. Somehow, I no longer thought of this world as home. I couldn't come up with the words to describe how I seemed pulled in two separate directions.

"Hmm," Sam spoke as jotted her comments down. "I'm wondering if there is an element of depression. Perhaps a chemical imbalance as the body adjusts to the change? I'll order some blood work."

As she wrote, a young man—in his late teens or early twenties with short, dark hair and a blotchy, acne-scarred complexion—came into the room carrying a food tray. He watched Sam intently as he walked, never moving his eyes from her face. The boy placed the tray on a table beside her then stood watching—staring actually. Sam's average height towered above the boy. He literally looked up to her, never refocusing his gaze.

"Thanks Corson," she muttered, her eyes fixated on her clipboard, although she no longer wrote.

"No problem Doctor Blakemore," Corson replied, still standing, staring.

I felt uncomfortable watching the pair. Corson stood close to Sam. He appeared to be waiting for further direction. Sam tried to ignore him. I wondered if this boy ever made his own decisions. I placed a mental bet on who could hold out the longest in this awkward standoff.

"Can I get you anything Doctor? Maybe some coffee? Or water?" Corson broke the silence—I won my own wager.

"That will be all, Corson, thank you," Sam replied, still pretending to focus on her work.

"Okay," he said, yet didn't move from her side.

"You can go now, Corson," Sam didn't attempt to mask her agitation.

Defeated, the poor boy nodded and slinked out of the room. When he left, Sam let out a huge sigh and finally looked up from her clipboard.

"Someone has an admirer?" I teased as she plopped down beside me on the bed and started to remove the sticky monitor leads from my chest.

"Ugh. Corson is our assistant. He tries...but most of the time he is just a little too helpful. He's like this pathetic puppy dog. I mean, at first it was sweet, but now it's just annoying. The boy just hovers."

"Did you two ever date?" I asked.

"Oh no! God no!" Sam recoiled in disgust. "I'm starting to wonder what you think of me! First off, creepy, stalker-ish boys aren't really my type, and even if they were, I'm over thirty, and he is just a baby...a weird baby... but a baby nonetheless."

I laughed.

"Besides," she continued. "We can't all have handsome, dark haired boys chasing us two hundred and fifty miles until their trucks run out of gas on the highway."

"Two hundred and fifty miles?" My jaw clicked as it dropped.

"Girl, that boy must really love you. I'm just glad we gassed up before we arrived at the hospice center."

I sighed. My last vision of Jake—kicking at the ground, then running for his truck—remained etched firmly on my brain.

"So tell me, who is he?" Sam prodded, elbowing me in the side.

Dr. Anderson burst into the room. "There she is!" he beamed. "Corson said you were awake. Welcome back!"

His voice held no repentance for killing me.

"Uh, thanks." I instinctively slid closer to Sam, placing her between me and the doctor.

"Hey, no hard feelings," he offered. "Just doing my job. Now, we should probably start the testing phase."

"Testing?" I asked.

"I think Senator Morris wanted to see her first," Sam interrupted. "He made a special trip from D.C. this week to meet Maddy. Besides, I think we can give her *one* day of rest before trying to kill her again, don't you?"

"Fine," Dr. Anderson glowered. "But we start first thing tomorrow," he said as he sulked from the room.

"Testing?" I inquired again.

"Don't worry about it," Sam said. "Just minor stuff really. I don't *think* we'll be killing you again."

She winked, yet I couldn't quite tell if that last statement was serious.

"But first," she continued, "we need to get you ready to meet the senator."

Sam walked over and opened a closet door along the far wall, just below a ceiling mounted television.

"So, I hope you don't mind, but I went through your belongings while you were recovering, and found it necessary to purchase some new clothes."

Reaching into the only bag I owned, Sam forced a look of disgust as she pulled out the pair of sweats I wore the morning I entered hospice care. "Really?" she mused. "Please tell me you aren't one of *those* people."

"What people?" I asked.

"The people who wear sweatpants everywhere they go... or worse, pajama bottoms," she cringed.

I laughed, "I promise, those were just my dying clothes. My friend Jenn would kill me—literally, I think—if I ever left the house wearing sweats on any other occasion."

"Good. Well, again, I hope you don't mind, but I bought you a pair of jeans, a few tanks and red button down shirt. I also bought you a second pair of jeans, a couple light sweaters, athletic shorts, some tees, three pairs of shoes and socks. They're all in the drawers below that shelf by the window. Oh, and I picked you up some cute undies too... no offense to your granny panties of course."

She held up the pair of white cotton briefs like a flag of surrender before tossing them into the garbage. I blushed with embarrassment.

Noticing, Sam added, "Hey, we're all friends here!"

I got to my feet and, grabbing a piece of toast from the food tray, walked to where Sam was emptying the remains of my past life into a waste basket.

It amazed me how losing one's ability to perform normal tasks, such as walking, could make a person so appreciative of the simple things in life. I cannot fully relate the feeling of joy in the simple accomplishment of walking unassisted.

"You look good," Sam commented. "I mean, when I first met you I thought you were pretty, for a dying girl, but now you are radiant!"

A mirror hung above a sink beside the closet. I sidled over and gazed at my reflection in astonishment. The reflection was mine—the person I knew before cancer began to eat away at my body—but there were definite changes too. Toned muscles replaced sickened atrophy, yet a feminine softness remained. I was never very physically fit, even before the cancer, but now it seemed as if my body displayed its ideal design.

Life returned to my eyes. My skin glowed, healthy and full of vitality. My dark auburn hair reflected a shine of youth that most people paid to imitate, yet no dye could ever truly reproduce—no matter what some advertising slogan promised.

"Another benefit of the change—you'll remain twenty-five-ish forever. That's about the point when human cells finally mature and, we think, our newly immortal bodies will stop in their aging process. Girl, you are going to have to watch out or you will have hoards of boys chasing you hundreds of miles!" Sam laughed. "But, in all seriousness, that reminds me..."

She came and stood beside me, meeting my gaze reflected in the mirror. "I feel it is my responsibility to warn you about Senator Morris."

Staring back at her reflection I asked, "What about?"

"Well," she paused, twisting her mouth while her eyes searched the ceiling for the correct words. "He is, shall we say, kind of snake-like."

"Snake-like?"

"I mean, don't get me wrong, his money paid for our research. He's the reason you are alive and the reason I have a job, so he can't be *that* bad, but..." she considered her words carefully. "He fancies himself a ladies' man. He's slick. A smooth talking charmer—snake-like. And looking at you, I know where he will set his sights next. If he offers you an apple, I wouldn't eat it, if you catch my drift." After a moment she added, "Not that I think you would."

"Great." A feeling of trepidation came over me. The thought of some old senator putting the moves on me wasn't what I feared; I knew I wasn't the type to be easily charmed. I could handle his advances. What frightened me was the chance I might have to reject him. I was never good rejecting anyone—not that I had much practice in the past—but I certainly didn't want to be forced into rejecting the man who indirectly saved my life.

"Don't worry about it," Sam comforted, sensing my unease. "Senator Morris is a big boy. He may hold grudges for awhile, but he eventually gets over them. Besides, you are going to make him a very, *very* rich and powerful man."

Sam smiled as I relaxed a bit. "Oh, and then there's Toby Caras, his assistant," she added.

"What about him? Is he a smooth talking snake too?"

"Not at all." Sam scoffed. "I don't really know much about him. I think Senator Morris prefers his aides to be seen and not heard. Toby always stands off to the side looking angry, or distressed, I can't really tell. Either way, he doesn't seem to be a pleasant man. Maybe he hates his job, maybe it's Senator Morris he hates, I don't know. It's too bad, though, because he's kind of handsome in a rugged Mediterranean way. I'm just telling you so you won't be surprised when this guy in the corner is glaring at you. He pretty much scowls at everyone, so don't take it personally."

"Great, so my afternoon will consist of meeting a snake who wants to seduce me, along with his assistant who probably hates me, as well as getting some rest to prepare for a battery of tests that threaten to kill me tomorrow. Where was all this in your spiffy little presentation and informational packet? Please tell me now if there is anything else I should be concerned about! Three-headed monsters, demons, ghosts..."

Sam laughed, "Don't worry. I'll stick by your side. You'd better get dressed, though. Don't want to keep your audience waiting. I'll step out for a minute so you can get ready."

"So much for sticking by my side!" I called after her.

"I'll be right outside the door." She turned and winked at me, then bounced out the door with the same awkwardly elegant stride I noticed at our first meeting.

I took one more look in the mirror. I never considered myself pretty, but in the girl staring back at me, I saw a light, a life in her eyes that wasn't there before. Sam was right, I was radiant, but I seemed to be radiating something other than physical beauty. Something in me changed. I couldn't put my finger on it, but something shone from within.

I disrobed—happy to be finished with hospital linens—and donned my new pair of jeans and red button down shirt, both of which fit my frame perfectly. Taking one last glance in the mirror, I inhaled a deep breath as I made my way to the door.

Chapter Sixteen

I found Sam, as promised, waiting outside my room.

"See," she said. "Right by your side. Dr. Anderson went ahead. He will fill Senator Morris in on all the technical mumbo jumbo."

Emerging into the hallway, I was surprised that it resembled an office building more than a hospital. The walls were painted a designer gray. The floor offered a carpeted pathway in a darker shade of the same color. The hall split in two directions, both ending a few feet away in symmetrical turns toward another end of the building. Four wooden doorways lined our small alcove. The door to my room was the only one adorning a window; it's marking announced "Patient." Beside me, a door indicated the room beyond was a kitchen, and across the hall, two doors revealed they housed laundry facilities and a research library.

Rectangular panels of fluorescent lights lined the ceiling, while well planned track lighting emphasized modern artwork hanging on the walls.

Sam led me to the right, followed by an immediate left at the end of the hallway. The next hallway resembled ours, only much longer. My room obviously sat in the back of the building. I glanced around taking note of each door as we passed; some were marked while others remained a mystery.

There was a gym, locker rooms for men and women, a pool, and in the next alcove, a set of double doors that announced the entrance to a laboratory across from a storage closet.

"Since this is your home now, I'll give you the nickel tour." Sam pointed out different rooms along our way, "Most doors are marked, and now that you are a part of our team, you are welcome to go wherever you wish within the facility. You've seen most of what will probably interest you: kitchen, gym, pool. My apartment lies down the other hallway, if you take a left out of your room."

"You live here?" I asked.

"Well, we spent so many long evenings engrossed in research that Senator Morris thought it would be a good idea if we all just settled in here for awhile. It won't be forever...of course I have to admit that it's nice to have another female face around here. The only people I've seen for months now are Dennis and Corson." She wrinkled her nose and stuck out her tongue. "And, of course, our three gate guards, Craig, Adam and Erik who have rotating shifts out front. Those guys are nice, but I only ever see them when I run out to the store and back. They aren't allowed to know what we're doing inside; their only job is to keep any unauthorized visitors out."

"Where are we?" I asked.

"This is the Research Institute for the Advancement of Regenerative Medicine, outside of Birmingham, Alabama—Senator Morris' home state. We are an unknown entity, and we like to keep it that way."

"Protecting your research from others who might claim it as their own?" I queried.

"That, and..." Sam stopped to look directly at me as she spoke. "There are lots of people out there, Maddy, who don't agree with what we are doing. They'll want to stop us. If they knew what we've uncovered..." She shuddered, glancing around as if someone could be listening. "There are lots of folks, especially religious folks, who would destroy everything we've worked for, especially down here in the Bible Belt. These people don't believe in science and would rather see others suffer in the name of some God than cure us all and finally bring peace to this world. To them, you are the Anti-Christ. Crazy, isn't it?" Sam laughed.

Until now, I hadn't thought about the religious implications of this miracle cure.

Checking her watch, Sam changed the subject. "We'd

better get moving. Senator Morris is probably getting a bit impatient by now."

We hurried down the hallway then took another right. The next hallway lead directly to a set of double wooden doors, Senator Morris' name proudly displayed in large letters beside the entrance.

"Ready?" Sam asked.

"No," I replied.

She chuckled and opened the door.

A row of large windows lined the wall opposite us. The view looked out across a treed landscape. The enormous room was wooden paneled. It had the feel of a high-end lodge where the designer took extra care matching the inlay of the wall paneling with that of the large, ominous wooden desk that commanded the entire length of the wall to our left. A high-backed leather chair behind the desk was currently unoccupied. To our right, a fire burned bright within a large fireplace—although outside summer temperatures must have been over ninety degrees. Beside the fireplace, a small wet bar lined with glasses and liquor bottles was set back into the wall. Directly in front of the bar was a round table set with four simple chairs, upholstered with fabric in the same shade of gray as the carpet.

In the furthest corner of the room sat a small desk facing its more ostentatious brother. Unlike the other, though, this desk was occupied. A grim looking man sat scowling, just as Sam had predicted. I immediately deduced this was the senator's assistant, Toby.

Dr. Anderson and another man—who I assumed to be Senator Morris—huddled together beside the assistant's desk, pouring over a stack of paperwork, engrossed in conversation.

Still unnoticed by the others, I took a moment to study Toby. Sam was right to say he was attractive. His jet black hair, olive toned complexion and muscular build—evident beneath his designer blue suit—could have landed him on the pages of Italian Vogue. His eyes met mine, both of us estimating each other's character. Unlike Sam's assessment, though, his face didn't appear stern or menacing as much as it seemed uncomfortable, on edge.

Standing, Toby cleared his throat, gaining the attention of the others.

"Senator Morris," Sam said with a smile, extending her hand as we approached. Dr. Anderson nodded and stepped aside to allow our introductions.

In his mid-fifties, Senator Clay Morris had light brown hair flecked with grey, bright blue eyes, and a tanned, leathery complexion—the result of years spent under harsh southern skies. He looked the part of a well-groomed Southern gentleman with a hint of cologne, cognac and expensive cigars hanging like an aura around him.

"My sweet Samantha," he said taking her hand in both of his. "You look lovelier every time we meet." Unlike most politicians from the Deep South, he made no attempt at hiding his thick southern drawl.

"Thank you, Senator," she said. "And may I introduce you to Maddy?"

The Senator turned his full attention, as well as his full charm, on me. "Ah, the woman of the hour. Dear Madeline, let me take a look at the woman who will win over the world."

Taking both my hands he lifted my arms, then twirled me as if we were dancing. "Grace and beauty." Turning to Dr. Anderson he added with a wink, "You've done good Doctor."

"You can thank Sam, sir," Dr. Anderson said. "She was the one who decided to go with the girl."

Senator Morris beamed. "Yes, I believe she made an excellent choice. People will follow a beautiful, young woman off a cliff if she says it's good for them! Women will want to be her and men..." He turned back to me and without any attempt at masking innuendo said, "All men will *want* her." He brushed my cheek with the back of his hand, lingering a bit too long in his caress. My throat tightened and closed. I made a conscious effort to avoid recoiling away from the senator's touch, keeping my reaction neutral.

"I'm Toby Caras," the man behind the desk jumped in, coming around to shake my hand. "I'm Senator Morris' assistant."

I was thankful for the interruption.

"Yes, yes, Toby," Senator Morris moved his hand from my cheek and used it to wave Toby off. "Come, Maddy, come with me."

Senator Morris took my hand and led me to his desk. He kept a loose grasp of my wrist as he turned to fumble with something inside one of the drawers. With his back to me, he stated, "Now, I have to see our success for myself."

He spun around. Something silver glinted in the light as pain scorched my palm.

"Ouch!" I cried. Looking down, I saw a large gash in my palm, crimson oozing from where the skin parted. Within moments gravity pulled the red stream toward the floor.

"What is *wrong* with you people?" Sam cried. "She is a *person* for goodness sake!"

Grabbing a towel from the bar, Toby rushed over and wrapped it around my throbbing hand. Although his face remained stern, uncomfortable, his eyes expressed concern. He seemed to be a man of internal struggle; there was something undecided in his nature. His exterior projected one message, his eyes reflected another.

"So," Senator Morris urged. "Let's see it. Is it healed?"

Blood continued to seep through the towel. I held out my aching hand for his inspection. Removing the towel, the senator's eyes narrowed. The gash remained.

"I don't get it. Why isn't she healed?" his brow furrowed.

"It isn't instantaneous, Senator," Dr. Anderson approached. "Although her body will heal much quicker now—after the change. The wound will scab over in a few hours and any scar will completely disappear by tomorrow."

The senator looked disappointed, "Well, we'd better work the kinks out before taking this to the world."

"With all due respect, Senator Morris," Sam broke in. "This isn't a kink. She is immortal, like the rest of us will be someday, but like us, she can still be injured. She feels pain."

"But nothing can kill her?" Senator Morris questioned.

"Nothing," Dr. Anderson stated.

"Except complete and total cellular destruction," Sam added.

"Complete destruction?" Senator Morris looked quizzical.

"Well, like if we burnt her body in an incinerator, killing off every cell's potential at survival. Then, I think, she would officially be dead. But short of that..." Sam said.

"What if we cut off her hand?" Senator Morris asked.

"It would grow back," Sam stated.

"Ah, but would a new body grow with the hand? Like a starfish? These are the questions that need answering before we go public," the Senator mused.

"No, as we've already seen in our lab tests, only the hand would be replaced on the existing body, not vice versa," Sam's voice carried a matter-of-fact authority that I doubted anyone could argue against. "Based on our experiments with mice, growth factors alert these mutated cells to divide and form, shall we say, a replacement part, until the injured part is completed. These cells, though, exhibit anchorage dependence to a site of circulation, not the extracted body part. In other words, cells will not divide unless attached to a circulatory system, or something with circulatory potential."

"What if we cut out the heart?" Senator Morris challenged. I found myself creeping backward, away from the group as they discussed ways in which to test their discovery.

"The heart would grow back where it belonged. The stem cells seek to fix what is wrong within the body, destroying the bad and repairing the good."

"But without circulation..."

"I don't think *circulation* has as much to do with the cellular division as the potential for it. An embryo's heart does not begin to beat until approximately twenty-two days after fertilization, yet the process of development is well underway. Like embryonic stem cells, these newly mutated cells seem to recognize when they have the potential to survive. The body knows that if it repairs the heart, the rest of the body will continue to function. The severed hand will have no function without a whole body, so cells won't attempt to repair what is already lost; the body is still the source of power. I'm sure we will find a more detailed explanation for this phenomenon in a few years as our understanding of these genetic mysteries becomes clearer."

I realized I'd traveled the length of the room and was bracing myself against the round table, as far from the group as I could get without completely exiting the office.

"Don't you worry about the implications..." I interrupted. "I mean, don't you worry what might happen...isn't anyone concerned that we might be playing God?" The words flowing from my lips shocked me more than the others.

Everyone erupted with laughter, except Toby, whose

eyes turned cold—although the rest of his expression remained level, indignant.

Senator Morris' voice boomed, "God? You certainly didn't have a problem leaving any God behind to become immortal."

Even though I remained undecided about God's existence, Senator Morris' words managed to pierce my heart.

"Not to worry my dear girl," he continued. "I believe our discovery proves there is no such thing as a Higher Power. Since time began, people created this idea of God to help alleviate their fear of death and suffering. Are there people who would wish to destroy our discovery, calling it blasphemy? Of course! The thing we must remember is that those people are religious fanatics. Those same people would want everyone to continue suffering for a God that doesn't exist—it's their way of oppressing the masses! Fanatics use God as a source of their own power and will do anything to stop those who threaten their control. We have conquered death, Maddy—science, not some figment of the imagination! This opens so many possibilities for the human race. In our new world there will be no war. People will learn to get along, because none of us are going anywhere. We will be free to love, to do whatever it is that makes us happy. There will be no fear of punishment by some invisible power. There will be no death, no suffering, no pain!"

My aching hand protested his point, but I stood silenced, thinking about a peaceful world without disease, without death. Freedom. It sounded extraordinary.

"Won't we run out of parking spaces?" I asked.

Sam burst out laughing. "What?" she choked.

"Well," I continued, "I had this foster mom once who said death was inevitable, because without it, the world would run out of parking. If we don't die, the world will quickly run out of space—there will be no room for future generations to inhabit."

"An intelligent question," Senator Morris nodded in approval.

"We've actually thought of this," Dr. Anderson joined the conversation. "And our answer is sterilization."

Sterilization? I never thought about sterilization. My dream of having children...was that gone?

"Am I? I mean...did you?"

"No," Sam interrupted. "We didn't tie your tubes. There was so much we weren't certain of that I didn't want to add another layer to complicate matters." Seeing the concern on my face she added, "We can only clamp the tubes anyway...if we cauterized or removed your reproductive system, your body would just replace what was broken and BAM! Fertile again. Besides, clamping would only be temporary, just to keep the world's population down until we discovered a way to expand into space or something. I'm sure that's possible...heck, we discovered immortality...what's a space station when you really think of it?"

"Oh," I said, thankful that I could still have children, but the thought lingered as to how soon that would change.

Exhausted, I slumped down into one of the chairs.

"She looks tired," Toby said, eyes focused, still cold and calculating.

"She's had a busy day—rising from the dead and all," Sam chimed. "I think maybe we should give her some rest."

"I think that's a good idea," Senator Morris said, walking over to take my good hand and help me from my seat. "Get some rest, my dear. I know the doctors will be putting you through many rigorous tests over the next few years. Take breaks when you can."

"Years?" I hesitated, throwing the Senator off balance as I plopped back into my chair. "I will be here for years?"

"Maddy," the Senator knelt down, wrapping his arm around my shoulders, stroking my hair with his free hand—I once again fought against the urge to squirm out from his awkward embrace. "You must understand that we cannot allow you to leave until we are one hundred percent ready to announce our findings to the world. There is so much we have left to discover. If word spread too soon, before we were able to mass produce the serum on a global scale, think how people would go crazy to have this for themselves—riots, fighting, mayhem—and we don't even fully understand if there are any long term side effects. Then there are others who would do anything to destroy our research—look for any reason to shut us down, especially if we didn't have answers about possible complications. We can't have that now, can we? It could ruin everything we've worked for. Until we fully understand what it is we've discovered, and there is a firm plan in place and enough resources to distribute this to the world, we must keep our research, and you, private."

"But years? I have to stay here for years?"

"I think," Dr. Anderson spoke from across the room, "that in a few months we may be able to let her out on day trips...under strict supervision, of course. It would be good to see how she interacts with the world in her new form. See if she, or anyone else, notices a change."

Senator Morris shot Dr. Anderson an austere look. Obviously, Senator Morris didn't enjoy his authority being undermined by anyone.

Returning his attention to me, the senator added, "You see, sweet Madeline, there is still so much for *all* of us to discuss." Rising, he helped me to my feet again. "Now, please, get some rest. I do so look forward to sharing your company on many more occasions. I have a feeling that we will be quite intimately connected in no time."

He raised my hand to his lips and kissed it as any southern gentleman would. Sam and I left the room. The sound of the men arguing followed us all the way down the hall.

Chapter Seventeen

I walked along East Bay Street in Charleston, following the familiar path I traveled my last night in that city. People bustled, a light breeze flowed from the water, everyone appeared happy...but something was wrong, missing. I couldn't put my finger on it.

I spun in a circle, trying to remember what I was doing there. Buildings loomed overhead. Someone bumped into me, a polite nod of excusal sent him on his way. I studied each person who passed. Somehow I knew I was looking for something, or was it someone? Each face held the same, polite smile, like those from the hospice center—almost robotic.

As I walked the thought occurred—everyone was

exactly the same age, in their mid-twenties. No elderly couples walked hand in hand, no children played in alleyways. Everything seemed right, yet nothing seemed right. I spun again, searching for a familiar face.

Across the street I saw them. Two young men— teenagers, with dark hair, light eyes and dimples—both the spitting image of Jake. One stood a bit taller than the other. They both watched me, sadness filled their expressions. I knew these boys.

A voice cried out in the street and suddenly the serene atmosphere was set ablaze, people stormed the boys from every direction.

The teens stood resolute, unafraid. Anger electrified the crowd as the masses descended. Someone picked up a stone and threw it, hitting the taller boy in his left temple, blood oozing from the gash. Another woman struck the shorter boy with her fist, splitting his lip. The young men continued to stare at me, quiet acceptance in their eyes. Soon, hundreds of people swarmed, beating their defenseless victims.

I couldn't move. Dumbfounded, I tried to call out for everyone to stop, but no noise escaped my mouth. My throat held tight, unable to form sound.

As quickly as they attacked, the crowd dispersed, returning to their monotonous existence as if nothing had occurred, robotic smiles in place.

Able to move again, I approached the two lifeless bodies lying in the street. I fell to the ground weeping as thunder crashed overhead. Through my sorrow, I knew these boys were meant for this fate. Another roll of thunder...

******

I woke. A flash of light illuminated the window as water streamed down the pane. A rumble overhead blurred the line between dream and reality. Looking around my room I knew the dream had ended, but the feeling of loss, fear and loneliness it projected still hung heavy on my heart, clouding my waking mind.

I lay motionless in bed for a long time, watching the symbolic war between light and darkness wage outside my window. Lightning punctured the sky—bright flashes blinded the earth below. Thunder echoed its anger amongst sinister clouds. As the sun worked to free itself from night's shadowy grip on the heavens, birds, early in their waking, chirped a warning for others to remain safely nested until a victor was determined.

It seemed, for a time, that the battle would continue throughout the morning, but ultimately the storm's tirade deteriorated into a trivial rant. Lightning retreated. Thunder's cry faded further and further into the distance, finally, exhausting itself completely. The sun broke through in the east—its rays melting the hazy remains of the climatic war. Birds called out a happier tune, once again free from the tyrannical rule of menacing skies.

As much hope as the sun's rising brings to each morning, I could not rise above my melancholy mood. So many questions lingered, questions I should have considered before making my decision to trade this world for any chance at the next. I never believed in God, or at least not in any real sense. To me, when I chose to believe (and that was rare), He was just the fix-it, go-to guy when something went wrong, and the one to blame if things didn't work out the way I thought they should. Now, with what should be no fear of consequence or an afterlife, no need for belief, I felt He was trying to speak to me, tell me something, but what that was I could not discern.

The quiet knock on my door forced me to return from my thoughts to the world in which I would remain eternally suspended.

"Good morning sleepy head," Sam's hushed voice called from the doorway. "Are you awake?"

"Who could sleep through that storm?" I called back, letting her know it was safe to enter.

"Storm?" she answered. "Wow, I didn't hear a thing. I guess I'm a heavy sleeper though. Are you ready for today? First day of testing!"

Her voice taunted. I groaned.

"Oh, it's not going to be that bad," she replied, coming to sit beside me on the bed. "Senator Morris left last night for his office in town and will be out all day, and I have a pretty good grip on Dr. Anderson. I'm sick of these guys trying to kill you behind my back! It isn't right!"

"Tell me about it," I huffed.

"Well, there will be none of that on my watch. You've risen from the dead, from both cancer, and, well....you know." She sliced her index finger across her neck. "I think we all know you can spring back from almost anything. Besides, this is why we have lab animals. Anything those boys want to figure out, like if we transplant one heart into another body which DNA will take over, can be done using animals, not humans. And in the spirit of not keeping secrets, I've printed out an itinerary for the day. I will provide one every day so you know what's coming."

Sam smiled, handing me the folded piece of paper. I opened it and read its contents:

7:30	Breakfast
8:00	Blood Draw
8:30	I.Q. Test
9:00	VO$_2$Max testing (running on treadmill)
10:00	Recovery/Nutrition analysis
11:00	Watch crappy soap opera with Sam
12:00	Lunch
1:00	Tour the Lab
2:00	Strength testing
3:00	Memory test
5:00	Dinner and movie in Sam's room

"Wow, looks like we will be busy," I said. "How disappointed is Dr. Anderson that I won't be tortured today?"

"Who said I won't torture you?" Sam laughed. "Didn't you read the part about the crappy soap opera?"

I laughed too, thankful to have her on my side.

"Okay, I'll step out so you can get ready," she said. "Wear comfortable clothing that you can run in… shorts and a tee should be fine."

As Sam rose to leave, Corson appeared in the doorway, looking lovesick as ever.

"Breakfast," he announced.

"Thank you," I said as he placed the tray on the table beside my bed. He didn't turn in acknowledgement, his attention never drifted from Sam.

"Good morning, Corson," Sam said with polite indifference.

"Can I get you anything, Doctor?"

"How about a cup of coffee?" Sam asked.

Pleased to have a mission, Corson bounded with childish joy for the door, "Of course! Right away!"

"Corson," Sam chastised. "Shouldn't you ask if Maddy needs anything else?"

The boy looked deflated, but managed to take his eyes from Sam, albeit momentarily, to glance over and ask, "May I retrieve anything else for you, Ma'am?"

Ma'am?

Even though my body now physically displayed characteristics at least three years younger than my chronological age, the word "Ma'am" made me feel decrepit. I wondered how old this boy really was.

"No, thank you," I smiled at Corson. He didn't smile back.

Turning toward Sam he beamed, "I'll be back with that coffee!"

Sam breathed a sigh of exasperation after Corson left the room. "I'll be right outside the door. Call when you are ready."

My first morning of testing began and, thankfully, there were no surprise changes to the schedule. Toby stayed at the Institute to monitor our progress during Senator Morris' absence. He popped his head in while Sam had me at full sprint on the treadmill, but when invited to join us in watching the soap opera, he respectfully declined stating that he would be attending to important business in his office for the rest of the day.

True to her word, Sam's soap opera was near torture, yet I was infinitely more pleased with that agony than having anyone spring from a dark corner to slice me open or chop off any extremities.

The only time I saw Dr. Anderson was during my tour of the lab. He was at work on a rabbit that was either sleeping or deceased, I couldn't tell. The lab looked exactly how one would expect a medical research laboratory to appear. The room was large and sterile with gray tile floors along with industrial metal cabinets, drawers and counter tops. A refrigerator sat in one corner with a sign posted on its door indicating that it contained biomedical material that required cooling. Countless cages lined the laboratory walls housing different types of mice and rabbits. A large work station with a sink, Bunsen burners, vials, and all kind of instruments and tools, was centered among the watchful test subjects. I knew the animals probably had no idea what was going on, yet my heart ached for the tortures inflicted on them in the name of science. Although, admittedly, I was certainly glad it was them and not I Dr.

Anderson now worked upon.

Our evening wrapped up in Sam's room with take-out Chinese food, red wine and a romantic comedy. Like an apartment, her room contained a living space with a couch, end tables, and a small television set. On the far wall, beneath a window overlooking the wooded landscape was a small dining table with two chairs. A kitchenette was stationed beside the table and adjacent was a door to Sam's bedroom and bathroom.

"Tomorrow we'll move you into the room next door. It's identical to my place. We get to be neighbors! You have no idea how glad I am that Dr. Anderson let me pick you over that other guy. I *so* needed another female around here!"

Sam's last statement—the fact that I was chosen for this experiment because I was female—hit me in the gut. I realized that by agreeing to become her test subject, I indirectly sentenced someone else to death. I felt guilty having been chosen, and yet somewhere inside, a part of me envied that man who was now, most likely, dead.

"What's wrong?" Sam asked, noting the look of sad contemplation on my face.

"Nothing," I lied. "Just a bit tired."

Despite the day's events, I was not actually tired. I replaced my frown with a smile and relaxed into the sofa while my new friend spooned chow mein noodles and General Tso's Chicken onto my plate. We talked throughout the evening comparing Dr. Anderson, Corson, and Toby to different characters in the movie.

"How are you feeling?" Sam asked after we finished our

meal and began working on our second glass of wine.

"A little tipsy, actually," I giggled.

"You've only had one glass!" Sam laughed. "Have you always been this much of a light weight?"

"I was never much of a drinker, but I must admit that I've never been quite *this* bad," I admitted.

Sam grabbed a spiral notebook from the end table beside the couch. "Must schedule alcohol tolerance test to see if mutated cells had any effect on your body's ability to process alcohols differently," she spoke as she scribbled. "Check blood alcohol level, blood pressure, heart rate, motor skills, processing and elimination…"

She jotted a few other things without speaking then looked up and said, "This is going to be so much fun! Drinking for science!"

I laughed, shaking my head.

"I'm serious," she said. "We still know so little about how the human body reacts to this mutation. There are so many questions!"

"Okay, well, since we are on the topic of questions," I said. "Can I ask one?"

"Of course! Mi casa es su casa…or whatever."

"Well," I began. "You all say you will bring this advancement to the world, that everyone will be changed. But you also say there are those who will want to destroy your research, so those individuals probably won't want to participate."

"Yes, that's probably true."

"So, how are you going to keep track of who is changed

and who isn't? Does the senator propose making it mandatory?"

Sam smiled, "We've discussed this. Although there will be resistance in the beginning, I believe, at some point, this will be mandatory for everyone throughout the world...not that I think we will have to force it upon people. Most individuals will welcome the chance to live forever. Think about it, we continually argue about medical costs and spend billions of dollars each year trying to fight disease. Now that we have unlocked our genetic healing potential, all these medical costs, drug costs, hospitals—they will all be a thing of the past! In one hundred years, when we look back at how we treated...say, cancer for instance...we will groan in disgust. Current treatments will be the equivalent to the act of medieval bloodletting. Chemotherapy will seem barbaric once we realize how easy it is to inoculate the human race against all disease. People will come to realize the gift science is giving them through this mutation."

"But not all people will accept it," I reminded her.

"True, but we figure those individuals will eventually die out over time."

"That could take hundreds of years, especially if those people continue to have children."

"That is true, but Senator Morris proposed a way of...*helping* that situation along. Of course, we would never *force* anyone to receive the mutation. That being said, we do need a way of keeping track of who has and who has not participated. The plan is to tattoo those individuals who receive the inoculation. That way, for instance, if you come across an auto accident, you can tell which person requires immediate medical care, and who we can let recover at home while waiting for him to heal on his own. It sounds harsh, but the people who refuse to be inoculated, although they will not be *denied* care—as long as health care still exists—they will face higher taxes, difficulty receiving services—they could be turned away from jobs because of the health risk they pose to themselves. I know it may sound like discrimination, but truly it is the best thing for humanity. Eventually, defectors will see the error of their ways...or their children will at least."

"Tattooing?" I asked, "What kind of tattoo?"

"Oh, nothing major," Sam replied. "Just little ones, barely noticeable. We were thinking of the number six—signifying that person received the full six genetic mutations—placed on the head, just above the hairline, and one very discretely on the right hand, here, between the pointer finger and thumb." Sam held out her hand, displaying the webbed fold of skin between the two digits.

"I guess that wouldn't be too bad," I said, yet something in her description disturbed me, like I'd heard it before.

"Hey," she said. "Let's change the subject. Tell me about Romeo. I still can't believe that he chased us hundreds of miles trying to rescue you from my evil grasp!" Sam finished her sentence with a sinister chuckle.

I blushed. "Oh, well, that's Jake. He's my..." I paused trying to determine the best way to describe him. "Coworker," was the word I decided upon.

"Coworker?" Sam's face mocked my description "I don't see any of *my* co-workers chasing after *me!*"

"I bet Corson would," I threw back at her.

Sam wrinkled her face in disgust, "Okay, but that's only because he probably wants to eat my liver with some fava beans and a nice bottle of Chianti."

Our laughter continued for several minutes. "Okay," I conceded. "I kind of like Jake, and he says that he kind of likes me, but I think he caved because I was dying. It's safe to say you love someone when you know there are no strings attached."

"Um, dying seems like a pretty big string," Sam said, suddenly serious.

"I guess," was all I could manage. My mind drifted to the last moment I saw Jake, his face twisted in agony as he turned and raced for his car. An image of the two boys from my dream, so much like Jake, lying bloody and cold on the ground flashed through my mind a second later. It sent a shiver up my spine.

"Hey, I'm sorry," Sam interrupted, seeing that I was upset. "We can let it drop. Do you want to finish the movie?"

"Yeah, probably a good idea. I don't want to stay up too late. I'm sure you have another fun day planned for me tomorrow."

"And the day after that, don't forget," Sam teased.

We returned our focus to Chinese food and the trivial plight of some lovesick boy, a standoffish girl, and the shy, female best friend who completed the love triangle.

Unfortunately, though, the movie wasn't frivolous enough to keep me distracted. My mind returned over and over again to Jake, and the two boys who looked exactly like him.

Chapter Eighteen

An uneventful week passed. I managed to keep all my limbs, didn't see any blood, caught up on soap opera character back stories, moved into the apartment beside Sam's and filled up on good food and wine in the evenings. In hindsight, all this was probably due to the fact that Senator Morris traveled to Washington D.C., for some very important vote, and although Dr. Anderson outranked Sam by sheer seniority, she seemed to maintain control of the facility during the senator's absence. Unfortunately, Senator Morris was set to return to the Research Institute at any moment. I wasn't keen on his checking our progress, certain he must have spent hours conjuring up more horribly gruesome scenarios that would need further study, or worse than that, horribly gruesome ways to try and seduce me.

Toby kept to himself, asking only for written details of the day's events in order to brief the senator. I went with Sam to deliver the paperwork on a few occasions and, as usual, Toby remained at his desk, glowering. He wasn't friendly, but he wasn't necessarily unpleasant either. He seemed to tolerate us—and the fact that he was just as trapped in this facility as I during the senator's absence.

This day, like every other, I found myself running sprints on the treadmill, hooked to electronic heart monitoring leads and a large breathing device that measured my oxygen intake and output. I didn't find it difficult, just awkward. Sam had me at a full sprint when the door crashed open. Toby charged in, agitated and anxious.

"You'd better get to the office," he said in a curt tone. "It isn't good."

Sam hit the emergency stop button on the treadmill and began unhooking me from the leads. "What's up, Toby? What's the big emergency?"

Staring directly at me, fire in his eyes, he said, "*She* is in big trouble. Senator Morris is back and in a complete rage."

"Me?" I asked, astonished. "What on earth did I do?"

"You'd just better come with me, quickly," Toby replied and started out the door.

"What did I do?" I asked Sam, her shrug indicated she had no idea either.

"Don't worry; I'm sure it's nothing. Senator Morris is known for having a bit of a temper. Did you steal his scotch or cigars while he was away?" Sam smirked.

"No," I replied, searching my memory for anything that I may have done in his absence.

"Well, there's only one way to find out what the heck is going on," Sam said as I followed her into the hall. The gym was located around the corner from the Senator's office, but even from a distance I could hear his ferocious tirade and items crashing about the room. Toby had not waited for us. I could hear his voice down the hall as he tried to calm the senator down.

"That doesn't sound like anger over a cigar," I said, apprehension pulling me backward, away from the source of mayhem.

Turning to stop me from slinking away, Sam said, "If we don't go, it will only be worse when he does catch up to us. Let's face it—this isn't a very large facility, not a whole lot of places to hide. Besides, I have no idea what you could have possible done to make him this upset. I've been with you this entire time. This is probably some dumb misunderstanding. I wouldn't worry about it. Tell you what; I'll keep myself between you and the senator. If he is being outrageous, he will have to go through me to get to you, okay?"

I felt better with her reassurance, although my resolve once again faded as we approached his office. It was not just a tirade but complete pandemonium transpiring behind the closed entry. Frustrated cries. Items crashing to the ground. Something struck the opposite side of the door, causing the entire frame to shudder.

Sam knocked then carefully entered, opening the door only slightly at first. When she felt we weren't going to be hit by any flying objects, she entered the room. Pieces of shattered glass lay strewn around the threshold. Across from us, I saw Toby and Dr. Anderson standing steadfast, condemnation highlighting their stark expressions.

"You!" Senator Morris charged like an angry rhinoceros. "Your lies have put this entire operation in jeopardy!"

As promised, Sam stood between me and the oncoming senator. Frustrated, he stopped short. I was glad Sam's presence somehow kept the senator at bay. He scowled, then leaning around Sam while shaking his finger violently at me he screamed, "You said you had no family! No next of kin! You *lied!*"

I had no idea what he meant. I stared at him blankly, unable to decipher the meaning behind his crazed rant.

"Do you *deny* that you're a liar?" he spoke through clenched teeth. Senator Morris continued shaking his finger, glaring at me with staunch ferocity burning in his eyes.

"Sir, I don't know what you are..."

"Liar!" he interrupted.

I looked at Sam. She glanced back over her shoulder toward me, obviously as confused as I was.

"Do you *deny*, then, that you are married?"

"Married?" I choked on the word.

"Yes, married. To a Mr. Jacob Kavanaugh."

I stood motionless. Stunned. Married?

"Well?" the senator forced.

I couldn't lie, "We were engaged, but only for a day. I didn't want to say anything because really, we hadn't married yet..."

"Liar!" the senator screamed again, this time forcing his way past Sam. Grabbing my hair close to the scalp, he dragged me across the room. Stopping in front of his disheveled desk he shoved a piece of paper in my face challenging, "Is this not your signature?"

I looked at the document. It did look somewhat familiar. I immediately recognized it was a marriage certificate. I saw Jake's signature, and two witnesses. Jenn's name was signed as the officiator—I recalled a time she applied online to become a justice of the peace when one of her other friends wanted a civil marriage outside the church. I looked at the signature line above the word bride, and there, in a very sloppy, yet recognizable form was my signature. Memories flickered in my brain. Morphine. Wills. Signatures. Jenn asking if I would marry Jake. I married him that evening without realizing.

"He tricked me," I stammered.

"So, this *is* your signature?" Senator Morris released my hair, backhanded me across my cheek, knocking me to the ground before he threw the paper back onto his desk.

"I...I..." I didn't know what to say. Rising to stand again, I shot Sam a pleading look as I backed away.

"Well, *Mrs. Kavanaugh*, unfortunately your dear husband is stirring things up at my downtown office." Senator

Morris cast a vehement look toward Sam before returning his attention to me. "Somehow my name was dropped at the hospice center before you deceitfully agreed to join our mission. This Kavanaugh fellow is making a lot of noise, demanding to see his wife. He's threatened to go to the media if we don't settle this matter quickly."

The ire in Senator Morris' soul radiated not only through his words, but seeped from his pores, infecting the mood of everyone in the room. I stood helpless, trembling.

Sam walked toward the desk, examining the marriage certificate for herself. She looked up from the paper. The disappointment in her face told me I was alone in this fight.

Without warning, Senator Morris relaxed his body position and took a deep breath. He took one step toward me, my immediate reaction was to flinch and back away.

I felt like the unwanted, five year old child, once beaten severely by my foster father for the heinous crime of forgetting to put the dishes away before school. Despite pleading with him that no one ever explained my responsibility, he continued to whip me with his belt, and then his fists until he tired. Bruised and bloody, I hid in my room, terrified, unsure where I could go or what I should do. A few hours later my foster dad apologized, offering me a flower and a borderline inappropriate hug. From that moment, I remained silent, never speaking, trying to avoid him and remain unnoticed. Thankfully, I spent only one miserable week in that house—I was removed after a neighbor called in a tip about suspected abuse. Though short lived, I never felt more confused and fearful in my life…until now.

"My dear Maddy," the senator said, his tone strangely calm and calculating, "You see how this little…*misstep* of yours has endangered all of us in this room? Everything we've worked for?"

I nodded, perplexed by his schizophrenic mood change. I didn't speak. Self-preservation.

"Don't worry," his voice was composed, silky sweet, eerie. "I know this isn't your fault. It's his. That wasn't kind of this Jake fellow to trick you. You have every right to be angry. If we had known you were married, there is no way you would be alive today. It was a very selfish thing for him to do."

I stood motionless.

"Toby," Senator Morris turned his attention to Toby who was standing across the room. "I need you to take care of this for me…for us." Senator Morris turned back to me, opening a drawer in his desk. "Don't worry, Maddy, this will all soon be over. It's not your fault, it's his. I hate that he's forcing my hand, but dear, this is the only way."

He pulled something black from the drawer. A gun.

"No," I mouthed, still silent.

"It's the only way," his voice expressed sympathy, but his eyes remained cold, indifferent. "Toby?"

Toby approached the Senator, accepting the weapon from his hands.

"No!" I screamed. "No!"

I lurched toward the senator, but something caught me. I was flailing, screaming. My head swam. "No!"

Corson grabbed tight around my torso, pinning my arms against my sides. I hadn't even noticed him in the room. I looked at Sam, my eyes pleading for her to help. She stared back, still holding the certificate, expressionless.

"No! God no!" I screamed, thrashing, as Corson dragged me from the room.

Chapter Nineteen

I hadn't noticed earlier that my apartment door locked from the outside. Corson threw me on the couch and before I could recover I heard the distinct click of the bolt engaging. I ran to the door, slamming my fists against it, screaming for Corson, Sam...anyone to let me out. I had to fix this. There had to be something I could do.

Senator Morris attacked Jake's character, condemning his trickery, when in reality, Jake married me for love. There was nothing evil behind his intentions. I was the selfish one. My desire to live, my actions, led me to this place and now because of me, Jake was sentenced to die.

"Please God," I pleaded. "Please, not Jake. I'll do anything, *anything*."

Exhausted, I slumped against the wall beside the door heaving sobs and begging God to forgive the apathetic attitude of my past. I promised Him a life of repentance and service if He would only grant me this one favor.

I lay helpless on the floor for hours, watching the day outside my window fade toward twilight. Shadows slowly crept toward me across the floor, devouring any light that remained. I both welcomed and feared the darkness—it called to me. It pulled me down, into myself.

There is no hope. Toby will kill Jake. Why would you allow yourself to think your life could be anything but miserable? No hope.

I heard a lock disengage; a sliver of light penetrated the room as the door cracked open.

"Maddy?" Sam's voice whispered. "Can I come in?"

I refused to speak. At this point I didn't care what she did. Lock me away forever, cut off all my limbs, remove my beating heart...nothing would be penance enough to bring Jake back, or to remove the guilt that coiled its dark, sinewy cords around my soul.

"Maddy?" she whispered again, the door revealing a larger beam of light, illuminating the spot where I crumpled on the floor.

I didn't look up, but I heard Sam enter and close the door behind her. I felt as she slid down the wall to sit beside my huddled mass.

"I'm so sorry, Maddy," she said. I remained unresponsive. A long moment passed before she spoke again. "Toby isn't a complete monster, you know?"

Her words knocked the breath from my chest. How could she possibly defend the man who was going to kill Jake?

"Listen," she continued. "I pulled Toby aside. I think we found a solution that will make everyone happy. No murder, okay?"

For the first time I looked up, sincerity creased the corners of her eyes.

Seeing she had my full attention, she continued, "Toby is not an unreasonable man. He doesn't want to kill anyone."

Did I dare to hope? I held my breath.

"Well, Jake is insisting that he sees his wife…"

"I get to see him?" I asked. My heart flipped in my chest.

Her face dimmed, "Not *exactly*."

Confused, I shook my head.

"He wants to see you, but he doesn't know if you are alive or dead. The last time Jake was with you, death was imminent," she paused as I absorbed her statement. "We have a crematorium downstairs in the basement, for the animals. Toby goes to Jake and gives him an urn of ashes, animal ashes, but we tell him it's you…that you passed on the way out here. We give Jake a fake death certificate; he accepts you are gone, that the marriage is over. Toby will have no problem selling the story. Jake can't blame us for your death—you were on your last breath anyway. Senator Morris won't know the difference as long as Jake is no longer threatening to expose us. Jake moves on and gets to live. It's win-win."

I contemplated her words, letting them sink in one by one. "Jake lives?"

"Yes. Toby likes the plan."

"But, I'm dead?" I said.

"Not really," Sam answered. "Jake just thinks you are."

"Yes, but..." I didn't want to reject her proposal, if Jake lived, that's all that truly mattered, but I still felt the sting of loss.

"What?" Sam asked. "I really don't see any other way."

I sighed. "It's a good plan. It's just that I imagined when I left this place that I would return to him. That Jake and I would finally live as husband and wife. Now, if he thinks I'm dead, he'll move on and..." I drifted off. My broken heart ached at the thought of him married to another woman.

Sam placed her arm around my shoulder, laying her head against mine she said, "He may still be there when you get out. The grieving widower may take years to recover."

"I'm sure he won't wait years," I stated.

"I wish you wouldn't sell yourself short like that. I'm sure he won't be able to move on for a long time. He chased you across two states for goodness sakes!"

I shrugged. "Okay, even if he is still single, what happens when he finds out I lied? That this whole time I was alive when he thought I was dead?"

"You can always throw the whole deceptive marriage thing back at him," she laughed. "Besides," Sam continued. "Marriage is highly overrated. Sure, you love each other, and at first think forever isn't long enough, but after a few years..."

"How would you know?" I didn't mean to sound insolent, but how could she even think to know how Jake and I felt about each other?

Sam sighed, "I'm just saying that now that we can actually live forever, you might find yourself wishing for the sweet relief of death to come release you from any marital obligation. Honestly, I suspect marriage won't even be a thing in the future. Who *really* wants to spend an eternity with someone constantly leaving his dirty underwear on the floor? Trust me, marriage is no honeymoon."

"So you have experience?" I asked.

I looked up to gauge Sam's reaction. She held her smile but her eyes grew distant, drawing memories from the back of her mind. "Yeah, I was married once."

Scooting out from under her arm, I sat across from her, listening.

"Paul. He was tall, blonde, blue eyes...handsome farm boy." Her childlike smile still reflected love. "He and I were high school sweethearts. We both attended the same college, and in our junior year he proposed. We married that summer—much to the dismay of our parents. I loved him, but he was a stubborn man. I was pre-med, he was majoring in theology. We both believed in God, so that wasn't the source of our troubles. Our troubles began when he got sick."

I watched as her eyes clouded and filled with sorrow.

Water glistened in the corners, though she did not let a single tear escape.

"I begged Paul to see a doctor. I knew that if only he would seek help..." she paused to collect herself. "He argued that God would heal him, that by accepting medical treatment he was casting his faith aside. The sicker he became, the more I pled with him to go to the hospital, and the more resolute he became to prove that God would heal him without the aid of medical science.

"I prayed and prayed for God to heal Paul. I begged God to reward his faithfulness. When it was obvious that wouldn't happen, I prayed for God to change Paul's heart, convince him to go to the hospital. His infection spread. At the age of twenty-two, just a month after he became ill, he died of sepsis, the result of infectious pneumonia. His death was completely preventable, curable, but it was too late."

Pain twisted Sam's face as she tried to keep her composure. I knew Paul's death still affected her more than she wanted to let on.

"God didn't answer a single prayer. When I looked at Paul's lifeless body, remembering the man whose faith got him nothing in this world, I realized if God did exist, He wasn't worth following. After that, I devoted my life to science. It's too late to save Paul, but now, science will save millions, and in some small way, I know I'm honoring him."

"I had no idea," I said, tears trickling down my cheek.

"Hey, it was a long time ago," she answered, suddenly upbeat. "We have the future before us, and it is going to be amazing."

I wiped my face with my shirt. "Speaking of the future," I said. "When is Toby going to tell Jake?"

"He left an hour ago," Sam replied.

I buried my face in my arms. I could almost feel Jake's heart breaking with my own.

I love you Jake. Please, please know that I'm still alive, my heart silently called. *Please, hear me. I'm still alive. I love you. Wait for me, Jake. Just wait.*

Chapter Twenty

Sunrise. Sunset. Sunrise. Sunset.

The repetitive anthem from Fiddler on the Roof played in my head as days blended into weeks. Every morning I woke to the same routine: testing, soap opera, lunch, more testing, dinner with Sam. I tried to remember that it wasn't a bad existence. Jake was alive and I wasn't being tortured. Nonetheless, this life held no more meaning for me than if I'd died back in Charleston.

As a child, I learned to survive in a world of emotional and physical turmoil. Reverting to my youth, I replaced every emotion with numbing emptiness. I found ways to keep constantly busy, even during breaks, because if I allowed my mind to wander, it always found its way back to Jake. For several days I imagined his reaction as Toby delivered the crushing blow.

I envisioned Jake delivering the news to Jenn, her sweet face warped by the loss of innocence experienced when death finally hits close to home. The strain on my heart became too much. Relief existed only in my anesthetized chasm of nothingness.

I muddled through each day, finding no joy in analyzing poorly acted daytime drama and in the evening, no comfort in bland comedy and equally tasteless wine. Sam expressed concern about my depression, but I refused medication. I deserved the crushing desolation, the solitary anguish in my heart. No amount of medication could ever fix the broken pieces caused by my selfish decision.

Senator Morris left for D.C. as soon as he learned Jake was out of the picture. I didn't know if Toby filled him in on our changed plan, but I wasn't going to press the matter to find out. I passed Toby in the hall a few days after he was dispatched to deal with Jake. He smiled at me but I could not force a smile in return. He tried to strike up a conversation—I'm sure expecting some sort of gratitude on my part—but I just ignored him. Although he spared Jake, Toby took the gun. He was willing to do whatever the senator asked and if it wasn't for Sam, Jake would be dead. There was no thanks, no forgiveness in that truth.

Dr. Anderson remained completely engrossed in his lab work, researching each of Senator Morris' strange questions on the small, defenseless animals he held captive in their cells.

Three weeks passed, nothing changed.

After an especially rigorous physical test, I sat eating my lunch in the communal kitchen, trying to ignore Corson's creepy, watchful pacing as he waited for his beloved doctor to enter the room. I heard the door handle turn prompting Corson to leap into position. Before the door opened, he was poised and ready for Sam's entrance, food tray in hand. I looked up as Sam strolled in, smiling.

"Put your food down!" she announced, passing Corson's eager stance to come sit beside me. "We are getting out of here today!"

Sam didn't notice that her announcement crushed Corson's optimistic mood. The poor boy stood there, holding the tray of food, looking dejected.

Despite the fact that I despised Toby, I didn't hold any hard feelings toward Corson for dragging me from the room that night and locking me in my apartment. Somehow I couldn't hold him responsible for his actions — probably because this boy, seemingly unable to make a decision on his own, appeared to do whatever he was told. Constantly looking for acceptance in those around him, he was easily led, hoping to gain approval and praise. I felt sorry for him.

"Getting out of here?" I asked, indifference weighing on my voice. The outside world had nothing more to offer than what these walls provided, now that Jake thought I was gone.

"Yes," she chimed. "We are going to...wait...do you wanna guess?"

I shrugged, "Not really."

"Okay, you are seriously taking the fun out of this."

"Fine," I said, trying to feign more eagerness. "Where are we going?"

Bringing her hands to her face, then fanning them out like she was announcing a Broadway spectacular, Sam replied, "The mall."

Sam pouted as I failed to display the appropriate amount of enthusiasm for the moment.

"Oh, come on Maddy. We are taking a huge risk leaving without Senator Morris' approval, but you have to get out of this funk! I think some fresh air and a change of scenery will do you good. We'll see a movie, have a late lunch, shop for clothes...it will be fun."

"Senator Morris doesn't know?" I was nervous, not so much for whatever consequences fell on me, but for those of my friend.

"Nah, we didn't run it by him, and we won't be saying anything about it either," Sam cast a critical glare at Corson. "...*ever*." He sheepishly lowered his head. Realizing his services weren't needed, he set the food tray on an empty table, then defeated, slinked from the room.

"Wait. What do you mean by, 'we didn't tell him?'" I asked.

"Well," Sam fidgeted like a restless child caught misbehaving. "Okay, just don't get mad..."

I shook my head, not willing to promise anything at this point.

"Toby has to chaperone."

"What? Toby?" The thought of spending any time with that man made my blood pressure spike and my skin crawl. "No way. I'm not going."

"Okay, I hate doing this, but you force my hand," she said, rising to her feet. "I am pulling rank on you. I order you to come with me."

I laughed, "You don't outrank me! I'm not on your staff."

"Fine, then I will go find my tranquilizer darts and when you least suspect it... bam! You'll be out like a light and won't come to until safely inside the Gap!"

"You wouldn't dare," I threatened, my mood slightly lightened by our banter. "Besides, I'll just spend all day ducking and weaving through the halls!"

"I shoot marksman. You'll never escape."

"I had no idea that a trip to the mall could turn this violent," I chuckled. "Okay, fine. I'll go. Just know that I hate it...at least the Toby part."

"Noted," Sam replied, smiling victorious.

I went to my apartment, fixed my ponytail and threw on a pair of jeans and light blue tee before I went to meet Sam at the entrance of the Institute. Sam wore jeans and a red knit top. Both of us looked completely underdressed beside Toby's gray pinstripe suit.

"This is what he wears to the mall?" I quietly grumbled to Sam as we approached.

"Give him a little credit. He's trying," Sam answered.

Toby waited beside the automatic sliding doors marking the entrance of the building. He stood there polite, trying to look humane, but I refused to be fooled by his compassionate pretense.

Stepping outside for the first time in months, the thick, southern air strangled my first inhalation, the sun dazing my senses with its blistering heat and blinding glare. Taking a moment to regroup, I wondered if hell relocated to the Deep South during the summer months.

"Come on," Sam encouraged. "Once we get the air cranked in the car you'll feel better. I'll let you ride shotgun!"

I followed my companions to the nondescript, blue sedan with government plates and got into the front passenger seat. I watched in horror as Sam climbed in the back seat as Toby took his position as driver. He smiled. I glowered. I hated this trip more by the second.

"How far is the mall?" I called to Sam over my shoulder.

"Only about forty minutes," she called back over the air now blasting from the vehicle's vents. "Unless we get held up by a train."

I reached for the radio, hoping to find some music worthy of the ire gnawing at my gut. Unfortunately, this car lacked a sound system of any kind. Frustrated, I hit the dash where a radio should have been before sitting back in my seat and fastening my seat belt.

"Sorry," Toby said, noticing my futile search for an FM dial. "No radio. Only senators get nice digs. We assistants get run down, government junk."

Furious, I glared out my window, refusing to engage my companion in the front seat, no matter how amiable he attempted to be.

I slouched in my seat, letting the warm air stream across my face praying it would cool off soon. The thought of sitting in a blazing hot car next to Toby for the better part of an hour, without a radio, became my own personal definition of hell.

We pulled up to the gated entrance where a young man in a security uniform, with dark hair and a slim build, stood in the door of the guard shack.

Toby rolled down his window, "Hey Erik, how's your afternoon?"

The man smiled, "I'm well Mr. Caras. Heading out for the day?"

"Yes," Toby replied. "But we'd like to keep it private. Senator Morris isn't around and we're kind of cutting work early, if you know what I mean…"

Erik smiled a knowing smile and said, "Amen to that! Have fun."

"Thanks, Erik," Toby said. "You on days this week?"

"Yeah," Erik answered. "I'm on days and Pete's on nights. It's Craig's week off."

"I think we'll be back before your shift changeover, but just in case, could you let Pete know we're out so he'll expect our return? He gets a bit jumpy at night."

Erik laughed, "I'll be sure he's aware. Hey," He stepped off the curb and leaned down, looking through the driver's window as he spoke across Toby, "You the new girl?"

I smiled, "Hi, I'm Maddy."

"Nice to meet you, Maddy," Erik winked. "Maybe if

you're free sometime..."

"She's married, Erik. Sorry," Toby interrupted.

"Too bad. Well, can't blame a guy," Erik said, shrugging as he stepped back onto the curb. "Have a nice time."

"Thanks," Toby said as Erik raised the gate allowing our exit.

My irritation with Toby skyrocketed. How could he possibly think it okay to say that I was married? Not that I was interested in Erik's advances, but how could Toby be so callous? He was the one who destroyed my marriage by proclaiming me dead. Furious, I glared out my window, refusing to look in Toby's direction for the remainder of the trip.

The Institute was definitely secluded from civilization. We drove miles down a long, empty, wooded stretch of two lane road before entering the highway. The car cooled to a manageable temperature, yet I smoldered. The afternoon traffic was heavy, but thankfully it wasn't rush hour. Stuck at a standstill under these circumstances would be the worst form of torture to date.

We made it a few miles down the highway before Sam called out from the back seat, "Hey, guys, I'm sorry, but can we stop up ahead?"

"What? Why?" I asked. I just wanted to get to the mall and get this day over with, no side trips.

"I'm sorry, but I think I drank too much coffee before we left."

"You can't hold it?" I asked, turning to give her the most evil glare I could muster.

"We're still a half hour away. Please...*please?*" Sam begged.

"You should have gone before we left," I griped. Toby's chuckle intensified my frustration.

"Sorry Mom. I promise I'll do better next time," Sam called out. I ignored her.

Toby took the next exit and pulled into a gas station.

"I'll be quick," Sam said as she hopped out and made a beeline for the restroom.

Toby and I sat in uncomfortable silence, listening to air hiss through the vents. I stared out the window, watching for Sam's return, not wanting to acknowledge our sudden seclusion.

"I wasn't going to kill him, you know?" Toby's voice broke the silence. I offered a breathless laugh while continuing to avoid looking in his direction.

"I know you don't believe me, but no matter what Senator Morris threatened, I wouldn't have killed Jake."

I turned to face him for the first time in weeks. His dark eyes peered into mine with solemn intensity. There was something in his voice, a slight accent. It wasn't obvious like Senator Morris' southern drawl, but there was a definite foreign edge that I hadn't noticed before. I couldn't put my finger on its origin.

"I'm willing to bet I hate this place as much, if not more than you do. I strongly dislike Senator Morris. He is a self-seeking, mean spirited man," he sighed. "But I was assigned here, this is my lot. Trust me, I'm no murderer."

I didn't respond. His accent grew deeper; I knew for

certain I'd never heard it before. Why now, did he choose to uncover its convincing Americanized mask?

He smiled, "You know, that Jake's a good guy. I liked him the minute we met. You're lucky to be married."

"Of course, thanks to you he thinks I'm dead," I reminded him. "So technically, we aren't married anymore."

"You think very little of me, don't you?"

It was an odd question. I didn't understand his point.

"Yes," I answered, feeling a twinge of regret. "Well, I mean...I guess." I could never stay angry with anyone...at least to their face.

"I hope you will think better of me in the future," he replied. "...and, in time, I hope you come to appreciate how important you are, that so many lives depend upon you."

"What do you mean?" I asked. Toby smiled and took a deep breath. I braced for his explanation.

The rear door swung open. "I'm ba-ack," Sam announced as she hopped back in the car. "Thank you, thank you, thank you! I feel like a new woman!"

Toby and I stared at each other for a long moment. I wanted him to explain, but understood Sam's return marked the end of our conversation, for now anyway.

"What?" Sam said, noticing our anxious behavior. "What'd I miss?"

"Just discussing which movie we are going to see," Toby said, his accent gone. "I wanted to see the new political thriller, but Maddy here wants to see that animated flick. Guess it's up to you to cast the deciding vote."

"Well, it's nice to see you two speaking to each other," Sam said. "Sorry, Toby, but I always have to side with the girl in the room, and since this is her day out, you're stuck with cartoons."

Toby shrugged, "Okay, I guess I will just have to suffer." Casting one more meaningful glance toward me, he added, "Better get going." He threw the car into drive and pulled away from the station.

As we drove the side street toward the highway my mind focused on three compelling questions. First, what was the origin of Toby's accent? Second, why did he choose to reveal it to me when we were alone? And finally, what *was* going on around here?

The light ahead turned red and we came to a stop. Sitting there, I felt uneasy, as if someone was staring at me. I looked to my right, but the couple in the black coupe were busy singing and dancing to whatever song pounded out a bass line on their radio.

Lucky fools with a radio, I sulked.

Still sensing I was being watched, I glanced around the car. Sam concentrated on her phone, messaging someone, and Toby's blank stare remained fixated on the storefronts beyond his side window. Perplexed, I glanced at the car waiting in front of us and immediately perceived the reason for my paranoia.

Dark, penetrating eyes in the car's rear view mirror focused their narrow gaze directly on me. I could tell the driver was male and that he was alone, but my lack of perspective from behind the vehicle did not allow me to determine more than that. I glanced away, hoping my lack of response to his stare would inspire the stranger to focus on another subject.

He's just bored, people watching...this is a long light, I tried to convince myself.

After several seconds I returned my attention to his reflection, shocked to see his eyes hadn't moved—they remained focused, menacing.

First in line at the light, the man should have been watching for it to change, but instead, his eyes never wavered. I wanted to ignore this impertinent intrusion, but I could not look away. A chill ran up my spine. I glanced around the car to see if Toby or Sam noticed the disturbing stranger's stare. Both remained involved in their personal distractions.

The light changed to green and as the surrounding traffic flowed into the intersection, those eyes remained focused a moment longer before their owner hit the car's accelerator, hard. He took off like a shot, cutting into the right lane before racing toward the I-459 on-ramp. I yearned to believe the bizarre incident was just the ogling of a creepy admirer, and nothing more, yet instinct warned me otherwise.

"Crazy drivers," Sam commented, noticing the car's wild getaway.

You have no idea, I thought as Toby accelerated forward at a less than harrowing pace, following the path of our peculiar traffic companion who, thankfully, was now beyond sight, probably miles down the highway.

Chapter Twenty-One

We arrived at the mall shortly after two o'clock. We groaned in unison as we approached the theater. A line stretched along the sidewalk almost halfway down the length of the building. Children fluttered around their parents, laughing and screaming. The three of us looked at each other, dismayed by the waiting crowd.

"Uh-oh," Sam said. "I think today might be the opening day for our movie."

"Now can we see my action thriller?" Toby ribbed.

"That may not be such a bad idea," I agreed. "But the wait will be just as long either way."

"Yes, but the theater will be empty," Sam said. "I'm not

sure I want to spend the afternoon listening to parents discipline their kids at the cost of ten dollars a ticket."

"We can always do something else," I offered.

"No," Sam said. "We're here, let's just get in line."

We took our position at the end of the line. The day had turned up its thermostat, further heating the stagnant, wet air stifling my lungs. I shifted uneasily, sweat beading along my forehead as I tried to ignore my discomfort. I was unaccustomed to the heat after remaining indoors as summer gradually built toward its sweltering climax.

A rumbling of voices stirred the crowd. A commotion erupted toward the front of the line. Someone called for help. Disoriented from the heat, I thought I heard another voice say something about dehydration, fainting.

Through the clamor I heard Toby, his voice strong and composed in my ear, tinted with foreign nuance, "Go. Go now to her. Get to the front of the line."

"What?" I said so softly that I wondered if it rose above the chaos sweeping through the crowd.

"Go, now."

Not certain how I got my legs to move, I found myself racing toward the box office. A group of people huddled around something on the ground. Without announcing my arrival, the assembly somehow knew to part, allowing me to join their circle. I saw a woman, in her mid-thirties with short blonde hair and a medium build, lying motionless on the ground. A small boy, about three years old, knelt beside her, fear and sadness distorting is sweet, youthful face. Blonde like his mother, his eyes were big, the whites stained red from the tears streaming down his cheeks.

"I think she passed out," a female voice said.

"She has a medical alert bracelet on," another voice chimed.

"Has anyone called 911?" a male's voice cried out.

"She's turning blue," the first woman said.

"Touch her," Toby spoke in my ear. "Reach down and touch her."

"But I don't know CPR," I said, this time loud enough to draw the attention of a few people nearby.

"Does anybody know CPR?" the male voice called.

"Touch her," Toby urged.

"But…"

"Do it now," he forced.

I looked down, observing the ashen face and gray-blue lips of the woman who had obviously been without oxygen for several minutes. Kneeling beside her, I glanced into the eyes of the small boy across from me. I didn't know what to do.

"Touch her," Toby encouraged.

Time seemed to hang, suspended in the moment. I no longer noticed the group surrounding us. Everything blurred away, leaving me alone with the little boy and his mother. The only thing I heard was Toby's prodding, "You can do this. Just lay your hands on her chest. Have faith."

Terrified, I stretched out my arms and carefully laid my hands upon the lifeless woman. Her rapid inhalation startled me backward. She opened her eyes, breath returned. The world rapidly rushed in around me while people who never physically left this space returned to my vision.

"Did you see that?" I heard a woman cry.

"Who is she?" asked another.

"I got it all here on my phone," a male voice answered.

"Me too," I heard other voices echo.

I looked up at the crowd pushing in around me—many extending phones and cameras in my direction—displaying more concern for capturing my image than for the woman returning to life below them. There, among the swarming mob was a face I recognized from my past, a face I was convinced could only have been a drug induced hallucination, but now, before me, he was as real as everyone else crushing in upon me. He smiled the same, recognizably foreign smile while an identical feeling of peace blanketed my soul.

"Wait!" I called as the stranger from my hospice doorway turned and calmly walked away through the crowd. I leapt forward, trying to stop his departure, but something caught the collar of my shirt, reversing my momentum. The man disappeared from sight. Stumbling, I lost my footing as people pressed in, forcing every type of electronic recording device imaginable toward my face. Staggering backward, my shirt collar was released and an arm grabbed me around the waist helping to support my weight while we rushed away.

I glanced up at my rescuer to find Toby, looking frustrated and overwhelmed, racing me toward Sam who was already across the parking lot, nearing our car. Wordless he sprinted, his arms wrapped tightly around me, my feet barely skimming the ground. The wail of distant sirens grew louder, announcing emergency crews were on their way.

Already in the back seat with the door open, Sam reached out as Toby hurled me into the vehicle beside her, slamming the door shut behind me. Toby climbed into the driver's seat and swiftly started the car. Throwing it into gear, we sped for the mall's exit.

"Crap," he said as we merged onto the busy boulevard. An ambulance and accompanying fire truck flew past going the opposite direction.

"Crap!" he announced again. "What on Earth did you do?"

"I have no idea," I said, my head wheeling. "I just did what you told me to."

"What?" Toby asked, incredulous.

"You told me to touch her," I said. "So I touched her. But I have no idea what I did."

"I didn't tell you to touch her!" Toby replied. "Crap! Everything is ruined!"

"It was your voice," I argued. "It had to be your voice. Sam, you heard him, didn't you?"

"Maddy," Sam said. "I didn't hear anything. One minute Toby and I are standing there with you, the next you are running for the front of the line. We didn't even know there was a woman in distress until you did whatever it was you did. What *was* that?"

"I don't know!" my voice cracked. "I don't know!"

My head was spinning; I swore I heard Toby's voice telling me to go to the woman. If it wasn't his voice, who did I hear?

A local news van equipped with a large satellite dish on top drove past, obviously heading toward the theater.

"Ugh," Sam said. "Media. This is going to be all over the local news."

"Oh, this isn't going to remain local." Toby reacted, anxious frustration punctuating every word. "Woman miraculously brings other woman back from the dead with one touch, then the mysterious healer gets dragged off and thrown into a government vehicle...The press will have a field day with this one. It will be national within an hour."

Toby made a sharp right turn and pulled into a crowded supermarket. Parking the car in the back of the lot he sat, both hands on the wheel, engine running.

"Ruined," Toby repeated under his breath. I dared not speak.

After a few minutes Toby turned to face us. "Okay, we have to figure this out. We need a plan. Senator Morris will know soon enough, but that's not the worst of it..."

Sam groaned.

"What could be worse?" I asked.

"Maddy, you are supposed to be dead." Toby said, worry creasing his brow. "Your husband will see the news—Jake's going to know. When he comes back for you Senator Morris will not be sympathetic, especially when Jake is supposed to be dead."

No. I had put Jake in danger again and now my friends were also going to suffer because of my actions. I shuddered with fear, "So what can we do?"

"Give me a minute," Toby said, pinching the bridge of his nose between his fingers. "I just need a minute to figure this out."

Chapter Twenty-Two

"Okay," Toby drew a deep breath. "Okay." He continued this mantra intermittently as he thought.

Sam and I sat silent while he strained to come up with an idea. I tried to think of what I could do, but nothing seemed logical. I considered intercepting Jake and running away with him, but sooner or later Senator Morris would come looking, and there was no doubt in my mind he would find us. Besides, that would leave Toby and Sam to deal with the consequences alone. I couldn't abandon them. I also couldn't abandon their research, especially if, as Toby alluded, so many lives depended on my participation.

I wished my new genetic makeup gave me super human intelligence. I desperately tried to access unused portions of my brain, certain I could come up with a solution, but unfortunately my mind didn't mutate into anything spectacular.

Super human strength was out of the picture too. Small framed Corson was able to subdue me and drag me from a room kicking and screaming. It seemed the mutation protected one from death and disease, allowing the body to reach its full potential, but only the potential it was genetically born to exhibit. Despite the disappointment over my lack of super human powers, it was a relief to know that even after the mutation everyone would keep their individual characteristics—at least we wouldn't be clones of each other in mind or body.

"Okay," Toby said once more. "I think I have an idea."

"Good, because I've got nothing," Sam said. I nodded in agreement.

"First I need to deal with the media. If they trace my plates those parasites will initially show at Senator Morris' office in downtown Birmingham, where the car is registered. If I can diffuse the situation, tell them that the woman fainted and Maddy happened to touch her at exact moment she came to, I think they would leave the story alone."

"What about the dragging me away and throwing me in the back of your car part?" I asked.

"Okay...that's more difficult. I'll just say that Sam and I were passing by on our lunch break and saw Maddy in distress, so we rescued her from the curious crowd closing in around her. We'll emphasize that we don't know her and we dropped her off in the next town so she could call friends to come pick her up. I think we can avoid this becoming a huge issue, keep it local. But, just to be safe, I think we need to keep Maddy away for awhile. Don't give anyone more reason to start prying or forming government conspiracy theories, at least more than they already will."

"I should probably call Dr. Anderson and alert him that we might have a problem...in case he needs to hide or move our research files," Sam said.

"Don't worry. I'll handle Dr. Anderson and the rest of the staff, I need you to focus on Maddy," Toby replied.

"But what if the plan doesn't work? What about Jake?" My throat tightened in fear mentioning his name.

"Yes," Sam interjected. "Jake is going to show in the middle of this media circus asking to see his wife...that will definitely add fuel to the fire, especially if he starts spouting off about how we were the ones who told him Maddy died."

"I know," Toby sounded flustered. "The plan isn't solid, there's so much I still need to work through, but I think our first step should be to get Maddy out of town and safely hidden until we see how this is going to play out. I figure we've got about 3 hours, at the earliest, before Senator Morris arrives, and that's only if he's near a TV as the story breaks. We may have a bit more time; at least I hope we do."

"So, where do we take her?" Sam asked.

"Someplace close—you don't have transportation and I can't risk getting too far out of town in case the reporters or

Senator Morris move quicker than I think. It also needs to be a place where locals don't spend a lot of time watching the news. I don't want anyone redirecting the media to your location if they happen to recognize Maddy."

After thinking for a moment Sam said, "I've got it! Hold on."

She picked up her phone. "Oak Mountain State Park, cabin rentals," I heard her say into the receiver.

When she finished the call, Sam looked up and said, "Good news, they have a cabin available. Thankfully it's a weekday, they're booked all weekend, so we'll have to be out by Friday, but at least it's a start."

"Where is it?" I asked.

"About twenty minutes from here, a little longer in traffic. The cabins are secluded—no televisions or phones nearby. I used to camp there as a child. I'm certain no one will bother us." Thinking for a moment she added, "I should probably run into the store to stock up on enough food to last us a few days, though."

"I'll go with you," I offered.

"No," Toby said. "I don't want to risk exposing you in public, especially if your face has already hit the news. People may recognize you. I don't think anyone got a good look at Sam. She should go alone." Turning to Sam he added, "You alright to go in alone?"

"Seriously?" she ribbed. "You think I can't handle a quick trip into the grocery store? I'm hurt."

Embarrassed, Toby replied, "Sorry, Sam. I'm not thinking right."

"No worries," she said, hopping out of the car.

I watched as Sam crossed the parking lot and entered the store.

Alone again with Toby, I was the first to speak, "I'm sorry, this is all my fault."

"No," he said. "There's a reason for everything, I just don't know what that is reason is right now." There was no trace of the accent he let slip earlier.

"Do you think it will work?"

Toby didn't answer. He was lost in his own thoughts.

"Toby?"

"What?"

"Do you think your plan will work?"

"I don't know." He rubbed his forehead and frowned, adding, "But it's all we can do right now." Looking me straight in the eye he emphasized, "Don't worry about Jake. Senator Morris won't touch him."

"How can you be so sure?" fear punctured my voice.

Toby didn't answer.

"What if we were just honest with the media? Couldn't we tell them who I am? Do you think we could convince Senator Morris to announce our findings? Do you think the world is ready?"

"No," Toby admitted. "Senator Morris likes to dot every I and cross every T before he backs anything with his political name—publicly anyway. He's not ready, and neither is the world."

"But this will save lives. Even you said…"

"No, Maddy," Toby grew more agitated. "You don't

understand." Sighing he regrouped, "Listen, it's not your fault. Things aren't going according to our plan. I just need time. I have to think this through carefully, but I do believe everything will work out, so try not to worry, okay?"

"Okay," I conceded, but fear is a vise that once clamped, is difficult to release.

We sat in silence waiting for Sam to return. I fidgeted, expecting that at any moment the news media would descend upon our car. I tried to remain calm, but I couldn't fight the panic now in control of my every emotion. A brief moment of relief washed over me when I saw Sam hastening toward us, four plastic grocery sacks in hand. That relief, though, only lasted a moment before I felt suffocated again with dread over events to come.

We drove out of town as rush hour traffic invaded the highway, slowing our progress toward the safety of the mountain retreat. None of us spoke, lost deep within our own worried thoughts. Unable to predict where the next few hours would take our lives, I imagined the worst while hoped for the best. My thoughts focused on Jake. I wanted to have faith that Toby could protect him—that everything would work out as predicted—but I could not find enough belief in my heart to maintain any level of optimism.

Forty minutes later we arrived at the entrance to Oak Mountain State Park. A young woman with spiky, purple hair and tattoos covering every inch of her exposed arms greeted us at the gate. Apparently bored by her routine, the punk rocker turned park ranger barely acknowledged our presence as she accepted our payment and handed us a map of the campsite, directing our vehicle to cabin three, along the shore of Lake Tranquility. Antsy, I wondered if I could allow myself to lounge by the lake while Toby handled things back in town. Before long I would drive myself crazy playing out every pessimistic outcome in my mind.

We drove down a narrow, forested road—cars belonging to other campers lined either side of the street.

"Are you both gonna be okay?" Toby asked as he parked our car on the side of the road as close to the cabin as he could get.

"Of course," Sam replied.

We would have to navigate several hundred yards to the cabin on foot. We climbed out of the car and wandered to the head of a wooded trail marked by a sign noting the path led to cabin three. Sam set the grocery bags on the ground and scrutinized our surroundings. True to its name, the secluded area was tranquil—that irony not lost on me.

Deciding I couldn't just wait around for Toby to diffuse the media time bomb, I devised a plan that began with me contacting Jake by phone before he saw my face on TV, or at least before he made it to Senator Morris' office. I surveyed the row of cars, wondering if perhaps I could steal another camper's vehicle—although I didn't know the first thing about hot-wiring. Of course, even if I did acquire a vehicle, I had no idea what to do after that—I hadn't worked through the rest. I didn't know if Sam would support my actions, but I felt I had to do something. Banking on the fact that she was female, and in love at one

234

time herself, I hoped she would at least let me try reaching
Jake.

"Honestly Toby, we'll be fine," Sam assured Toby
who watched me skeptically. Checking her phone, a
discouraged expression crossed Sam's face. "No reception.
It says on the map there is a public phone somewhere in the
campsite. I'll have to set up times to call you from there."

"Okay," Toby said, studying his watch. "It's just before
four o'clock now, how about we set up a call time of seven
thirty? That gives me a chance to get downtown and start
putting out fires. I'll also have a better idea when Senator
Morris will show, if he hasn't already arrived by then. You
have my number?"

"Yep, right here," Sam flashed her phone in his direction.

Looking at me, Toby added, "Maddy, it's really going to
be alright. Just don't go anywhere, okay? You need to stay
here, no matter what is happening. It won't help the
situation if you try to take matters into your own hands.
I've got this."

I blushed, realizing my search for a getaway car wasn't
as covert as I'd hoped. Toby kept his eyes focused a
moment longer, emphasizing his assertion. Self conscious, I
looked down at my feet. I knew he meant well, but I
couldn't promise anything.

Toby sighed, "Okay, seven thirty. I'll be expecting your
call. Keep an eye on Maddy."

Picking up the bags of groceries Sam said, "Don't
worry, we'll be okay, won't we Maddy?"

I shrugged my shoulders and nodded in half-hearted

agreement.

"Seven thirty," Toby repeated.

"Got it," Sam answered as she turned and headed down the trail.

Chapter Twenty-Three

The cabin was nice enough. Each single-story, tan structure sat several hundred yards from another of its kind, offering complete forested seclusion to campers looking for an escape from their hectic, modern lives. Though rugged, all cabins offered modern amenities that might be missed by those looking for a mountain getaway, but not adventurous enough to sleep in a tent. Cabin number three featured a small porch, two large bedrooms, one bath, a kitchenette with refrigerator and a comfortable living space. Low grade hotel furnishings decorated the space, along with portraits hanging in every room that showcased the surrounding woodland and lake views. On most occasions I would consider this my type of camping—I'm certainly not one for roughing it—but my mood cast a shadow of gloom over any redeeming quality found in this wooded mountain retreat.

Okay, on second thought, perhaps the pleasantly unexpected air conditioning lifted my spirits, but only a fraction above complete despondency.

Sam bustled about putting groceries away while starting a pot of boiling water for the spaghetti she announced was on the dinner menu. Offering me a mountain themed soda—one she took exceptional pride in procuring for our adventure—Sam finished a can of her own, commenting afterward how she wished she had picked up some rum to go with it. I declined the drink, but she insisted, pointing out that I hadn't had anything to eat or drink since earlier that day. I sipped it slowly, and though I didn't like anyone telling me what to do, I had to admit I did need something on my stomach.

I tried to ignore how each minute that ticked off the clock increased my fear, along with my morbid curiosity over how things were playing out in the world beyond. I focused my attention outside the window. Although afternoon crept toward evening, the summer sun refused to ease in his relentless scorching of the earth below. Lingering in the sky, he opted to share the vast expanse above with the rising moon. Anxious, I felt time closing in around me. I had to break free and get to Jake...soon.

Sam placed dinner on the table, and begrudgingly I picked at the spaghetti on my plate. Continuing to stare out the window across the lake, I refused to give in to Sam's pleas that I eat something. She argued I would need my strength if things went poorly and we had to make another getaway. Unfortunately, my appetite didn't agree. My mind focused on Jake. I had to see him, warn him. I also had to figure out how to get Sam to go along with the plan. Unfortunately, each idea that popped into my head ended with Jake's fate determined at the hands of Senator Morris.

Sam finally gave up trying to get me to eat, realizing that I would not be much of a dinner companion. We sat in silence, the air conditioner's constant drone dulling my senses against the backdrop of its white noise. Lost in my trance, Sam's sudden leap from the table startled me out of my own chair.

"What? What is it?" My heart raced, unable to restrain my fear of whatever unseen force propelled Sam from her seat.

"Nothing," Sam laughed, shaking her head. "Nice of you to return to the land of the living though."

Returning my chair to its upright position, I collapsed back into my seat, not amused by her remark.

"Oh, come on Maddy. Stop being so nervous! See, it's seven fifteen. I am going to walk to the payphone and check in with Toby. I bet everything worked itself out by now, you'll see. Do you want to come?"

Apprehension gripped me. Unable to move, I shook my head in reply, avoiding eye contact.

"Okay, I'll be back soon. Don't you go anywhere," Sam sighed and I heard the door to the cabin close behind her.

Alone, I was unable to sit still. Restless, I twisted the

remaining spaghetti on and off my fork, but quickly became bored playing with my food. I stood up and paced the length of the room. Returning to the table I looked at the clock on hanging on the wall, it read seven twenty. I changed my mind—it might be best to hear any news first hand, before Sam had a chance to sugar coat it. I paced the floor once more, trying to determine if I should leave the cabin and catch up to her. Maybe she would let me call Jake, warn him. I looked up at the clock again—seven twenty one.

"Ugh," I murmured, deciding I wouldn't be able to sit patiently and wait on Sam's return.

Rushing to the front door, I jerked it open and stepped outside. The humid evening air streamed in, blanketing me in its thick coat, instantly causing sweat to bead over my entire body. Woozy from the heat's effect, I considered returning to the inviting cool of the air conditioned cabin, but my heart, pounding its anxious rhythm in my chest, hurried me forward.

The sun, deciding it was time to surrender, allowed the moon to take his rightful place as owner of the night, while deep purple chased the orange evening sky toward the horizon. Dusk's entrance transformed my forested surroundings into a two dimensional world of blue-gray shadows, obscuring my vision across the camp. I stopped at the edge of the porch, sweeping the lakeside with my eyes. Realizing I hadn't looked at the map, I didn't know where the campsite's solitary phone was located or which direction Sam traveled to find it.

The campground was oddly quiet in that moment. No birds chirped. No boats on the lake. No happy campers picnicked nearby. I strained to hear Sam's footsteps in the stillness.

Something rustled from behind the cabin. Catching movement in the corner of my eye, I jumped backward.

Turning to face my intruder, breath caught in my chest, my knees buckled. I had to steady myself against the cabin wall. A mirage, it had to be a mirage.

"Maddy," a voice choked. "Oh God, it's really you."

"Jake?" I asked, certain now this was a dream, that I was actually inside the cabin face down in my spaghetti plate. I pinched myself—it hurt. Jake chuckled. It was the same, warm laugh I would recognize anywhere.

I glanced around, no sign of Sam or anyone else nearby. Cautiously I moved forward, afraid my vision would vanish if I approached too quickly.

Arms extended, Jake beckoned, patiently waiting for me to make a decision. He didn't disappear as I drew near. A strangled sob caught in my throat as I threw myself forward into his arms, nestling into his torso. The heat from his embrace, the happy chuckle that rumbled through his chest, the smell of his cologne—I rejoiced knowing every detail was real.

I looked up into his hazel eyes and dimpled smile, not once considering where he came from or how he found me. He was safe with me for the moment, and in that moment, his security was all that mattered. We held each other, our eyes expressing what words could not.

Without warning, Jake refocused his attention, removing himself from my gaze. Glowering, he scanned the campsite, "Maddy, we don't have much time."

"Much time for what?"

"Shhh," he said, raising his hand to my face. "Don't be afraid. Things will be different when you wake. I love you."

A cloth covered my nose and mouth. Something burned the back of my throat, dizzying my senses. No time to react, a wave of nausea washed across my body just before my unsteady world went black.

Chapter Twenty-Four

I felt my eyes flutter, yet darkness remained, preventing a clear view of my surroundings. I struggled to free my mind from the muddled blanket that swathed its consciousness, trying to remember where I was and how I got there, but when I moved, my spinning head ached in pain, begging me to remain still. Nausea swept through my abdomen in small, daunting waves. A trace of some unrecognizable, acidic flavor lingered in my dry mouth, increasing the queasiness.

"Ugh," I uttered.

Shivering as the warmth of sleep began to leave my body, I reached for a blanket. My futile search alerted me to the fact that I was not in bed. My aching side suggested the support beneath me was hard, but not cold like cement or tile would be given the chilled temperature that hung in the air. Where was I? Only half waking, part of me remained trapped in the fog of a dream. Something important clung to the fringes of my memory, but I couldn't focus. The haze weighed heavy on my mind, clouding my ability to think.

Gradually emerging from my dreamy cocoon, I felt a hand gently stroking my hair. I realized my head rested on something soft and warm, different from the firm slab I felt beneath my hips. Strange fingers caressed my head, my hair, my cheek…they lingered across my skin with a familiar, loving touch.

I raised my arm, reaching for the fingers now tracing smooth, peaceful lines along my jawbone. The hand I met was warm in contrast with the cold air and when touched, it automatically entwined its fingers with mine. In that moment my mind jumped awake, hit with the realization that I did not know whose hand I gripped. Startled, I sat straight up, yanking free from the grasp of my anonymous companion.

Still woozy, I was caught in a spinning whirlwind as blood rushed from my head, threatening to send me toppling back into the blackness of sleep. I swayed backward; the hand I tried to escape now reaching out to catch me, steadying my torso and preventing my fall.

With eyes fully open, the room focused into view. Although dim—lit by a single light only a few feet away—the space felt familiar, though I didn't know where I was or how I came to be there. A memory fingered on my brain—

trees, a lake. The hand on my shoulder burned, reminding me of the stranger who, moments before, caressed me in my waking. My head, still aching, turned to observe the person sitting beside me now.

My heart raced, pumping much needed blood through my body, pulling me completely out of my disoriented state. Jake, his hand holding me upright, looked at me smiling, but his eyes held a look of trepidation—of what, though, I was unable to determine.

I had never been happier to see anyone in my entire life. I flung myself into his arms, catching him slightly off balance. A light chuckle rumbled in his chest as he wrapped himself around me, holding me close. I worried this all might still be a dream.

I buried my face into his chest, smelling his cologne, feeling his body heat warm my exposed skin. I didn't want to let go of him, stricken by the irrational fear that he might turn into smoke and disappear.

"Whoa, take it easy Maddy," he breathed. "I missed you too." I realized I locked him tight in a death grip.

Blushing, I let go and sat up, looking into those devastating eyes that sparkled despite the dark gloom surrounding us. As I righted myself, I once again tilted too far backwards, forcing Jake to reach out and catch me with both hands. He put one arm around my shoulder for support as he continued to stare. He seemed cautious, keeping me at a safe distance. I couldn't understand why he wasn't sweeping me up and carrying me away.

A memory flickered. A cabin. Jake, I saw him earlier...

As if sensing the return of my memory, Jake edged away, his arm still supportive, yet he managed to increase the distance between our bodies.

Yes, I saw him, outside the cabin. I ran to him...

My mind snapped back into place. I remembered the cloth he held to my mouth, the sting as I inhaled its chemical soaked fumes. It was the taste of the toxin that still lingered in the back of my throat.

My mood changed. My anger grew fierce.

"Maddy, listen..." Jake started.

"What did you do?" I growled, removing, well, more like throwing Jake's hand from my shoulder. He slid even further from my reach.

"Maddy, if you'd just give me a second to expl..."

"Are you *insane?*" I interrupted. "Do you know what you've done? Senator Morris is going to hunt us down! He wants you dead. You've left my friends to deal with the consequences. Sam is probably worried sick! Do you know how much danger you've put yourself in? How much danger you've put my friends in? What were you thinking?"

"Maddy, please, just let me speak."

Jake's stern gaze silenced me.

Defiant, I folded my arms across my torso. I glared, waiting for his explanation when something dawned on me, "Wait, how did you know I was alive? And how did you know where to find me?"

Jake smiled a crooked smile, "Well, if you'd just let me explain."

"Sorry," I conceded, unfolding my arms and slouching back in my seat.

I noticed we sat on a bench—a wooden bench. Finally taking a moment to observe the room around me, I realized we sat in the front pew of a church. A rounded light, the space's only illumination, hung from the ceiling positioned above the altar. It cast a warm, conical glow directly below. I could make out the distinct lines of a crucifix hanging slightly behind the altar. Glancing toward the back of the church, I couldn't determine the area's true depth as everything beyond the first three pews faded into shadowy gloom. Along the walls, floor to ceiling stained glass windows glowed depictions of Biblical events, lit only by street lights beyond—their radiance indicating that darkness of night cloaked the world outside.

Taking both my hands in his, Jake brought my attention back to his stunning, yet serious eyes.

"Maddy, the day you left—our wedding day—you have no idea..." he choked and looked away, his face twisted in pain. Guilt overwhelmed my heart seeing him. With a deep breath, Jake suppressed tears that threatened to erupt and quickly regrouped.

Sighing, he continued, "I know it was wrong for me to trick you into signing the marriage license, especially when you weren't in a position to refuse, but I had to make it legal...for me. I knew you didn't want the fuss, but Maddy, I did. I love you. I wanted our marriage to be real, in every sense of the word. I was glad I did it too, because our marriage gave me leverage to demand information about what had happened to you, what they had done. Do you know how crazy I would have gone, not ever knowing what happened? Not being given any explanation? If you had just disappeared..."

I put myself in Jake's position, knowing if the roles were reversed, and he had disappeared without explanation, I'm not sure I could have lived. I hated to imagine what I'd put him through, and what he might have become had he not tricked me into signing the marriage certificate. Even though Jake deceived me, I couldn't be angry. I wanted to tell him how sorry I was and that I would promise to make it up to him for the rest of eternity, but words didn't come.

"I didn't know what to expect when I received a call from Senator Morris' assistant. He told me to meet him at this seedy bar in downtown Birmingham. When I walked in, the place was all but deserted, like it hadn't seen business in years. It was dark, the windows were covered in gray film, and the floor looked like it hadn't been swept in months...hardly a hot Congressional hang out. I knew there was a chance I had stumbled into something dangerous, but Maddy, I would go through hell and back for you. I refused to be intimidated.

"When the guy showed, he was nothing like I expected. I pictured the senator sending some brute to deal with me, but instead, the gentleman who sat down beside me at the bar dressed in a nice suit and tie. He handed me an urn and a death certificate, told me you had passed, then immediately got up to leave. It was so strange... anticlimactic, I guess. Before the man exited, though, he turned around and with a sympathetic stare said, 'One day, you will not be so angry.' I was left sitting at the bar, too numb to even cry."

Jake's face took on a somber expression as he remembered that night. I too thought back to that night, remembering Senator Morris' original plan. I wondered if I should tell Jake that his instincts were correct, that originally he was marked for death. Such information could prove important depending on the level of damage control Toby was able to accomplish over the past few hours. For the time being, though, I chose to keep that information to myself, deciding some things were better left unsaid unless necessity warranted.

"I'm so sorry," I said. "I never wanted to hurt you."

"Hey, it's okay. You're alive. That's all that matters."

"I guess it was a good thing the about the news story, huh? I still don't understand, though, how did you know to come to the cabin?"

Jake's brow furrowed. "The news?" he puzzled.

"Yes," I answered. "The evening news. The woman I touched who came back to life...everyone had my picture. That's why I went into hiding at the lake."

"Maddy," Jake said. "I have no idea what you are talking about. I haven't seen the news today. Besides, I knew you were alive weeks ago. I knew that night at the bar."

"What?" my incredulous expression drew a smirk from Jake.

"You aren't the only one keeping secrets," he flashed a crooked, knowing grin in my direction.

"I don't understand," I breathed, searching my mind for anything I'd missed.

"Well, after this Toby guy left," a sneer tugged the corners of Jake's mouth as he mentioned Toby's name, "another man came and sat beside me, offering to share his bottle of wine as well as some interesting information. He knew all about Senator Morris and his research. He also knew about you, Maddy."

My jaw dropped. Heart racing, I struggled to determine the meaning behind Jake's words and who could be stupid enough to defy the senator. Lost within my thoughts, I didn't notice a figure emerge from the shadows behind the altar.

"I guess now would be an appropriate time to introduce myself," the thick, unmistakably foreign voice announced. I jumped at the sound.

The stranger came to stand in front of the altar beneath the solitary light radiating a soft glow from above. I scrutinized his appearance. Dressed in black, he was young—perhaps in his forties—with a medium build, olive colored skin, dark hair and a long beard. His dark pupils opened wide in the dim light, popping against the whites of his eyes and the bronzed backdrop of his face. There was something oddly familiar about those eyes. Images flashed in my head as I tried to connect where I had seen them before.

Reading my perplexed expression the man answered my thoughts, "Yes, you have seen me before."

A lump caught in my throat realizing the truth behind

my foreboding instinct—his were the same dark, menacing eyes that, hours ago, glared at me through a car's rearview mirror.

Chapter Twenty-Five

"What is going on here?" my voice quivered as I glanced around, deciding if I should make a run for the door.

"I apologize if I've scared you," the man spoke. "My name is Father Nikoli Petros. I promise, Maddy, there is no reason for your fear. I am here only to provide information; the rest is up to you."

"How do you know who I am?" I whispered, looking between the stranger—who took a seat on the first of three steps leading to the altar—and Jake, who grasped my hands while keeping a safe, yet comfortable distance beside me on the wooden pew.

"My brothers and I have been waiting for you," Father

Nikoli spoke.

"I don't understand," I breathed, shifting uneasy in my seat. Sensing my discomfort, Jake slid closer, placing his arm around my shoulder.

"I am a priest from the Island of Patmos, perhaps you've heard of it?"

I shrugged, embarrassed that I didn't recognize his home.

"Patmos is the Holy Island where Saint John wrote the Book of Revelation," Jake spoke in my ear.

"Jake," I turned from the priest, trying to keep my voice hushed. The man's intense stare loomed across from us, intruding into our conversation. "Listen, I don't know what to believe. The others warned me that religious leaders will want to destroy our research. Knowing we can now become immortal, they will lose their control over the masses. Scaring people with the idea of God is their only source of power."

Laughing from his seat, Father Nikoli said, "Maddy, do you not hear yourself? You know the Truth. You have seen it."

My thoughts swirled. When I was close to death I found myself believing in God—I even cried out to Him—yet how could I really be certain He existed? Of course, there were the visions...and the place I entered after I died. Had I really seen Heaven? My heart told me I had, yet my mind convinced me otherwise. Doubt wrapped itself around my consciousness. Faced with a choice, it was difficult to determine which reality was true.

"Besides," the priest continued, "it is not I who wishes to control anyone. If I were you, I would be more concerned with who, or what, wishes to control you and the rest of the human race!"

"Please, Maddy," Jake pleaded. "Just give him a chance to explain. Hear him out, but…"

"But what?" I forced.

"You need to be a bit open minded. What he is about to tell you will make your brain hurt. His warning is beyond anything I thought I knew about the Apocalypse."

"Well, that should be easy enough as I never understood anything about it myself." A twinge of frustration lined my words as I angled my body to face the priest and said, "Okay Father, I'm all ears."

Nikoli smiled, "I suppose the best place to start would be the beginning…the very beginning."

I settled back in my seat and took a deep breath, trying to remain open minded.

"The Book of Genesis tells us that God created man in his likeness. Adam was the most blessed of all God's creation—formed in the trinity of body, mind and soul. In the beginning, our bodies were immortal, our spirits obedient, our souls everlasting. During that time, before our fall, we walked with God, able to perceive Heaven around us—our soul and spirit always aware, always with Him.

"But there is one, one who walked with God yet decided to rebel against Him. Lucifer, a once beautiful archangel, was cast out of Heaven after trying to overthrow the Lord

God. Bitter, he watched as God created the Earth. Seeing how God favored Adam, Lucifer became jealous and resentful of man. In another attempt to overthrow God, this Evil One tempted the woman, Eve, and her husband, promising to give them what God could not, promising they would become like God—knowledgeable of all things good and evil. Selfishly, they defied the Lord's command not to eat from the tree of knowledge. And so we became knowledgeable, and cursed.

"Lucifer hoped this would be the end of man, but although God was furious with Adam and Eve, He could not destroy His beloved creation. Instead, He cursed them both, banishing them and their offspring from the Garden and keeping them from everlasting physical life; severing the connection between body, mind and soul—our trinity. So we wander, separated from God in these earthly vessels. God took from us our immortal bodies, limiting our years, until, of course, His final judgment. Despite how often we disappoint Him, though, God still loves and treasures us, as a father loves his children. He sent to us our souls' salvation through His Son, Christ Jesus, and soon He will come again to build a New Jerusalem where we will be made anew in everlasting life."

"So," I started, somewhat snide, still clinging to my disbelief. "God made us immortal, but because Adam and Eve were tricked into defying Him, we are cursed to die until He comes again? Where is the proof?"

"My dear girl, you are the proof!" Father Nikoli leaned forward. "Each person has the potential to become immortal—that secret locked deep within. Despite His wrath, God's immortal fingerprint remains on our DNA. He knew that one day man would grow knowledgeable enough to decipher its code, to discover the Holy Grail."

"I thought the Holy Grail was some chalice that contained Christ's blood. That if you drink from it you never die...or something like that," I said, gleaning my knowledge from Hollywood. Jake tightened his arm around my shoulder.

Father Nikoli smiled a crooked, knowing smile, "Yes, the Holy Grail is tied to Christ's blood, and through it immortality could be possible, but not for the reason humans have speculated. You see, if one were to analyze Christ's blood, it would show evidence of genetic mutation."

After an immeasurable moment, I asked, "So, Jesus' DNA was changed...different from the human race?"

Father Nikoli leaned forward, meeting my fixed gaze with equal parts fear and awe. "Let me ask you Madeline, how long did it take your body to heal after the doctor injected you?"

"Three days," I gasped. Jake exhaled loudly. I realized we both had been holding our breath.

"And, do you still feel pain? Do you still feel, human?"

"Yes," I trembled, my mind racing.

"Throughout the Bible there is evidence that God has altered certain lives during our separation from Him. Many Biblical figures lived for hundreds of years, far longer than others of their time. People have been healed for unexplained reasons. Despite our disobedient nature, God still loves us. Is it so impossible to accept that God, through the Holy Spirit, can alter someone's DNA, curing them of disease, or prolonging their life?"

I considered his words carefully, knowing they made more sense than I wanted to believe.

"But..." I paused, choosing my words carefully, "If my DNA is now changed like Jesus, does it mean I am like Him? Why do I not see God the way He did?"

Father Nikodemos smiled, "Ahh, therein lies the rub. You see, Jesus was God's Blessed Son, changed by the Holy Spirit. He was the Trinity—God's Trinity—His eyes opened, like God's, knowledgeable in the way Adam and Eve had hoped to become after they partook of the forbidden fruit. But He remained in human form until the resurrection when, through the Holy Spirit, the final change took place. You see, you have undergone six genetic mutations to create in you an immortal body, but this new body, like Christ's human body, is not immune to pain or suffering. You still bleed, you continue to feel pain, the change you experienced allows your body to heal but it does not make you impervious to dying—only permanent physical death...for now.

"You may heal, but your exile from God continues, and that, dear Maddy, is the greatest sin of all. Your soul has not been returned to Him, and He is going to come one last time and bring judgment on all those who inhabit this Earth. Our lives are not everlasting until all seven changes occur; the final change coming only from the Holy Spirit.

Seven, not six, is God's Holy Number."

I leaned my head against Jake's shoulder, overwhelmed. "How do you know all this? How do you know about my six mutations?"

"Maddy, my Brothers and I have guarded a secret, long kept since the time of John and his revelation. We have waited patiently and watched. There is... somebody on the inside. Somebody sent ahead to watch for you, knowing the time was near," Father Nikoli paused. "Our informant alerted us to the fact that researchers discovered the Holy Grail and that a woman, similar to Eve, now walked among us. We had to wait until we could get you away from the others. We couldn't risk anyone being alerted of our plan before we got to you, knowing that there are those who would be watching for us too. Of course, God works in mysterious ways. I have to admit, it was quite a pleasant surprise to learn the Lord blessed you with a husband. It provided a natural way of gaining your attention, easily drawing you away when the time was right. From that point everything fell into place. God's way is always better than anything we could hope to plan."

Looking up, Father Nikoli smiled as if sharing some private joke with the heavens. I glanced upward, trying to perceive any celestial being hovering in the space above. All I saw was a dark ceiling.

I cast an incredulous glance at Jake. He kissed the top of my head in reassurance.

Father Nikoli rose from the steps and took a Bible from the altar, then walking to the choir section, he retrieved a chair—the back legs hopping against the carpet as he pulled it along the floor—coming to sit directly in front of our pew. The three of us now huddled close together, the tiny chapel unbearably still, as if millions of unseen ears hung on each revelatory word.

"To this day Satan remains determined in his attempt to overthrow God, seeking to take God's power and control the human race. Satan will use our selfish desires and our fear, to turn us from God in these, our final hours—our hardened hearts and ignorant minds will unknowingly, yet willfully follow the Evil One."

He opened the Bible toward the back. "Maddy, John received many heavenly visions of our final days and was told to prophesy to all people. Centuries passed as scholars tried to determine the meaning behind much of what John writes. People have interpreted many earthly events as signs of the end times—earthquakes, floods, famine—yet some things remained so outrageous in our vague human sight, that many dismissed parts of John's prophesy as incoherent ramblings or partial truths, often claiming John was irrational or didn't understand what he had seen. For example, in chapter eleven, John testifies that God's two witnesses will be slain and the whole earth will gaze upon their dead bodies for three and a half days before these men rise again. No one understood how this could occur. In John's time, and until recently, it seemed preposterous—the idea that the entire world would be able to pilgrimage to the site in only three days, but now—with the internet, satellite television, cell phones—images from around the world can be streamed to a small screen you carry in your pocket. In present times, this prophesy doesn't seem so farfetched."

I fought against the hysteria rising inside my chest as I listened to the priest explain the inexplicable.

"Our limited human perspective continually keeps us from seeing God's full plan. We are ignorant, often believing prophesy only to the extent which we understand how it fits into the world we know. We are not always able to see with the eyes of God," the priest sighed. "Two millennia ago people saw signs in the night sky proclaiming the arrival of their Savior. Interpreting prophesy within the limits of their earthly understanding, they looked for a mighty king—a warrior who would unite the nations of Israel and secure their freedom.

"When a lowly carpenter stepped forward, claiming to be the Son of God, despite his miraculous works, many could not believe that he was the King promised them by God. Even Christ's own disciples did not, at first, fully understand the Lord's role. Many did not understand God's gift in this poor carpenter until His resurrection. Now, almost two thousand years later, we can see God's Prophesy fulfilled. The lowly carpenter proved to be a man far greater than we may have hoped, greater than any human king leading an army. God gave His saving grace to all people, giving us what no mortal ever could—true eternal life."

"But now we've unlocked the genetic key to immortality," I pointed out. "So who says we won't just find the seventh change and return to God ourselves? I don't remember prophesy about genetic mutation anywhere in the Bible."

Nikoli sat back in his seat, the chair emitting a faint squeak that penetrated the stillness hanging in the air. Suddenly I felt like we were inside a tomb rather than a chapel. A creepy sensation crawled across my skin, bumps raising the little hairs across my flesh.

"You are half correct," he continued. Although Jake's arm tightened around me, I still felt the world tumbling as my head reeled. "There is no direct mention of these events, but there is another piece to this puzzle. Even with its revelation, our earthly knowledge will confuse such prophesy, the Devil using our own minds against us. You see, there is something else, a secret alluded to in chapter ten of Revelation. The only information John relates publicly to mankind is that the Angel of the Lord, after showing him details of a scroll, instructs John to eat the scroll—that its taste would be sweet as honey, yet turn his stomach sour. John tells us that the angel commanded he keep the details of this Little Scroll from the world, yet what no one knows is that the angel instructed John dictate this vision to his trusted disciple, Prochorus.

"Though many—with limited comprehension of God's magnificent design—tried to interpret the mystery of the Little Scroll, only those of us guarding its secret understand that the Little Scroll represents the tiniest part of ourselves, our DNA.

"Prochorus, and the brothers who followed him, were

charged with protecting the truth of the Little Scroll, knowing there would come a time when man discovered its secret of our own accord. We now see prophesy fulfilled, and as John alludes, immortality without God will prove sweet for a time, but in the end, it will turn stomachs sour when God comes in judgment. Those who follow evil will realize they cannot hide from God's power."

"Why hide it, though?" I stammered. "Why wouldn't God warn the people He loved?"

"Ah," Nikoli relaxed in his chair. "You forget that humans did not discover DNA until very recently, late in the last century. Who would believe even fifty years ago, let alone in John's time?

"God was careful to keep John's visions powerful, and cryptic, yet close enough to our human comprehension regarding the workings of the universe—allowing our frail minds to accept John's visions on our most basic level. Unbeknownst to the world, John's prophesy is so exact that, without knowledge of modern genetics, he drew a precise representation of what we now know is a human DNA double helix—six points of light shining within, a seventh burning brighter than the rest. At the time, neither John nor Prochorus knew what this picture signified, only that it would be man's last challenge here on earth. If John or Prochorus could not comprehend the gravity God's revelation—knowing it came from God Himself—how much more would others doubt John's vision? Having no understanding of genetics or our wondrously complicated human design, many—seeing John's squiggly lines and seven points of light—would have faulted John's prophesy as incoherent, or even blasphemous, and discredited the entire book. Even now, many will doubt. None of us have the ability to see our world through the eyes of God, although we grow closer daily."

"But at the time DNA was discovered, why not bring this prophesy to light?" I flushed trying to keep up.

Father Nikoli drew a deep breath, "You must understand, Maddy, we must allow humans' free will to flourish. God's prophesy tells that we are not to know the time of His return. We could not interfere with that plan, only to watch for His signals. Humans must be free to make their own decisions. The crux of His final judgment is revealing who among us will choose God and who will turn away. Mankind had to discover immortality, and now we must make our choice.

"My brothers and I kept this secret, watching for the signs, waiting. God knew that someday humans would think they'd discovered how to live eternally without His Grace, but He is a loving God who wants to give mankind one more chance before the Evil One's rise to power. Through his letter to Prochorus, John foretold that when man unlocked the door to physical immortality, that you, Maddy, would be the first—a daughter in the likeness of Eve—to become physically changed, no longer mortal. Through you, God intends to give one final warning to the people of this earth—their salvation hinging on this final test. We are standing at the threshold of Eden—so close, yet still not inside. Many will think they've outsmarted the One who created us, falsely believing that they alone determine humanity's fate. Unfortunately, realization of the Truth will come too late; no one can enter the garden without God. He alone holds the key."

Father Nikoli folded his arms in his lap, his expression grew dark and sullen. "This test will not only determine which of us disbelieves, but will also determine those who call themselves Christian and yet are only lukewarm in the faith. When tempted with physical immortality, many will ignore God's promise that through Christ, and only Christ, will we gain everlasting life. These Christians will turn away in their ignorance and fear, giving their bodies over to Satan—their fate sealed as Tribulation begins. One cannot pledge allegiance to both sides, although many will try. Members of the church who choose immortality will not be raptured, but rather will go on to face the final battle. For those who return to God and repent, these individuals will be charged with leading others until the day of His final judgment. Those who continue to ignore God's Word will be damned in the lake of fire, the only way—as I understand it—your new human body can now be destroyed."

Jake's eyes widened with fear. I wrapped my arms around his torso, hiding my face against his chest. His heart pounded against my ear.

Now, more than ever, I felt alone, fearful. This was my fault. I spent my life denying God's existence, but now, after conquering death, had I lost the chance at being a part of His kingdom? Something inside my heart shifted.

Everything I doubted, everything I spent years refusing to believe seemed to snap into place in that one moment. I remembered crying out to God when I felt my life slipping away. Deep down I realized I needed God, but I chose to turn away time and time again. Now I was damned.

"What have I done?" I cried, burying my face deeper into Jake's embrace. I heaved a sob of frustration and sorrow, "I'm changed, there's nothing I can do. My soul is lost."

I wished I had died back in Charleston. At least I would have a chance at true eternity. It struck me how many more would feel this anguish if Senator Morris' work became public. Mothers, fathers, husbands, wives—so many souls lost.

Father Nikodemos interrupted my self-loathing, "Madeline, you *are* changed, but do not fear; your soul is not lost. John prophesied your arrival, and now through you, God will grant mankind one final chance. This is your penance…"

Chapter Twenty-Six

"My penance?" I asked, picking my head up from Jake's chest to look at Father Nikoli. "I turned away from Him. Why would God grant me forgiveness?"

I felt Jake shiver beside me.

"Madeline, God loves His people and though we don't always realize it, His Will—even if it seems wrong in our vague human observation—works for the good of all. Don't you see? You had to be orphaned and alone—no faith to rely upon—in order to have the opportunity and the reason to agree to become immortal. You had to doubt and turn away. If you were a true believer you would not have chosen this path for yourself, instead rejoicing in the chance to live with Him in Heaven. God needed you to change physically before He could open your heart and change you spiritually. He will employ your sin for His good. You will guide others away from evil and into His Truth. God often uses the least among us for His greatest purposes—you are no exception."

"But I don't know anything about God or the Bible. How can I possibly lead others?" The gravity of my situation pressed in around me. I was no leader. I barely knew the Bible. How was I supposed to go and preach to the world?

"You don't have to be an expert on theology. You will testify based upon your own experience and Maddy, you will not be alone. With the Holy Spirit's guidance, we will help you learn the way in which God wants you to prophesy. Of course, this life will not be an easy one. You will be persecuted by believers and non-believers alike. Some will say you are a false prophet while others will discount your testimony. Many will forget God for a time. Unfortunately, science will become humanity's new deity— those who bring these scientific discoveries to the world will be worshiped as kings themselves."

"So, we must believe that science is bad...because it goes against God?" Jake asked, hesitation punctuating his voice.

"Of course not," Father Nikoli sighed. "Science is a gift from God. The danger comes in how we give credit to what science discovers and what we choose to worship. God is responsible for all good things, and science gives us a glimpse of how great His love is for us and how beautiful our design, but we must never forget that God is the only One who is infallible. Why is it that there are two patients who receive identical care for an identical disease, yet one lives while the other dies? If science is exact, should not both patients live? What we overlook is God's hand at work. One person's life can change so many others around it, in both life and death. God has a plan, science does not. The danger comes when humans no longer see God in the revelations science provides."

"So, scientists working on medical cures, for instance, do not necessarily go against God," my words hovered somewhere between a statement and a question as I recalled my conversation with Sam about her husband's disdain for medical science.

"No, but in the wrong hands..." Nikoli paused, gathering the appropriate words. "Providing a cure for sickness and disease is not wrong. In fact, God charged us with loving and caring for each other, and wanting to save another's life is part of this love—it reflects God's love for us. Our desire to save others from death should provide a glimpse of God's desire to save our souls and keep us from death. Unfortunately, as I said, many will forget God during this dark time.

"Humans, unfortunately, are capable of being tempted against their better judgment. You must understand, many who will profess the goodness that comes from immortality will not do so with evil hearts. These people will be tricked into believing there can be a utopian society relieved of death. But we know that without God, utopia will not exist. Satan will twist human minds until they accept his ways. Satan will profess that mankind is freed from the bondage

270

of religion. He will convince the human race they can do whatever they desire including sexual acts, drugs, gluttony, greed—anything and everything that defiles the goodness of God. But there are those who will not be satisfied with simple human desires. There are many who will be free to commit crime, rape, torture—without Grace, or consequence, evil will flourish."

I imagined the world, uncontrolled and uninhibited. I knew firsthand of the evil lurking within some human hearts—those who enjoyed the suffering and pain of others for no greater reason than the pleasure they experienced watching another cry out in anguish. Even after the mutation, some individuals will remain stronger than others. The strong would continue to prey on the weak. Now however, there would be no recourse against wrong doing, no way out if you were the one trapped in the affliction of another's sick diversion. A cold chill ran down my spine considering how much more agony one person intent on harm could impose on another, knowing that even after tormenting that person to death, their victim would rise again only to suffer greater misery and fear the next time, and the time after that.

"You can imagine how this revelation terrified John and Prochorus," Father Nikoli's brow creased, his eyes narrowed. "The Lord disclosed Satan's intention to use mankind's longing for eternal life, combined with our selfish desires, to enslave us and turn the human race away from God. Even now we see people turn away from God, rather than run toward Him, during times of famine, war, natural disasters and sickness. Many have already lost faith, forgetting God's promises. True followers will not be swayed, they will stand righteous. Unfortunately, the Devil will bring forth this new path to immortality and for those who have no faith, or whose faith is tepid, they will follow the path of evil. Only those who truly love the Lord and trust in Him will find salvation and eternal life. The truth, though already revealed, will be confirmed too late for those who abandon the way of God."

A chill ran up my spine as I remembered my desperation to be healed. How ready I was to try anything, Immortality—the thought never crossed my mind that it could be evil. I didn't stop to consider how my life, and my suffering, might all be a gift from God. How He might be using those struggles to draw me closer to Him. I couldn't comprehend how many people would jump at the chance to live forever. How many, already abandoning God to worship science, will refuse to listen? And how many more, currently claiming to believe, will readily throw their faith aside for the blind promise of physical immortality?

"But I still don't understand where I fit into the picture," I spoke. "Shouldn't I be the first to be damned? Shouldn't I be the example?"

"Maddy, despite your choices, God loves you. He will use you as proof of His love and grace—His willingness to give second chances. You are to go forth, Maddy, and warn people of the signs they should already know to watch for. But, due to ignorance and hardened hearts, they will miss the signs, as you already have."

I tried to swallow the lump lodged like a boulder within my dry throat. "But you said the Little Scroll was a secret. What have I missed?" I rasped.

Turning the pages of the Bible, Father Nikoli found the passage he searched for and read it aloud, "He also forced everyone, small and great, rich and poor, free and slave, to receive the mark on his right hand or on his forehead, so that no one could buy or sell unless he had the mark, which is the name of the beast or the number of his name. This calls for wisdom. If anyone has insight, let him calculate the number of the beast, for it is man's number. His number is 666."

Looking up at me, Father Nikoli added, "Unfortunately, early on it was mistranslated as 'hand *or* forehead' when it should have been 'hand *and* forehead,' thus compounding the confusion Satan hopes to manipulate in his favor. When the time arrives, people will be looking for the number 666, not recognizing that they have already been marked."

Terrified, I tightened my grip around Jake, remembering information I so nonchalantly ignored weeks earlier. "Sam mentioned that Senator Morris planned to mark everyone's right hand and forehead with the number six, to identify who has been changed and who's DNA has yet to be altered. But she said the mark would be a six on one hand, and a six on their head," I pointed to the locations. "John said the number is 666. Where is the other six?"

"Their DNA," Jake whispered.

I looked up at him, dumbstruck. Like coming out of a

dream, everything snapped into focus. Hand...head... DNA...666.

"This is why John warns the number calls for wisdom, but unfortunately people will allow themselves to be deceived, wasting time calculating a single man's number that equates to 666. They won't notice it belongs to every man until it is too late." Father Nikoli slumped in his seat, a heartbroken expression distorting his handsome features.

"What do I do?" I asked, tears flowing.

"You must prolong mankind's discovery of our immortal body."

"How do I do that?"

"First, you must return to the lab and destroy all traces of the mutation serum and the research that supports it," Father Nikoli said.

Still weeping I said, "But if we are meant to discover these changes, what good will it do if I destroy the research? Won't Satan find a way around my efforts?"

"Time, Madeline, all we are buying is time, and God willing, a second chance for those who have yet to be delivered, before it is too late. You must go forth and prophesy to all people about the changing tide, the new flood. You must warn all nations of what you've seen and what you have become. Many will turn away, yet there is still the opportunity for some to find salvation. Yes, it is only a matter of time before people discover the key to their physical immortality. Once this mutation is brought forth and given to the world, the End Time will begin. No one can stop the events that must occur, but thanks be to God,

He is giving humankind one last chance. You will delay the Devil's rise to power and warn others before it is too late."

Sitting forward, taking my hands in his, Father Nikoli added, "I must, in good conscience, inform you of one more role you will play in this final mystery."

More, I thought, *How could there be more?*

"Chapter eleven, The Two Witnesses," Father Nikoli stared me squarely in the eye.

I nodded, remembering his earlier mention of the martyrs who would be resurrected before the watchful eyes of the entire world.

"Maddy, the two witnesses, they are your children."

Chapter Twenty-Seven

I choked when Father Nikoli mentioned children, pulling free from his grasp. Supporting my elbows on top of my legs, I leaned forward and rested my head against the palms of my hands. Jake gently rubbed my back, likely worrying that I was about to throw up, which, at that moment, was a strong possibility. I remembered my dream, the two boys standing on East Bay Street, people surrounding them, stoning and beating them to death. Did my dream prophesy my future?

Shaking my head I glanced up, "There is no way. You said the Two Witnesses would be resurrected, but I would never let my children become like me. I would not allow them to become immortal."

Father Nikoli laughed so loud it made me jump. "My dear," he took a moment to catch his breath. "You speak as if you have any say in the matter! Did I not clarify that God can do wondrous things? Besides, it is already written that these two men will prophesy against the Devil. Rest assured they will not carry his mark. But just because they are not inoculated by his hand, does not mean your sons won't carry the mutated genes."

"What?" I looked at Jake, his expression as perplexed as my own.

"Because you are changed, your offspring will also be changed. People will not believe, though, that God could perform such a miraculous thing, again placing their faith in science alone. Your children will prophesy and be given great power to torment those who follow the Devil and his ways. Your sons will be hated among men, but after their resurrection, a great earthquake will shake the city and the terrified survivors will have their eyes opened and give glory to God. His will be done."

Maybe it was my imagination, but Jake seemed to sit a little taller in his seat, a wry smirk upon his face.

"What?" I asked him. "What's with the look?"

With fatherly pride he said, "That's my boys."

I shook my head in disbelief, feeling a warm flush rise in my cheeks. Even though Jake was officially my husband, I hadn't yet come to grips that we were actually married. I remained jittery thinking about our first kiss. Now, here he was, the beaming, proud father of our unborn children. Flustered, I buried my head back in my hands. It was bad enough being embarrassed in front of Jake, but sitting before a priest made things even worse.

"Sorry," Jake snickered. Keeping my face hidden, I managed to throw an elbow at his side. Deep down, I enjoyed that he could still tease a smile from me, even as we literally faced the end of world.

"Ah, young love," Father Nikoli remarked. Mortified, I refused to look up.

"So, how are we going to get into the lab and destroy the research?" Jake asked, thankfully taking charge of the conversation and changing the subject.

"Preparations should be under way at this time," Father Nikoli replied. "But I must tell you that it will be dangerous. Despite our efforts, we were unable to determine every person's allegiance. Of course, we believe there is at least one who will fight to the death to protect this discovery."

A chill ran up my spine as I remembered Senator Morris pull the gun from his desk, ordering Toby to murder Jake in cold blood. Could Senator Morris be possessed by the devil? What about Dr. Anderson, or even Toby himself? Although Toby didn't kill Jake, he readily took the gun. Perhaps he had every intention of killing Jake until Sam confronted him. Perhaps Toby was the possessed one. Could the strange accent I heard in the car be the demon within? Did demons work that way? My mind wandered back to every horror movie I saw in my youth. Images from those films flickered in my brain working to confuse my judgment.

"I must advise that, although I cannot condone the taking of any life, the use of force may be necessary. If your own life is threatened, you should be prepared to do whatever is necessary. The research must be destroyed," Father Nikoli said, reaching into his robe and retrieving a hand gun, placing it on the bench beside Jake.

"I can't die," I countered, looking up to meet the father's gaze. I didn't want to kill anyone, no matter what evil force controlled them.

"No, Maddy, you *can* die," Jake reminded me.

"Jake is right," Father Nikoli agreed. "Despite your immortality, your body remains vulnerable. If you happen to be killed it will take three days for you to recover, during which time the enemy will flee with the inoculation and the research. You must not be afraid. If it comes to pass, the Lord will erase all doubt from your mind giving you the strength to do what you must, but I will pray He keep you from any situation where deadly force is necessary."

My eyes remained focused on the small black object, sitting ominous beside Jake. "Don't worry," Jake reassured. "Father Nikoli taught me how to use it. I've become quite proficient over the past few weeks. I'll take care of us. We'll be okay."

"Wait...us? We?" I asked, realizing Jake intended to join me in this fight. Turning to stare him down I added, "I don't think so. Even though I can die, *I* will recover, you don't have that luxury. I have to do this myself."

"Maddy," Jake returned my stern gaze. "I am your husband, we are in this together. I am not going to let you do this by yourself. I'm invested in this too."

"But..." I started.

"You aren't going to win this argument," Jake interrupted. "You can win every fight for the rest of eternity, but I won't let you win this one."

"I'm going to remember you said that," I grumbled, folding my arms across my chest. "Eternity is a very long time."

Smiling in victory Jake returned his attention to Nikoli, "Can you at least tell us who your informant is? So we have some idea who is on our side."

"You two are very good together, you know that? It's like you've been married for years," Father Nikoli chuckled. "Maddy, I think Greek blood flows in your veins. You remind me of my own sisters." A pensive smile tugging at the corners of his mouth, he added, "Perhaps, though, one should assume you are born with Jewish blood."

Perplexed, I opened my mouth to question his assumptions about my heritage, but Father Nikoli quickly redirected the conversation toward the topic at hand. "Unfortunately," his soft eyes focused on Jake, "I cannot tell you who my informant is, that information cannot be compromised. You are our first line of defense, but if, for any reason, you are unable to complete this mission, we need our insider to continue the operation without threat of being discovered."

"I wouldn't tell anyone," I argued.

"We," Jake corrected. "*We* wouldn't tell anyone."

I pouted making mental note to ensure Jake never won

any argument for the rest of eternity—ever.

"Maddy," Father Nikoli said, directing his answer toward me. "I believe with my whole heart that neither of you would intentionally compromise this person's identity, but the Devil loves deception and plays upon our weak human emotions. In the heat of the moment, the slightest slip of the tongue or wrong look could destroy everything we've worked to accomplish." Smiling patiently, he added, "Of course, whatever the outcome, we must accept it is part of God's plan."

My brow creased, "So what happens next? I can't just walk into..."

Jake cleared his throat. Rolling my eyes in an over exaggerated fashion I corrected, "We just can't walk into the Institute now. How am I going to explain my disappearance? When I show up with Jake..."

I trailed off, trying not to imagine Senator Morris' reaction.

"Simple. You were worried about Jake," Father Nikoli stated. "You worried what would happen to him, so you ran off when the opportunity presented itself. Somehow you convinced another camper to drive you into town, where you called Jake's cell phone and arranged to meet him and tell him the whole story."

I thought back to my arrival at the camp site, how I observed the vehicles lining the street, looking for a chance to go after Jake, to save him from any encounter with an irate Senator Morris. Father Nikoli's story seemed plausible enough to work.

"What if they don't believe me?" I asked, skepticism plaguing my hope that the story wouldn't be convincing enough for the others. I thought about Sam, worried about her reaction. I hated that I disappeared without giving her any explanation. I prayed my actions did not endanger her life.

"You must have faith, Maddy," Father Nikoli said. "Faith that everything will be in place when you arrive. Have faith that God will provide exactly what you need when you need it."

Staring into Nikoli's patient, determined eyes, I decided there could be no argument against faith. Shrugging, I said, "So once we are in, how do we know what to destroy?"

Father Nikoli rose from his seat and retreated toward the space behind the altar, disappearing into the shadows. He reappeared, a stack of paperwork in his hands. Sitting once again before us he began paging through the documents.

"The information provided states that the mutation serum can be replicated ten times from the contents of one vial without having to start from scratch. The lab keeps ten vials on hand at all times to assist with research and animal testing. Because animals do not seem able to defy death, the complex needs constant replenishment with each new set of specimens imported into the lab. Your first target should be those vials—destroying the contents will, at very least, slow the reproduction of any new serum. I believe these will be located within the refrigerator."

He handed us a photograph of the laboratory, the

refrigerator in the corner circled for identification. I nodded, remembering the refrigerator.

"What else?" I asked, my body, rigid with anticipation. I shifted uneasily in my seat, taut muscles aching, unable to relax my posture.

Jake seemed equally as tense.

"My insider will hack into the laboratory's computer system and destroy the research files stored internally. The Institute keeps its own mainframe inside the building for security purposes. As a backup to those efforts, if you have the opportunity, I want you to head downstairs and destroy the entire system. Smash it to pieces. Also, if you notice any external storage device that might hold key information, demolish that too. Things may be chaotic, though, as it becomes apparent the Institute's security is compromised. Remember, the vials are your first priority. If all trace of the immortality drug is destroyed, it will take those who discovered it much longer to duplicate their research."

"Smash vials, smash computers, force if necessary… got it," Jake said.

"Yeah, like it's going to be that easy," I countered, slightly annoyed by his over- confident demeanor. "There is so much that can go wrong. What if the lab isn't empty? I can't see how anyone is going to let us walk up and destroy anything."

"Maddy is right to be cautious," Father Nikoli stated. Caging his eyes directly on mine, he added, "But you also must keep faith that the Lord will protect you and that He will be victorious. My contact is preparing for your arrival. I truly believe everything will be in order for you to accomplish your mission. If something does go wrong and you have to get out, head to the airport and await further instruction. Here, take this..."

Father Nikoli handed me a small cell phone, "Call the only number listed when you've finished. Remember, Maddy, this is only part of what God expects you to achieve. When everything is said and done, your testimony to the world is truly the only thing that matters. All we are trying to accomplish is buying a little more time."

I looked up, stunned, as the chapel's stained glass windows glowed. For a moment I thought it was a sign from God that things would work out, but hope gave way to disappointment as I realized the illusion was nothing more than the sun dawning in the morning sky. Exhaustion, fear, and apprehension worked the fringes of my weary nerves as I tried to focus on our task at hand. I drew upon the few Biblical stories I could remember, reminded how light always conquered darkness. I said a quiet prayer that the day's events, and ultimately my life, would follow suit.

Chapter Twenty-Eight

Before exiting the church, Father Nikoli prayed, offering a blessing on Jake and myself.

Outside, the early sun set the sky ablaze with azure hues, while cheerful larks chirped their morning song high above in the magnolia trees. The night's warmth lingered. A hazy mist drifting from a nearby pond blanketed the ground—an omen of the day's impending heat. Dawn projected stillness, peace and hope—a new day with endless possibilities. Although I took momentary solace in this beauty, a cold shiver resonated through my body as I contemplated the fates of all those who today, like any other day, awoke underestimating just how close mankind was to its own undoing. Would people listen to me? Would they believe? Did I truly believe? A gnarled pit of fear rose from my stomach, tightening its noose in my chest, whispering to my heart that I could not possibly do what God now asked of me.

Glancing around the empty parking lot, I took note of the chapel's private location, surrounded by dense woodland. The main street and surrounding homes—if there were any—were hidden from view. One exception was a small, two-story, white house sitting beneath the shadow of the tallest magnolia tree near the lot's exit. I assumed it was the pastor's home. Although it was five-thirty in the morning, a solitary light burned from a lower level window, yet no one seemed aware of our presence. We remained alone in the stillness of the early morning. Next to the church, a black four door sedan—that I recognized from the day before—sat beside Jake's blue truck, both just beyond view from the pastor's house.

"Peace of God be with you," Father Nikoli said as he kissed the top of my head.

"Thank you," I replied.

Shaking Jake's hand, he offered the same blessing.

Climbing into Jake's truck, I felt the familiar tug of fear and anxiety that I experienced as a small child who, every few months, climbed into Ms. Shirley's car, ready to be transported to another foster home. Would I be good enough? Would I be loved? No one wanted me enough to accept and love me before, why should this time be any different? I felt small and inadequate. Doubt crept into my mind forcing me to wonder what God saw in me, why He trusted me with such great responsibility. Was I truly good enough in His eyes? I didn't know the slightest thing about religion. How could I prophesy as He asked?

My eyes focused on Jake, studying a map with Father Nikoli against the hood of his car. I reminded myself that God sent at least one person into my life who loved and accepted me and was willing to do anything for me. That alone should be proof of His existence.

Yes, but that was when you were dying. A voice inside argued. *Do you truly believe you are good for him? Do you really believe in God? Why would God want to warn others about the gift you've been given? Why would He forgive you and not others? If He is truly against immortality, what you've done is beyond redemption. You are damned and will only curse Jake's life along with your own. You aren't cut out for this. You will always be a forgotten, unwanted child.*

"No," I whispered to myself.

Come on, Maddy, you know better. Do you really believe God would punish people for wanting to live forever? If He exists, He loves everyone. Surely He would not condemn those for choosing immortality as you have. If you tell others of what you've become, people will wonder why you refuse to share your gift. They will love you even less if you keep them from what is rightfully theirs. In fact, people will hate you. Just think, Maddy, how loved you will be when you deliver this miraculous cure to the world. That's all you've ever really wanted, isn't it Maddy? To be loved?

"Stop it," I breathed, teetering on the edge of insanity.

It's not too late, Maddy. Come back. Claim what is rightfully yours. This is a gift, not a curse.

The driver's door shut, startling me from the battle raging inside my head. Father Nikoli stood waving as Jake started the engine and backed out of the parking space. Waving in return before he put his truck into drive, Jake turned to me and said, "Ready to do this?"

"I hope so," I shrugged, looking down at my hands folded neatly in my lap, as we drove out of the church's parking lot.

I watched in silence as we made our way through wooded side streets, passing several small, bungalow-type homes along the way. I glanced at Jake who concentrated on the road. I wondered what he was thinking, but didn't ask. I returned my attention to the world beyond my window pane.

I wonder if anyone inside these homes is sick. I wonder how much he or she would give for the chance you've been given. How thankful family members would be to hold onto those they love... to not be forced into saying good-bye. Healing. Healing doesn't seem like such a horrible thing to offer.

The landscape continued to blur past as we pulled onto the interstate. I was surprised to see traffic. Although early morning hours kept most people in outlying areas tucked safely inside their homes, the interstate flowed with delivery vehicles and urban commuters not bound by the traditional schedules of their more sleepy suburban counterparts.

After drifting through traffic for twenty minutes we exited the interstate and slowly made our way past the populated outskirts of town onto a vaguely familiar, secluded two lane stretch of road.

Maddy, I know you hear me. Don't destroy this gift. That is what immortality is, a gift. Humans discovered the key. We didn't need God. We have a right to return to our Eden.

"Stop," I shouted without realizing.

Jake immediately pulled over to the side of the road. Keeping the engine running, he threw the truck into park and stammered, "What? What's wrong?"

Tears welled in my eyes as I looked into his alarmed expression.

"I don't know if I can do this," I murmured. I wasn't sure where the words came from—they just flew off my tongue. "Jake, I'm not strong enough for this. I'm not this amazing prophet with some ardent belief in God. I'm still not sure I believe. I'm the same abandoned, unwanted child who was at death's door a few months ago. The only reason I'm alive is because I chose to go against God. If immortality is truly a sin, I don't deserve to be forgiven. Let's face it; I'm just not good enough...for Him...for the world...for you."

A pensive smile spread across Jake's face as he turned and stared out the windshield.

"Tell me what you're thinking," I prodded, unsure I wanted an answer. "I know you are disappointed in me."

Turning back to look me in the eyes, Jake said, "Is that what you think? That I'm disappointed?"

Shrugging, I said, "I would be."

"Maddy," Jake unbuckled his seat belt then turned his body sideways to face me. "If you weren't afraid I would be worried. This is no small thing you are being asked to do, but I know you are strong enough. I know why God chose you. If anyone should feel inadequate, it's me."

"What on earth do you mean?" I asked.

"Maddy, here I am, some guy, nothing special, who fell in love with this amazing woman. A woman who struggled her entire life, yet never gave up. A woman, who faced hardships one can only imagine and still chose to rise above and make something of her life. She put herself through college, found a job, escaped the cycle of despair. She is a strong woman who has the power to overcome any challenge in life, and as it seems, even death itself! This same woman, beyond any rational explanation, agreed to marry me. Now, come to find out, she is God's chosen messenger and I am blessed enough to stand by her side and support her.

"For the life of me I still don't know what I did to deserve the honor of being your husband and now... Don't you see? I am in awe of you. I guess I might be feeling the way Joseph did when he learned that Mary was blessed in the eyes of God. I always knew you were special, but it is so much more humbling for God to announce that my wife is chosen to do great work— His work—for all humanity. I can only hope that I'm good enough...for you and for Him. I will always endeavor to be the kind of husband you, and He, expect of me."

I stared at him in stunned silence. How could Jake think he was not good enough for me? Didn't he know that I was the lucky one?

"That reminds me," he continued. Reaching into his

pocket he pulled out a tiny, sparkling object. "I believe you left his behind, Cinderella." He smiled as he slid the engagement ring onto my finger. As Jake's hand held mine, I noticed a gold band adorning his ring finger. I touched it then looked up into his eyes.

A coy smile formed across his face, accentuating his dimples. I'd forgotten the feeling his dimples could ignite within my soul. "Well, we are married now. I had to show the world. Here..." Jake pulled another object from the same pocket. "I got you a matching band."

He started to place it on my finger, but I pulled my hand away.

"No," I said. Jake's shocked expression forced me to glance away. I toyed with the diamond ring decorating my finger. "Jake, when you first asked me to marry you, I agreed to be your wife as long as we didn't make it official, in the legal sense."

"Maddy, look, I'm sorry I tricked you. I didn't mean to upset you. We can..."

"Just let me finish," I interrupted, my eyes once again meeting his expectant gaze. "I'm not upset. It's just, well... before, I thought as long as our marriage wasn't on paper— that it wasn't recorded in some county ledger—it wouldn't be real. I figured a simple religious ceremony wouldn't be significant. You'd get your wish and I would get mine."

Looking away, Jake's bewildered eyes studied the gold band in his hand.

"But I was wrong, backward. If I am going to devote my life to God, I want to do it completely. We may be married in the legal sense, Jacob Kavanaugh, but I realize now that we aren't officially married. I want be married in the church. I want to pledge our love for each other in front of God, our family and friends... and I won't take no for an answer."

Jake looked up, his dimples unleashing their full, heart racing power. "You mean it? You want to get married in the church?"

"Absolutely," I beamed. "Hopefully your parents can make it to this wedding. And, of course, I will have to get Jenn that blue bridesmaid dress. I'm going to make sure it has a giant bow, right on her backside."

"You never cease to amaze me," Jake laughed as he carefully tucked the gold band back into his pocket. "I love you Madeline."

"I love you too," I said, smiling up at him.

"Forgive me for this," he said. Before I could react, Jake reached out and, wrapping his arms around me, he kissed me. No time to over-think, the moment flowed naturally as his soft lips pressed against mine. I was less shocked by his kiss than by my heated reaction to it. I felt the seat belt strain against my chest as I wrapped my arms around his neck, pulling myself closer into his embrace, kissing him with fervent urgency. I didn't want to let go of this moment.

By the time we separated, my head was swimming with giddy euphoria. I felt the flush of color rise in my cheeks as I realized I could spend the entire day sitting in Jake's truck kissing him. As if thinking the same thing, Jake said, "I guess we'd better get going…can't just sit here all day."

A shy, yet accomplished smile flashed across his face. I gave a heavy sigh, hoping I could bring myself back down to earth and concentrate.

"Okay, let's get this over with," I stated.

Jake put the truck into drive and pulled back onto the empty road. "According to the map, the Institute should be up ahead, just past the curve in the road."

"God, please let this work," I breathed.

"Amen," added Jake in the same hushed whisper.

Rounding the corner, the gray concrete walls of the Institute came into view. The dense woodland pressed in from all sides, squeezing me close to a claustrophobic hysteria. The first obstacle blocking our path—the guard shack and gate—loomed before us. My breathing accelerated, I tried to keep from hyperventilating.

"Relax," Jake comforted as he placed his hand on my knee. "Act natural. We can do this."

I was thankful to have him by my side, glad that he didn't let me do this alone. Slowing as we approached, I realized something was off. No one stood in the shack. Erik wasn't around to check our credentials. Everything was still.

"Something's wrong," I said as Jake stopped in front of the guard shack. "Someone should be here. It's manned twenty-four hours a day. No one is allowed inside the gate unless approved."

"Maybe the guy is just on break. Stay here," Jake said as he put his truck into park and cautiously got out, drawing the gun from beneath his shirt.

Holding my breath I watched as he neared the tiny booth. Straining to listen for any noise, I grew irritated with the hum of the truck's engine; it seemed to scream our arrival against the eerie silence surrounding us.

Jake edged along the curb and peered into the windows of the small structure. I exhaled loudly as he lifted his hand to his mouth, his body convulsing as he retched, color drained from his face. Quickly sliding the guard's door open, Jake reached inside, a second later the gate rose as he sprinted back to the truck. Throwing the gun onto the dash, he jumped into the driver's seat.

"What?" I asked as Jake drew deep, jagged breathes, steadying his shaking hands against the steering wheel.

"The guy inside is dead," he said through staggered inhalations. "Shot in the head."

I felt the bile in my empty stomach rise to my throat as I pictured Erik, lifeless in the tiny, hot shack. Looking out my window I tried to avoid seeing his body as we drove cautiously through the gate. Something in the bushes caught my eye. A human foot protruded from beneath the dense thicket. I knew that foot belonged to another dead guard.

"I think they're expecting us," I said, trying to subdue the panic accelerating my heart. Common sense begged me to turn and run. Jake kept silent as we parked outside the Institute's main entrance.

Chapter Twenty-Nine

Stillness. Not a single sound emanated from the Institute or the woodland beyond. The swish of the front door sliding open trumpeted our arrival, yet no one stirred inside. A sudden chill enveloped my body as the entry transformed into a demon's mouth, beckoning us forward, ready to swallow us into the depths of hell—although that vision was only the projection of my paranoid imagination.

Jake led me into the front hallway, gun drawn. After leaving the bright morning sunlight it took several moments for our eyes to adjust to the darkened shadows inside the building. A stream of cool air washed down from one of the vents above. Sweet at first, the air soon turned metallic, the sickening scent of rusted iron overtaking my senses, gagging me.

"Blood," Jake said as I tried to regain my composure, moving from beneath the vent. "The guard shack smelled the same way, only ten times worse in the heat."

I gagged again, trying to block the images of people I knew lying dead in the corridors beyond. The enemy waited for us down one of these halls. I envisioned the evil look in Senator Morris' eyes at our last meeting. The smell of death lingering in my nose, I remembered his willingness to kill. I breathed a little prayer for Sam, hoping she was not sacrificed at the hands of the evil senator.

My eyes were still adjusting to the dimmed light as we moved down the main hall toward the lab. Approaching the double doors to Senator Morris' office, something caught my foot, tripping me, sending my body flailing forward. Jake's arms grabbed for me as I fell, but not in time to prevent my impact against Senator Morris, who lay slumped against the wall, blood oozing from beneath his lifeless body.

A mortified scream strangled in my throat as Jake jerked me up with his free hand, the gun outstretched in front of us with his other.

"Senator Morris isn't the one," I choked, a hoarse whisper. "But how could it not be Senator Morris? He was in charge."

"I don't know," Jake answered, staring down the corridor, his voice steely and calm. "Unfortunately, we've lost the element of surprise. We have to suspect everyone. Anyone could be our enemy. I am willing to bet whoever it is waits for us in the lab."

He turned to meet my eyes, gun still pointed down the hallway, both of us prolonging the inevitable, neither of us wanting to proceed. The eerie calm of the building was punctured by the sound of breaking glass and a muffled scream…a woman's scream.

Sam.

Overcoming fear, I raced to protect my friend, hurrying toward the sound of Sam's voice. Her screams suddenly went silent. The sinister hush of the building crept back in; the soft thud of our footsteps against the carpet rhythmically punctured the soundless void as we neared the corridor leading to the laboratory. Turning the corner, I saw the laboratory's entrance. Halfway down the passage, light poured from the lab's open door into the deserted hallway. Nothing stirred—no sign of life.

Ignoring concern over my own safety, I rushed toward the door, Jake close behind. Inside the lab, a mosaic of shattered glass covered the steel counter tops, papers were strewn across the floor. A small fire smoldering in a trash can sent white smoke rising into the space above, creating an eerie fog that encircled the room. The buildings fire suppression system must have been disabled, because water should have been raining from above.

I brought my hands up to my mouth, muffling a startled cry. The scene before us was a macabre eradication of my prime suspects. To our right, Dr. Anderson sprawled backward in his lab chair, shot in the chest three times. His eyes, wide with fear, remained open, staring toward the ceiling. The shock he felt while gasping his last breath remained twisted on his face, frozen in time with his infinite stare. Beside him on the floor, partially blocked from view by the large, island work station, Toby laid face down, unmoving, his Italian loafers soiled in a pool of fresh blood.

Sitting atop the center island, a rack holding ten test tubes with brightly colored tops rested on a metal tray, left for the taking. I didn't need to read their markings to know these were the vials of serum. I knew someone, or something, was challenging us to come forward and destroy the vials. Whoever—or whatever—left them there seemed to be taunting us. I knew destroying the serum wouldn't be that easy.

I noticed the laboratory animals—watching huddled in their cages—didn't move. No mouse squeaked or rabbit clicked acknowledging our presence. They were too silent, motionless, instinct alerting them of danger. Instinct told me the animals weren't the only ones watching us with intense curiosity, waiting for our next move. I could feel an evil force close by. Glancing around, I tried to perceive the concealed threat. Again, nothing moved.

"Maddy?" A weak voice called from the far end of the lab, behind island workstation. "Maddy, is that you?"

Jake steadied the gun in front of him, aiming it toward the voice. Sam reached a bloodied arm onto the counter and pulled herself up, bracing against the stable platform. She looked horrible. Dark circles loomed beneath her eyes, blood stained her lab coat and smeared across her face.

"Oh thank God it's you," Sam breathed.

"Sam!" Worried for my friend, I started toward her. Jake caught my arm and held me back, keeping me beside him. He obviously felt the threat lurking nearby as well. "Sam, what happened? Are you okay?"

"I'll be okay," she stuttered. Weak, Sam slipped against the slick, steel counter but caught herself and readjusted her stance. "Oh Maddy, this is so horrible. Things got out of control. Corson went crazy. He shot everybody. He kept shouting something about how he won't be stopped. I tried..." she coughed, her breathing labored. "I was late. If I had just been a little faster...I was so worried. You have to believe I tried to save them, but I was too late. You have to believe..."

Tears brimmed in her eyes as she looked at Dr. Anderson and Toby lying dead beside her. Jake kept his grip tight on my arm.

"You did what you could," I reassured. There was so much blood. Fearing for Sam's safety I said, "Sam, we need to get you out of here. You need medical attention. Where is Corson now?"

I shuddered remembering Father Nikoli's warning that the Devil loves deception. Corson was the last person I assumed could be Satan's pawn, but it did make sense. He seemed so unassuming, who would suspect Corson of deceit? Despite keeping a low profile, I realized Corson was always involved, always watching. He could be present in the same room without notice—like the evening he pulled me from Senator Morris' office. Corson seemed to appear out of thin air. With that thought, a chill ran down my spine as my eyes searched the room for any sign of his presence.

"I don't know where he went. He bolted from the room when he heard you coming." Sam spat. "But we'd better get out of here before he comes back. Corson's crazy, I tell you! I don't think we have the power to stop him."

Jake relaxed his grip on my arm but remained alert, tense. "Let's destroy the serum and get out of here," he said, motioning toward the waiting vials.

Releasing my arm, Jake drew his gun in front of him, then backed toward the edge of the room providing a clear view of the laboratory door, and a clear shot if necessary. I cautiously approached the vials, prepared to smash them into a million pieces.

"Wait!" Sam cried as I picked up the tray. "Maddy, listen, I know this is going to sound crazy, given what it is you have to do, but please, listen. Let's not destroy the serum. This is my life's work. Soon enough the world is going to discover it anyway, until then, we can just keep this between us."

My heart ached for Sam's dilemma. I knew it would be difficult for her to let go, but she knew we needed to protect mankind.

"Sam, I know this is not easy, but we have to destroy the serum. The human race is not ready for this. They need more time," I argued, stepping back from the counter, tray in hand.

"No, please, wait," Sam begged, raising her hand,

motioning for me to stop. "I know you are trying to save mankind, but think of me. I didn't just undertake this assignment for the world, I did it for Paul. There's a chance I can bring him back, Maddy. You of all people should understand what I'm telling you... I love him. I can bring him back. Together, with this serum, we can bring him back. We can live as happily married couples, maybe even in the same town. Wouldn't that be wonderful? Our children could play together."

I stood holding the tray, watching my friend, blood trickling down her arm. My heart ached looking into her despondent eyes. I pictured two-story homes with white fences, barbeques in the backyard, leisurely walks with baby strollers side by side, play-dates at the park—I could see it all.

"Maddy?" Jake's voice came from behind. "We have to do this Maddy."

Ignoring him I watched Sam's face, twisted in pain, glancing between me and the vials.

"I thought you could only save someone from death if they received the serum within an hour," I countered. "Paul's been dead over ten years, Sam. Think rationally. You know you can't bring him back."

"Maddy, that's just it. I think I can bring him back. The Bible says that 'at the last trumpet the dead shall be raised imperishable,' and 'that a time is coming when all who are in their graves will hear his voice.' All will be raised, not just in spirit, but their actual bodies. That means there must be a way. God doesn't want this serum released to the world, but you know as well as I that He wouldn't be angry if we just kept this for ourselves. Our little secret."

"Maddy," Jake spoke, impatience spiking his tone.

The tray in my hands started to shake. Doubt slithered into my conscience.

Just one vial couldn't hurt.

No, I argued with myself. *We have to destroy it all.*

But Sam has been a loyal friend. You, of all people, should understand trading immortality for love.

But God expects...

God, God, God. He loves you no matter what. He forgave all of your past sins, He will forgive you again.

"Maddy?" Jake's voice broke in again.

Shaking, I turned toward the trashcan. "I'm sorry Sam, but I have to do this. Paul will return, but in God's time. You have to believe you will be together again, have faith..."

"No!" Sam shrieked in a shrill, piercing timber that echoed against the laboratory walls. "Maddy, stop!"

I turned to see her quickly hobble toward me, using the workstation counter for support.

"You are not so prim and proper! *You* chose immortality for yourself, to stay with your beloved Jake. You have no problem destroying my work, keeping others from the gift you have been given because hey, you've got yours, who cares about others?"

"Sam, that is not true..."

Stopping to catch her breath, Sam leaned against the counter. "Maddy," Sam said, slumping over. Looking up at me, eyes serious, voice calm, she said, "God isn't the only one, you know? There is another. He makes good on his promises, doesn't keep anyone waiting. He can give you anything you want, when you want it. *He* is the one who made your life possible. *He* is the reason you are here, now, with your beloved Jake. Don't you see how much more Lucifer loves you than God? God would have separated you two. Lucifer kept you together. Don't you see how much more he loves all mankind? He only wants what is best for us. He only wants us to be happy, free from God's tyrannical rule."

Nausea washed through my stomach. What was Sam saying? No, no she couldn't be the one. She couldn't.

"Maddy, you can join us. You and Jake, think about it. You will have everything you ever wanted. Who knows when God is going to get around to His little Tribulation thing? And if you are afraid of the outcome just remember, God is the one who wrote the book, of course He says He is going to win. Lucifer and his followers, though, know better. Do you think God would cast Himself in a bad light?" Sam chuckled as she inched closer to me.

"Maddy, don't listen to her. Destroy the serum. Do it now!" Jake pleaded.

My eyes remained focused on Sam, bloody and broken, slowly creeping toward me, still bracing herself against the center island. "No," I whispered, shaking my head. "No Sam, I've made my choice. It's not too late, though. Sam, come back to God. He loves you. Please, come back..."

Sam's eyes burned with rage, "You are quick to do

God's work when everything is safe and secure, but if you were in my shoes, if it was your precious Jake that needed saving, I bet you wouldn't throw those vials into the fire!" She continued toward me, weak but persistent, almost close enough to touch. I took a step back, my hands shaking violently, the glass test tubes clinking within their rack.

"You shouldn't be so eager to judge me! I know you have your doubts. Why the sudden change of heart? What proof did they give you that God even exists? You can't fool me. I know you would do anything to save Jake, anything! Why should you be forced to choose between God and the ones you love here on Earth? Why should any of us? *My* lord would never force you to choose! No Maddy, I am positive you would turn away from your precious God if Jake's life depended on it," Sam howled.

"No," I mouthed, shaking my head. "No."

But my heart questioned everything. I started to recognize the truth in what Sam was saying. If forced to choose, could I love God—trust His will—more than I loved Jake?

Without warning, a deafening explosion rocked the tiny room. I instinctively raised my hands for protection. The tray slipped from my grasp sending the vials crashing to the floor.

Chapter Thirty

Moments after the explosion, I remained standing. I had survived. I felt no pain, though my ears were ringing, the blast temporarily deafened me. Assessing the damage, I realized nothing had changed, nothing was out of place. Everything in the laboratory looked exactly as it had moments before the explosion. Sam remained propped against the island's countertop, dangerously close to me, a wicked smile tugging the edges of her mouth. She recognized my confusion.

I glanced down at the vials now scattered at my feet. One...two...three...four. Four survived their impact with the tile. Six shattered, their contents slowly trickling toward a drain in the floor about three feet away. Glancing back up at Sam, I saw she was speaking, but the ringing in my ears persisted, drowning out all other noise. Her eyes focused on something at the laboratory's entrance. I realized she wasn't, in fact, talking to me.

Turning, horror flooded my soul seeing Corson in the doorway, a gun dangling at his side, mirroring the same evil sneer of the woman across from him. Corson's attention remained fixated on Sam. As my ears cleared, I began to make out pieces of their conversation.

"You did so well, my love," Sam said. "You have made our master proud. He will reward you greatly."

His sneer morphed into a lovesick smile. "We can finally be together?"

I turned to Sam. She was no longer slouched but standing tall, wiping the blood from her face, seemingly unharmed.

"All in good time, dearest. Be patient. All in good time." She returned her attention to me. "Well?" she asked.

At a loss for words I shook my head, trying to understand what was going on.

"Whatever you ask of God, God will give you. So, dear Maddy, how much do you truly believe? Go ahead, ask. Let's see if your God will provide." Sam motioned toward Jake.

Turning to face him, my heart ripped into pieces and plummeted to the pit of my twisted stomach. I realized the explosion came from Corson's gun, the sound amplified by the room's metal framework. Corson's aim hit its mark; Jacob's lifeless body lay crumpled on the ground, his own gun still clutched in his right hand, finger on the trigger. Jake never had the chance to defend himself.

Shock took over. My mind blanked. My body and soul numbed. I stared helplessly at Jake, unable to move.

I felt an arm wrap around my shoulder. Sam held one of the vials in front of my face, diverting my attention. "Have you said your little prayer yet?" she whispered. "Has God answered your plea? Please, Lord, *please* bring dear Jake back to us!" she mocked.

My eyes refocused on Jake. How could this happen? Flashes of our future life together streamed through my mind. We were going marry in the church with everyone present. Our sons were supposed to be great prophets. But now…

Despair, fear, isolation—thousands of emotions swirled inside me, dragging me into darkness.

"What? What's that I hear?" Sam continued to ridicule. "Oh wait, that's right…nothing. Jake's still laying there, Maddy. Do you see some miraculous healing light surrounding him? No? Where is your God? This, Maddy…" Sam once again held the vial before me, her tone softened. "This is what will save him. I can start an IV. Jake will be healed in three days. You will be together forever, Maddy. This is your only choice."

Frozen, I stood powerless. I couldn't force myself to move. Unbearable, disheartening pressure closed in around me, crushing me. I couldn't think, couldn't speak. Icy fingers worked their way into my soul, wrapping me in the bondage of darkness. I tried to cry out, but my mouth would not move. I felt trapped, something gripped me from within and wouldn't let go.

"That's a girl," Sam coaxed. "Just give in. Just say yes to my lord and you will be free. He loves you. I love you. I'm still right here with you, still your friend. Where is your God? He's not answering your prayer." Leaning her head against me, she whispered in my ear, "*We* haven't left you alone. *We* will bring Jake back to you. Now, I'm going to walk over and get my supplies. I'll get Jake's IV started immediately; we'll push the serum into his body. Trust me; you are making the right decision. This will all soon be over."

Removing her arm from my shoulder I heard Sam say, "Here my love. Will you hold this for a moment while I get my supplies?"

Paralyzed, I stared down at Jake, terror overwhelming my heart. I fought internally against the sinister entity holding me hostage. The more I struggled, the more forcefully it crushed me in its grasp. I realized whatever possessed me, its power was far greater than any human could fight against alone.

"Give in," it whispered inside my head. "Give in to me."

I closed my eyes, trying to focus my thoughts as its evil voice resonated in my mind.

"No," my mind replied.

"You have no strength to defeat me. Give in," it provoked. "Give in to me. You will be great and powerful. I will give you everything you've ever wanted, starting with Jake. I will bring him back to you."

"No," something stirred inside my soul. Stronger I cried out, "No. Never"

The pressure released momentarily, only to return with merciless, virulent force. I struggled to breathe as it strangled my body.

"Give in to me!" the voice wailed. "You belong to me!"

Powerless, feeling the life within me draining away, I allowed myself to stop fighting, to let go. I could not defeat the strange entity controlling my body, but I would not allow it to control my soul. With my entire heart I cried, "There is only One I devote my life to. Only One whose vision for my life is greater than what I could ever imagine. The Lord gives and the Lord takes away, but it is all part of a greater plan. If He takes Jake from me, I trust in His Will. I believe in God. I devote my life to God. I will never be yours. Never! Jesus, please help me!"

A bright light filled my mind and with a brilliant flash it proceeded to radiate, almost burn, through my body. I saw a vision of Heaven—remembered its indescribable, unmatched beauty. I knew I was saved.

Something pulled violently against me, the vile spirit's grasp unmatched against the force that, in one swift instant, released me from my demonic prison. An angry voice howled, snarled, growled, and screamed out in pain. I felt it fight to grab hold of me one last time, but the light burning inside me easily pushed it away. Accepting defeat, the evil presence vanished.

The bright light faded, then disappeared, but the feeling of peace and freedom left in its wake remained. I knew God strengthened me, giving me the power to bring an end to Sam's operation. Opening my eyes, I saw Jake, collapsed on the floor, home in Heaven. I missed him desperately, but I couldn't mourn for him now. I had to complete my mission. I trusted God's plan. Comforted, I realized that with God, hope remains eternal. I believed that Jake and I would someday be together, forever.

Cautiously, I turned from Jake, searching the lab for the two people I knew I had to stop. Sam, her back turned to me, worked across the room preparing the supplies for Jake's IV, while Corson, only inches from where I stood, leaned against the center island watching his beloved with his usual tortured, lovesick expression. Corson's gun sat beside him on the counter. No one noticed I was released from Satan's spell.

Corson guarded one of the unbroken vials in his hand, rocking it back and forth absentmindedly, the contents sloshing from one end of the tube to the next. The other three vials remained unattended on the floor. I inched backward toward Jake, trying to remain silent, unnoticed. I felt my heel bump against his body and slowly lowered down, keeping my eyes constantly focused on my former friend. I groped for the gun clutched in Jake's dead hand. I shivered, feeling the coolness of his skin. My fingers brushed against the gun's textured magazine. Fumbling blindly, I tried to dislodge his grip on the weapon, but to no avail.

My heart beat frantically—I was running out of time. Sam was plugging the IV tubing into a saline bag and I knew at any second she would turn around and discover that I no longer stood helpless in a catatonic state. Glancing away, I focused all my attention on prying Jake's hand free from the gun. I plucked each of his fingers from around the black metal, at last releasing it into my hand.

Quickly rising, gun drawn, I charged at Corson hoping the element of surprise would work in my favor.

Before Corson could react, I was beside him, holding Jake's gun against the side of his head. "Give me the vial, Corson. I don't want to hurt you."

Corson froze. Sam spun around from her work. To my astonishment she let out a light chuckle. I tried to steady my violently shaking hand.

"Maddy," Sam laughed, pulling a gun from beneath her lab coat, aiming it toward me. "Do you really think I care if you kill Corson?"

I put Corson between the two of us. Still shaking, I repeated, "Corson, give me the vial and no one gets hurt."

"Samantha?" Corson pleaded. "Samantha, please…"

"Here, Maddy, let me help you." Sam pulled the trigger.

The explosive sound of the gun's discharge reverberated through the laboratory milliseconds before Corson fell to the ground in front of me. My ears were ringing again. We stood facing each other for a long moment, guns drawn. When my ears cleared, Sam smiled.

"I shoot marksman, remember?" she laughed, shaking her head in dismay. "Oh Maddy, I so hoped it wouldn't come to this."

"I will shoot," I countered, my aim bobbing between

Sam's head and gut thanks to my unsteady hand.

Keeping her aim, Sam retorted, "No you won't. Look at you! You don't have a killer instinct. Face it, Maddy, you've lost. If God can't help you win this one tiny battle, how can you possibly believe He will win an entire war?"

"Drop the gun, Sam!" I forced, my voice faltering. "I don't want to hurt you. Remember, I can't die. Drop the gun!"

Erupting with laughter Sam said, "Maddy, I'm not stupid. You can't even keep your gun steady! You aren't going to win. Besides, I *can* kill you! And once I do, I will take your body down to the incinerator so you won't return. You can go dance on a cloud with your precious Jake."

"Sam, drop the gun!" I ordered.

Staring me down she challenged, "Make me."

Trembling, I drew a deep breath. Looking into Sam's vengeful eyes, I said a silent prayer, then squeezed the trigger. The gun recoiled in my unskilled hand, kicking the barrel upward, my shot leaving a hole in the ceiling panel above Sam's head.

Sam roared with laughter.

"See Maddy, I told you!" Surveying my damage to the ceiling she added, "See, you can't do it! You can't kill me!"

My palms sweaty, arms shaking, I couldn't take a second shot. Lowering my gun I made a silent apology to God. I wasn't the hero He expected. I failed.

Sam continued laughing toward the ceiling, her aim locked steady. Closing my eyes, I anticipated the next explosion. It startled me, nonetheless, when it erupted. I waited for the impact of the bullet against my chest, waited to feel the searing pain as it ripped into my heart. My only solace came in knowing that soon I would be with Jake.

"She may not be able to kill you," a familiar voice sounded beside me, "but I am."

I opened my eyes to see Toby standing beside me. Across the room, Sam was dead, a direct shot to the head.

Chapter Thirty-One

"Are you okay?" Toby asked, lowering his weapon.

I whimpered a yes as my knees buckled. The adrenaline dissipated from my body, leaving me exhausted and weak. I gagged as the putrid, metallic smell of blood filled each inhalation. My stomach curdled while the blood-stained laboratory slowly swirled around in my vision. There was so much death in the room. My entire body shaking, I braced against the countertop, taking deep breaths through my mouth, trying to avoid the stench and keep from passing out.

Looking back toward Sam I asked, "Is she..." I retched, unable to finish my question.

Walking across the room, Toby knelt beside Sam's body.

Checking her carotid artery for a pulse he confirmed, "She's dead."

"But wha..." I stammered. "How..." I couldn't pull an intelligible sentence together. The tremors in my body grew. I tried, without luck, to swallow the dry lump lodged inside my throat.

Looking up, Toby's brow furrowed, "Are you sure you're okay? You don't look so well."

"I'll be okay. Just give me a minute," I managed to choke out.

Toby rose and came to stand beside me. He placed his hands on my shoulders, helping to brace my convulsing body. Tears welled in my eyes as the reality of my world folded in on top of me. I looked up at Toby, trying to steady my thoughts, trying to remember every question lost within the frenzy of my mind.

"I thought you were shot. You were on the floor covered in blood. Toby, how are you not dead?"

Smiling, Toby said, "First, allow me to introduce myself...formally. My real title is Father Tobias Caras." Making sure I was steady, he removed his hands from my shoulders and stripped his suit jacket from his body. Turning around he lifted his white shirt to reveal a vest with two circular, shiny, silver holes punctured in the back.

Craning his neck while unsuccessfully trying to observe the damage to his back, Toby said, "Sam was right about one thing...she's a good shot. The impact darn near knocked me unconscious. Thank the Lord I had the sense to throw myself against Dr. Anderson and let his blood stain

317

me after being hit. I didn't want Sam noticing I wasn't bleeding." Toby's accent returned as he spoke, which I now recognized held the same nuances as Father Nikoli. "Of course, God's timing is impeccable. Seconds later, Corson ran in to announce you and Jake were at the gate, so I doubt she would have noticed one way or the other." Toby lowered his shirt and held his suit jacket in front of him. Sticking his finger through one of the holes he sighed, "Too bad, I really liked this suit."

Jake.

There were so many questions I needed Toby to answer, but my mind couldn't focus on them now.

Turning to view Jake's crumpled body, a glimmer of hope sparked in my heart that maybe he too was wearing a vest, but the blood stain running down his shirt, as well as his waxy-gray complexion forced me to accept that Jake wasn't coming back. I saw only the shell of the man I loved.

I wanted to be strong. I wanted to believe there was a reason behind everything, to accept Jake's death as God's Will, but my heart broke, leaving me with overwhelming anger, fear, and crushing despair. I suddenly, desperately wanted him back. With those emotions also came guilt for not trusting God. I fought to convince myself that grieving Jake was sinful—he was in Heaven with God, it was selfish of me to want him back—and yet I could not control how I felt.

Moving from the counter, I stumbled over to where Jake lay crumpled on the ground, then collapsed on my knees beside him, convulsing as pitiful sobs rocked my body.

Toby came and knelt beside me, placing his arm protectively around my shoulder. I tried to shake him off, tried to hold back the tears, but I had lost control.

"You've been through a lot. It's okay to let your emotions out," Toby comforted. "You were very brave back there, but you're safe now. It's okay. You need to let go. You need to grieve."

"No," I said, violently shaking my head. "No, I'm supposed to be strong. I am supposed to accept God's plan, be happy for Jake...be happy that he's in heaven. It's sinful for me to want him back. But why can't I be happy? Why can't I keep from wanting him back?"

I doubled in two, covering my face with my hands. The shame of my emotions crippled me more than the emotions themselves. How could I be God's messenger if I didn't rejoice in His plan? How could I be so weak?

"Hey," Toby said, gently lifting my chin, forcing me to meet his stare. "Listen, God doesn't expect you to be superwoman. There is nothing wrong with what you are feeling right now. You are human, you need to grieve. God doesn't expect you to always understand His plan, and a lot of times He doesn't even expect you to *like* His plan. He just expects you to trust Him. Hiding your emotions would be foolish since He already knows your heart. You've had a very traumatic day, to say the least, and yes, God expects great things of you, but that doesn't mean He expects you to forego all emotion. It is your emotion, Maddy—your love—that will help you connect with the world. Don't ever feel like you are less than perfect in His eyes—anger, fear, guilt and all. He created you that way and He intends to use you just the way you are. All He wants for you is to rely on Him in a time like this. Turn to Him. Trust in Him to care for you."

I fell into Toby's arms, sobbing against his shirt. "I just wish He didn't have to take Jake from me. I don't know how I am going to do this alone. I just want him back, Toby. I just want him back."

Toby wrapped his arms around me and let me sob until the tears dried and my shuddering subsided. Exhausted, I remained in Toby's protective embrace until my mind numbed.

"I know you hurt," Toby said, "but always remember you are never alone."

Sitting up, wiping my tear streaked face with the back of my hand I said, "I know, but I can't help feeling a little angry. After everything I've promised God, I don't understand why He had to take Jake away from me. I thought our sons were supposed to be the witnesses. I'm just so confused."

"Maddy, I wish I had an answer for you, but I believe, in time, God will reveal His full plan. Perhaps He wanted to make sure you could put His Will before everything else in your life." Toby's eyes focused across the room at the three vials lying on the floor.

The thought crossed my mind that the serum could be my last chance to save Jake. Perhaps God would allow me this one transgression. But then my thoughts returned to Sam, how she traded her soul for the false hope of bringing

Paul back. I wouldn't trade my soul. Toby's words resonated. Perhaps God was testing me one more time to see if I could put Him above everything else in my life, including Jake.

Looking back at Toby's pensive stare, I said, "I have to do it."

He nodded as I stood and cautiously crossed the room. Standing over the vials, the thought of saving Jake entered my mind once more, but I shook it free. Looking up toward the ceiling I said aloud, "I trust You. I may not like it right now, but I trust Your plan."

Taking a deep breath, I stomped hard on each of the three tubes, hearing the glass crack beneath my shoe. I exhaled after the last vial broke, not realizing I had been holding my breath. I watched as the serum oozed from the broken containers and spread across the floor. It was done.

I relaxed a bit, feeling like I'd just passed a difficult exam, yet somehow the task felt unfinished. Something pricked my memory.

Corson. Corson still held one of the vials in his hand. I turned to the spot where he collapsed after Sam shot him.

"No!" I gasped.

Corson was gone.

Chapter Thirty-Two

Spinning in circles, I searched the lab for any sign of Corson. Dr. Anderson was sprawled backward in his chair, Sam was dead where she lay, but there was no sign of Corson or the remaining vial.

"What?" Toby was instantly beside me. "What's wrong?"

Pointing to the spot where Corson should have been I said, "He's gone. Corson has the last vial. Oh God, what do we do?"

Toby's body went rigid; his eyes scanned the laboratory.

"He must have escaped when you were comforting me," I said, once again plagued by guilt. "Oh God, because of me Corson got away."

Toby frowned, "No. It wasn't because of you. I should

have been more alert." Pointing toward the door he added, "He's injured, there's a trail of blood leading out the door. Stay here."

Toby drew his gun and edged out the laboratory door.

I stood motionless in the room, glancing toward Sam and Dr. Anderson with the eerie feeling that at any moment one of them would come back to life. Doctor Anderson's eyes seemed fixed directly upon me, but neither he nor any of my lifeless companions moved. I strained to hear any noise coming from the hallway but the only sound was the constant drone of the central air blowing from the vents above. I continued to scan the room, looking repeatedly between Dr. Anderson, then Sam, then the door.

I jumped when Toby reappeared in the doorway, his dark eyes narrowed, a grim expression lining his face.

"Erik's car is gone, but Erik is still in the guard shack."

I shivered remembering the poor young man who I'd met only yesterday, now dead.

"Corson must have stolen Erik's car," Toby stated the obvious. "Who knows how far away he is by now, but he's injured—he'll probably need medical treatment soon."

"He has the serum," I said, glancing over to where Sam had been setting up Jake's IV supplies. Those too were missing. A shiver traveled down my spine realizing what Corson intended to do.

Toby noticed the missing supplies too. "Crap," he said under his breath. "We are going to need help. I'm going to have to make a few phone calls outside...no reception in here." He pulled a cell phone from his pocket.

Glancing over toward Jake, I said, "I think I'm going to stay here with Jake, if that's okay?" I didn't want to leave his side, not yet. "I want to say good-bye."

Toby's smile reflected that of a patient father, and for the first time, I could picture him as a priest. "Of course," he replied. "Are you sure you're okay?"

"Yes," I nodded. "But, Toby?"

"Yes?"

"Could we move *them* before you leave?" I motioned toward Dr. Anderson and Sam. "You know, with all the genetic research going on, I keep picturing the two of them coming back to life and sneaking up on me. It kind of creeps me out."

Toby chuckled, "Sure. We'll put them in the next room until we can dispose of their bodies. I can to bind them up if you think it will ease your mind."

"No," I smiled at his offer. "Just getting them out of the room will be enough."

Carrying a dead body was more difficult than I expected. Sam's body was heavy, limp and awkward, not stiff like I assumed. Toby informed me that rigor mortis didn't usually set in until several hours after death, so unless I wanted to leave her in the lab and wait, we would have to do the best we could to lug her body into the small storage room across the hall.

Toby allowed me to hold Sam's feet while he struggled to lift her torso, his arms hooked beneath her arms. After maneuvering her into the hall and laying her body in the empty storage room, we decided to wheel Dr. Anderson out in the chair he currently occupied. I needed to lift his feet to keep them from dragging on the ground, but this method of transportation worked far better getting him out of the laboratory with much less effort. Unfortunately, Toby's white shirt now looked like it was red tie-dyed thanks to his contact will all that blood.

"Thank you," I said, feeling another twinge of guilt after glancing at his shirt, although I reminded myself that it was already ruined with two bullet holes in the back. "Now I feel like I can be alone with Jake. I know that sounds ridiculous but..."

"No," Toby said, grimacing as he noticed the red stains. "That doesn't sound ridiculous at all. To be honest, they kind of creep me out too." Looking up and smiling he added, "You sure you're going to be alright while a step outside?"

"Yes, thank you," I blushed.

"Okay, I'll be back as soon as I'm done talking with Niko. Probably about five minutes. Will that give you enough time?"

I nodded.

"I'm right outside if you need me." Toby ensured the storage room door was locked then winked at me before proceeding down the hall toward the Institute's main entrance.

I sighed as I watched Toby disappear around the corner. Making one last, careful assessment of the lock on the storage room door, I turned on my heel and walked back toward the lab. From the laboratory's entrance I could see

Jake's lifeless body.

I knew he was gone, somewhere else, somewhere beautiful. Although I was certain he wouldn't hear me, I needed to say good-bye, needed to tell him I loved him one more time. Taking a deep breath, I crossed the room, unsure of exactly what I would say. Kneeling, I leaned over and gently kissed his forehead. Jake's skin was waxy and cold against my lips.

"I know you can't hear me," I whispered as I moved to sit cross-legged beside him. "But I have to tell you how much I love you. I don't know why God took you from me..." An agonizing flush of heat rose in my cheeks, tears suddenly streaming uncontrolled. I choked as sorrowful sobs once again erupted from my chest. Minutes passed before I could speak again.

Picking up Jake's hand, I held it to my heart. "I can't say that I'm okay. I miss you so much. I don't know how to do any of this without you. Deep down, I know you are somewhere amazing, and that someday, in God's time, we will be together again, but it hurts so much inside. I feel like half of me is gone, and I don't know how to put myself back together. I want you with me."

I heaved a sigh. Still crying I looked up toward the heavens and said, "God, why couldn't Jake stay with me? Please God, I know it's selfish, but I want him back."

From the corner of my eye, I saw something move in the doorway. Though I should have startled, a sense of peace filled me instead.

It didn't surprise me to see him standing there—

perhaps that's what they do, control your emotions, taking away all fear—but there he stood, the man from my hospice doorway. The same man from the crowded theater and now, naturally, as if I expected him, he was there in the laboratory only a few feet away. He smiled as he drew near. I didn't question his presence. I didn't run in fear. I could only watch as the silent stranger came and knelt beside me. His eyes were human, yet there was something far more powerful in his gaze, like he stared directly into my soul. He concentrated on me a moment longer, as if reading my thoughts, then he closed his eyes and leaned forward, kissing me on the forehead. I too closed my eyes and leaned into the stranger's calming embrace.

In my mind, I traveled through flashes of light, colors unseen by the human eye, songs sung by unfamiliar tongues with chords and harmonies almost too beautiful for my ears. And there I came to stand, in a brilliant, white light. I felt God's peace blanket me. The singing quieted to a dull murmur. I knew Jake was there.

"Thank you," I said, feeling God's reply in my heart.

I knew God was giving me the opportunity to say good-bye to Jake, but I didn't know how to start.

"Heaven is beautiful," I said.

"Yes it is," Jake replied.

"I'm so sorry, Jake. I'm so sorry I got you into this."

"Don't be," he said. "It's pretty cool being able to see Heaven. I'm sorry I couldn't protect you like I promised. Thank God for Toby! Geez Maddy, you really are a terrible shot!" Jake's laughter rang in my ear. It was so close I could almost feel him beside me.

I laughed too. I was going to miss his teasing the most.

"Yeah, I bet that's one ceiling panel that will think twice before messing with me."

"Maddy, open your eyes," Jake said.

"No," I said, shaking my head. "No, I just want to spend a little bit longer here with you. I'm not ready to go yet."

The light in my mind swirled and danced.

"Why would you want to stay here?" Jake asked.

The light dimmed. I felt God's laughter echo in my soul.

"Open your eyes, Maddy," Jake said.

Hesitantly, I opened one eye to the dim laboratory. The stranger was gone. I was leaning forward into nothing.

Heart pounding, stomach free floating, I opened both eyes as I turned my body back toward my husband.

There was Jake, sitting beside me, smiling. He was alive. My soul flooded with joy as I threw myself against him. His body was warm against my cheek. Wrapping his arms around me Jake pulled me closer. The tears flowed as my ecstatic heart beat a song of thanksgiving.

"Is it you?" I finally asked, reaching my hand up to touch his face. "Is it really you?"

Jake laughed and pulling me deeper into his embrace, he kissed me. The kiss may have lasted seconds, or hours, my spinning mind couldn't tell.

When we finally separated, Jake whispered in my ear, "So, the Big Guy sent me a message to give you. He wants you to know He's proud of you, Maddy, and that you are more than worthy of being His chosen messenger—

of course, He also wants you to know that He already knew that." Jake chuckled and I blushed. "Oh, and He wants to know when the wedding is. He heard the rumor that He's invited now."

Looking into Jake's joyful eyes I beamed, "I'm pretty sure He already knows the date."

I threw myself into Jake's arms again, content upon holding him for the rest of my life; the joy of that moment is still the closest place to Heaven I've been inside this human existence.

Looking up toward the heavens, I breathed the words, "Thank you."

Chapter Thirty-Three

How do I know that God exists? Well—disregarding the angelic visitations, miraculous healing, demonic possession, visions of Heaven and Jake's resurrection—God officially became real the day I wed the man I had been praying for my entire life.

Inside the courtyard of a Greek Orthodox monastery, surrounded by whitewashed archways and a bell tower reaching toward the azure heavens, I sat dressed in a white, flowing gown while Jenn pinned flowers in my hair. Despite everything that had happened over the past few months, this was officially the moment God completely stole my heart. I realized only He could take my youthful fantasies and multiply them beyond anything I ever thought possible; that His love story is so much deeper and more beautiful than any silly fairytale any of us can create.

I recalled how months ago, standing atop a rooftop deck, I dreamed of Cinderella and Prince Charming, wanting so desperately for my life to end happily ever after, yet believing it never would. Now, changed in this new life, my fairytale would begin with a heart devoted to God, and the man of my dreams waiting for me on the roof of this castle-like monastery overlooking the sapphire blue Mediterranean Sea.

We would marry near the spot where, almost two thousand years earlier, God revealed my future existence to John. I smiled in wonderment, puzzling over the fact that God knew me even then. It no longer mattered that my parents abandoned me, that I wandered lost in my life for so long, because God loved me thousands of years before I was born. He was always at my side and He had a plan for my life—in that I've found comfort and healing.

A light breezed danced across the open courtyard as I listened to Jenn prattle on about the beauty of the scenery; the wonderful surprise she received finding out I was alive and that she was going to Greece; her joy at finally seeing me and Jake marry (although she did, in fact, marry us first); how happy she was to discover the bow adorning the backside of her bridesmaid dress was just a joke (because no one should ever be forced to accentuate their bottom like that); along with her observations as to how attractive Greek men were and if there might be good nightlife on the island. I smiled as she went on and on. I truly loved my dear friend and was thrilled she was with me on my big day.

I was also happy that Jake's parents were able to attend. At first they thought Jake was insane when he recapped the story of how we came to be honored guests of Orthodox priests on a faraway Greek Isle, but after meeting me and the monks here in Patmos, their eyes were opened. God moved them to help in our ministry from their home in Texas. Sabrina, my hospice nurse, was also here. She too was thankful to be included in our big day, and excited to help minister in South Carolina.

I watched the sun drift toward the horizon, knowing that at any moment my newfound brother, Toby, would arrive to escort me to where my groom would be waiting at the chapel's entrance. Father Nikoli would be presiding over our nuptials.

"Oh Maddy," Jenn sighed. "I can't believe it. This is just like a fairy tale!"

"Yes," I smiled. "God is amazing."

"A-hem," a voice came from behind. "Is the bride ready?"

I turned to see Toby standing in his black cassock. He was beginning to grow out his beard, yet it couldn't hide the broad smile gleaming across his bronzed face.

"You look beautiful," he said as I rose to meet him.

"Why, thank you, Brother Toby," I blushed.

Jenn excused herself to make sure everything was ready for my arrival. Smiling, Toby reached out and handed me a sugar cube.

"What is this for?" My quizzical look made him laugh.

"Tradition," he grinned. "A blessing for a happy and sweet life. You can tuck it in your bouquet."

"Thank you," I said, turning it over in my fingers.

"Well, are you ready to meet your groom?"

I was more than ready to see Jake, but realizing this might be the last moment I could capture Toby's undivided attention, I decided to ask the questions that had been plaguing me in the week since leaving the Institute.

"Toby?" I asked as he led me toward the cloister's exit.

"Yes?" he said.

Stopping him, I turned to look up into his eyes. "I need to know what happened at the Institute. Were Senator Morris and Dr. Anderson part of Sam's plan? And what about the news story? And how are we going to catch Corson? And..."

"Whoa, hold on," Toby smirked. "This is your wedding day, can't these questions wait?"

"Please Toby?" I pouted. "After tonight Jake and I will be in training with your brothers until we are sent off to begin our ministry. This may be the last time you and I are alone. I have to know."

"Okay," Toby sighed. "I'll start with what happened at the theater. I thought for certain your face would be plastered across every evening news channel, but the media is mostly concerned with ratings, and while I hate to sound as if I rejoice in this fact, a devastating earthquake hit Asia a few hours after our incident. Your story was pushed off to make room for the disaster coverage, and then it was eventually forgotten. Or at least, it will be until you appear to the world with your message."

"Oh," I said. The thought entered my mind that perhaps God orchestrated the earthquake to protect my identity. A pang of guilt struck my heart.

"No," Toby answered, studying my face. "It wasn't your fault. God's Plan is so much greater than any of us can understand. Don't blame yourself."

"How do you do that?" I asked.

"Do what?"

"How do you seem to know exactly what I'm thinking?"

Toby smiled, "I don't know if you realize it, but you express every emotion on your face. One needs only to look at you to know what you are thinking. By the way, don't ever try lying, you would be terrible at it... that, and it's a sin." Toby winked. "The fact that you feel everything so deeply, that you can't contain your emotions, is probably one of the reasons God chose you as His messenger. You are genuine and people can tell immediately by the way you wear your heart on your sleeve."

"Is that a good thing?" I asked.

"I think it is," Toby grinned.

"What about Senator Morris and Dr. Anderson? Were they part of the conspiracy?"

Toby thought for a moment. "I'm not sure if we'll ever truly know. I don't like to speak ill of anyone, but I must say that they weren't very nice people, and though I definitely believe they fell for the Devil's deception, I don't know if they intentionally sold their souls. Sam, of course, was in control the entire time. She was the one on whom Satan bestowed all his power, but she did a darn good job making it look like the Senator was in charge—good enough to keep me guessing anyway." Toby shook his head in dismay.

"I don't know how, but someone, or something, tipped her off that we got to you. Or maybe she saw Jake in the woods, I don't know. Either way, she didn't know who the informant was, so Sam decided to take everyone out. This is only speculation, of course, but I believe she contacted Senator Morris and the other guards, calling them to return to the Institute. She left me a frantic message that Senator Morris needed me back at the Institute immediately. Before returning, I tried hacking into the computer's mainframe from my remote location in the Senator's Birmingham headquarters. Something was wrong with my access but I couldn't tell what. I should have suspected...I didn't realize the extent of the problem until I arrived at the Institute and found the guards, Senator Morris and Dr. Anderson already dead. I knew our plan was compromised.

"I walked in on Sam ransacking the laboratory, making it look like the research was destroyed—of course I didn't know that's what she was doing at the time. Looking like she'd been attacked, Sam gave me the same line about Corson going crazy and, like a fool I believed her. I couldn't, or didn't want to believe that she belonged to Satan. I ran over to check on Dr. Anderson who was still spurting blood—of course he was already dead—and that's when she shot me in the back, twice. Moments later,

Corson rushed in stating you and Jake arrived. Sam knew she didn't have time to hide the vials, so she planned to manipulate you instead."

Toby's expression grew distant as he spoke, "I lay on the floor listening as Sam and Corson decided you wouldn't be strong enough to resist her master. She was confident you would side with her, not anticipating the extent God's love entered your heart. Of course, we humans are given free will to choose. Sam hoped you would willfully abandon God. Forgive me, Maddy, if I knew she planned to kill Jake, I would have done my best to stop her. I'm sorry."

"What about Corson?"

"We can't find him," Toby said, a solemn look clouded his handsome features. "I'm not sure if we ever will. I'm sure in God's time though…" He trailed off.

I shuddered, thinking that somewhere the Devil's immortal pawn lay in wait, preparing for the coming war.

"What did you end up doing with the bodies?" I asked. "Won't the Senator be missed by his family, not to mention his constituents?"

"After we took you and Jake to the airport, Father Nikoli and I returned and watched the bodies for three days. When no one came back to life, we felt it was safe to release the guards and Senator Morris to their families. We blamed their deaths on a rogue gunman who disagreed with the Senator's policies on stem cell research and the treatment of the animals inside the Institute," Toby smirked. "Of course, we pinned the deaths on Corson, hoping someone would turn him in. Unfortunately, that hasn't happened. Sam and Dr. Anderson had no recorded next of kin, so we incinerated their bodies as...well...a safety precaution. Finally, we figured the test animals were no threat so we released them into the woods just before destroying the Institute."

We both stood silent for a time in the walled courtyard. I looked toward the sky and watched a sea bird gracefully soar as warm hues of pink and purple stained the wispy clouds above.

I took hold of Toby's arm. "Thank you," I said.

"For what?"

"For everything." I leaned my head against his shoulder.

"Just doing my job," he replied. "See, I told you someday you wouldn't hate me."

"No, what you said was someday you *hoped* I would think *better* of you," I corrected, laughing. "...better than an evil, murderous monster."

"Oh, well since you've set the bar so high..." Toby smiled. "Am I better now in your esteem?"

"Do you think I would allow an evil, murderous monster to walk me to the chapel?"

He kissed me on the top of my head. Regret flashed across his face. "I did kill a woman," he confessed.

"God forgives you. You were *protecting* another woman, as well the entire human race, remember?"

Toby sighed. He was a good man and I knew he would struggle with the fact that he took another person's life until the day that he died. I also knew there was nothing more I could say.

Changing the subject, I announced, "Hey, we have a wedding to get to, remember? You don't want the groom thinking I skipped out again!" I locked my arm into his and started tugging Toby along.

Smiling again, Toby relaxed and pulled me back to match his slower pace. "No, we definitely can't have him thinking that."

As we proceeded to the small chapel in the setting sun, Toby commented, "God must be with us. We've had such beautiful weather since your arrival. Usually September is stormy and wet."

I spotted Jake immediately, standing in front of the chapel door, his light eyes sparkling against the dark frame of his hair. He wore tan slacks, a button down white shirt and a blue blazer. Holding a bouquet of white roses, a smile stretched across his handsome, dimpled face as I approached.

White-painted walls surrounding us glowed a brilliant orange as they reflected colors from the sky. I walked forward to meet Jake as our friends and new family surrounded us, receiving us with joyful fanfare.

There was another among the small crowd that evening. I felt his presence before I saw him. I searched the sea of faces surrounding us, finding his familiar eyes watching, unnoticed by the others. He smiled at me, and though I looked away for only a moment, when I turned back he was gone, like I knew he would be. I felt God's love, peace and joy continue to wash over me as I took Jake's hand in mine.

"I'm glad you made it this time," Jake teased.

"I wouldn't miss this for anything," I smiled back, accepting the bouquet and gently placing the sugar cube inside.

I heard the voice of God speaking softly, telling me He was with us, reminding me that He wouldn't miss one moment of my life for anything. Taking one more glance around at the happy faces of those I loved, my elated heart swelled in appreciation for all God's gifts, knowing He blessed me more than I deserved.

I took Jake's hand in mine, and looking into his joyful eyes and dimpled smile, we stepped into the small chapel.

Epilogue

The small town of Monroe, Washington, sits nestled in a beautiful valley along the banks of the Skykomish River. Among the foothills of the Cascade Mountains, it is surrounded by forested hills and farmland. At first glance it hardly seemed the place to introduce our apocalyptic ministry to the world, but, as in all things, God made His path ready before us.

A family friend of Toby's, Pastor Scott—who recently acquired leadership of a small church within the town—became intrigued by our story on a visit to Patmos shortly after our wedding. Overwhelmed by the gravity of our message, Pastor Scott encouraged us to begin our missionary work in his small corner of the world, persuading members of his congregation to offer assistance in any way possible.

Despite its rural locale, the residents of Monroe welcomed us into their churches and their community. To the casual observer, if the hand of God wasn't evident in the scenic beauty surrounding the town, it was more than obvious in the hearts of the people who lived there. A spirit of brotherly loved flourished. Churches of every denomination were thriving as they spread God's Word through outreach to the elderly and poor, ministering to those inside prison gates and creating programs for endangered youth. Jake and I were true missionaries, relying solely on God and the kindness of people within the communities we entered, and the lovely citizens of Monroe did not disappoint. Opening their homes and their minds, they welcomed our message, and soon our prophesy began to spread. Before long, pilgrims from neighboring communities visited the town to hear our warning about the future.

It was an unseasonably warm November in Western Washington. Hills of dark evergreen were spotted with fiery leaves still clinging to their deciduous hosts, the colors blazing to life against the sun's setting rays.

Jake and I sat on a bench outside the Community Church after a long day of speaking at several different venues. We were discussing dinner plans when we noticed Kara, Pastor Scott's wife, bouncing toward us, her dark brown hair bobbing against her shoulders as she approached. Her petite frame and uplifting spirit reminded me of a woodland sprite, full of contagious joy, yet something about her made me suspect a mischievous side made its appearance on occasion.

My other friend, Michelle, was by her side. Her smile reflected as much warmth as her soft hazel eyes. Michelle and her husband, Danny, offered to take us into their home when we first arrived in town. Despite the fact that her husband worked full time and she was frantically chasing after four children from morning until night, Michelle went out of her way to ensure our comfort. She quickly became one of my dearest companions, and though Jake and I now occupied a space within one of the local churches, and spent the majority of each day ministering, I still managed to see her several times a week.

"A letter came for you!" Kara announced as they both sat on the bench beside us.

"A letter?" I asked. "Who would send us a letter?"

Jake shrugged looking equally as perplexed.

"Why don't you open it and find out?" Michelle prodded. She and Kara exchanged meaningful glances.

"What are you two up to?" I asked, raising my eyebrow.

"Oh, just open it," Kara said.

Pulling out the handwritten note I read through it before revealing, "It's from Toby."

"Well," Jake said. "What does it say?"

My brow furrowed. "He and Father Nikoli rented us a house in Leavenworth, Washington, next week. He says it's a wedding gift from all the brothers. They think we deserve a honeymoon."

"Why do you look so glum?" Michelle asked. "I think it's wonderful. You'll love Leavenworth! It's the cutest little Bavarian town just on the other side of the mountains."

"Oh, it's not that I don't appreciate it. It's just..." I frowned, trying to determine how to continue. "It's just that we don't have time. We need to get our message out to the world. I'd feel so guilty taking any time for fun when God's people are counting on us. I can't abandon our mission right now."

Kara smiled, "Toby thought you might say that, so here!" She handed Jake another letter.

"Why do I think you two had a hand in this?" I asked, looking between the women.

"Whatever do you mean?" Kara feigned innocence.

Michelle interjected, "All we did was suggest a place you might enjoy for a getaway. The honeymoon was really Toby's idea. I think it's sweet." I loved Michelle's conscience. She couldn't deceive anyone in even the smallest way.

"It is a very kind offer, really, but we just can't right now," I said.

I forgot the letter in Jake's hand until he chuckled.

"What?" I probed.

A twisted smirk tugged at his mouth. Kara and Michelle grinned too.

"What?" I asked again, trying to grab the note from his grasp. He pulled it away before I touched it.

"Remember when I promised you could win every fight for the rest of eternity?" he asked.

343

"Yes," I answered. I felt a flush of heat rise in my cheeks.

"Well, just remember, your argument isn't with me." Jake stared me down, waiting for me to capitulate.

I threw up my hands, exasperated. "Oh, just get on with it."

Clearing his throat, Jake read, "I am guessing that Maddy is hesitant to go on vacation, arguing she doesn't have time, or that she feels guilty taking time off when God expects so much of her."

I shook my head. "How does he do that?"

"You are kind of predictable," Kara smiled. "But in a good way," she added when I folded my arms across my chest, trying to pout.

"Anyway," Jake continued. "Please inform Maddy that even God needed time to rest, and yes, yes, He only took *one* day, but remember He is God. He can recover in a day. We humans take a little longer. After much prayerful reflection, we at the Monastery of Saint John of the Apocalypse, feel God spoke to us very clearly saying you, Maddy, should take your husband away for a week and celebrate your marriage. To not do so would be one of the gravest sins against His Will...okay, I made that last part up, but please go and enjoy with our blessings! You can return to your ministry the next week. In God's Grace, Your Brother, Toby."

"You can't argue with that," Kara smirked.

"Yes," Michelle chimed. "Like Toby said, it's God's Will for you."

Looking up from the letter, Jake said, "Well, what do

you say? Are you up for a honeymoon?"

Shaking my head in defeat I surrendered. My frown changed to a grin, "I guess if it's God's Will, I could use a romantic week alone with my husband."

*****

Although reluctant to leave our ministry at first, as our honeymoon drew towards its end, I wasn't ready to return to a world of chaos and impending doom. I loved the charm of the picturesque Bavarian town back-dropped by the soaring eastern peaks of the Cascade Mountains. On the first night of our stay, Jake and I traveled through the charming streets, indulging in rich German food as well as the compliments of people admiring our newlywed status.

Our accommodations were breathtaking, to say the least. Toby and his brethren had generously rented a two-story home that sat on over ten wooded acres. It offered four bedrooms and three bathrooms—the master containing a large jetted tub overlooking the swift flowing Wenatchee River—a sitting room with wood burning fireplace as well as sweeping floor to ceiling mountain and river views from almost every location. A dozen roses and bottle of champagne waited for us in a huge kitchen. The lodge provided ample cooking and living space, so Jake and I decided to stock up on a few necessities and enjoy the private seclusion of the woodland retreat. I realized this was the first time in our life we spent any time alone together, and I finally understood why everyone was so insistent we take the time to escape and enjoy our marriage.

I woke on the last morning of our stay with a feeling of sadness...and hunger. I sat up in bed and noticed the sun had yet to make his appearance, though he sent ahead a soft blue hue in the waking sky. The clock read six thirty in the morning. It wasn't like me to wake so early without an alarm. My stomach growled.

I looked down at Jake sleeping peacefully in our bed. I didn't want to wake him, so I decided to lie back down and watch the sky changing colors outside our window. After a few minutes, my stomach growled again, loud enough this time to rouse Jake.

"Hey," he said, sleepy eyed and stretching. "What are you doing up this early?"

My stomach answered before I could.

Jake laughed, "Was that you?"

"Sorry," I blushed. "For some reason I'm starving this morning. I didn't mean to wake you."

"Wow," Jake propped himself up on his elbow. "You must be really hungry if it woke you up! How about I go down and fix some bacon and eggs?"

I grimaced and stuck out my tongue. Maybe it was the fact we had eggs the day before, but they just didn't sound appealing to me.

"I feel like something sweet. Like a pastry maybe?"

Jake thought for a moment then said, "I don't think we have anything like that here. I could run out to the bakery..."

"Let's walk and enjoy the morning," I offered. My

stomach voiced its aversion to the idea.

"It's over a mile away, Maddy," Jake said. "That's a long walk. We have to go around to the bridge. Are you sure you don't want to eat something here? We can get something sweet on the way out of town."

Ignoring my stomach I insisted, "No, I want to enjoy the scenery before we have to leave. I think a walk in the crisp air will do us good."

"Are you sure?" he asked.

"Yes, please? I really would rather walk on a beautiful morning like this."

Jake laughed, "Okay, let's take a walk."

The sun finally peeked over the horizon as we left the house and started out across the wooded valley. The tranquil world remained hushed during this waking hour. Rays of sunlight spilled through the trees, casting a filtered haze across the landscape. A herd of elk grazed in an open field, oblivious to our presence as we walked above them along the road. One in the herd perked up his ear and sniffed the air as the breeze shifted, but he seemed to find no threat in our passing. Jake and I enjoyed the silence, walking hand in hand, listening to our footsteps strike the pavement and watching white puffs of breath float from our lips.

We had walked about a half a mile and were admiring the soaring mountains when he appeared.

"Good morning," the man said.

Jake and I both jumped. We hadn't seen anyone on the road seconds earlier. It only took a moment for me to assess the nature of our visitor.

"Good morning," Jake replied, oblivious to the man's true identity.

This stranger was not the man I'd seen on so many other important occasions, yet my soul was charged with the same electricity that came from the other before him.

He looked as if about to speak, but instead glanced toward a steep rising hill in the distance. A shrill cry of anguish erupted from a somewhere high in the ridgeline above. I couldn't determine if the stranger responded to the howl, or if the shriek was in response to the stranger. Jake pulled me close, using his body to shield me—although I knew this was not necessary.

After several seconds, the tormented cries subsided and the stranger returned his attention to us on the road. "Forgive me," he said.

"That's okay," Jake replied, hesitant. "I think whatever that was distracted us all. Poor animal—sounded like it was being tortured to death."

"Indeed," the man said.

"Well, have a nice morning," Jake offered as he proceeded to walk around the man, holding me close with his arm.

Focusing his attention on me as we passed, the stranger announced, "You need not fear. You are protected." Then, with a knowing smile he added, "He is protected."

My belly fluttered in response.

"Excuse me?" Jake asked, stopping to face the man.

I continued to stare. Not yet. It couldn't be happening

yet.

"Do not fear," the man said again. "God's love and protection surround you all."

Another flutter.

Jake looked at me, eyes wide. I glanced back at him as I felt my belly flutter again. I returned my attention to the stranger, but as I suspected, he was gone.

"Wait, what?" Jake spun in a circle. There was no sign of our guest.

"Remember when I told you about my angelic visitor?" I asked Jake, recalling a night in Greece when I told him of my visitor from the hospice room, the theater and the laboratory. I failed to mention the wedding.

"Was that him? Why didn't you say something?"

"No, that wasn't *my* angel," I replied.

Jake brow creased in confusion. "I don't get it," he said. "Why did he say I was protected?"

Smiling I replied, "He said we all were protected."

Jake shook his head, still not grasping the proclamation's meaning. Taking his hand, I placed it on my stomach.

"We *all* are protected," I emphasized. I watched Jake's thoughts drop into place one by one.

He looked at my belly, then my face, then again to my belly. I watched him repeat this action several times in comic fashion.

"I think that was *his* guardian," I added.

"Does that mean...I mean are you?" Jake stammered.

"I think so," I replied. Feeling the flutter again I added,

"On second thought, I know. I guess that's why I'm so hungry."

Jake's dimpled grin emerged as he took me in his arms. "Well," he said, kissing me softly. "I guess I'd better hurry and get you both something to eat."

Throwing my arms around Jake's neck I kissed him again. Holding on to one another, we couldn't stop laughing. There, on that empty road, Jake and I realized our baby meant the end was near, but we were not afraid, for with God, there is no end for those who believe — only a new beginning.

Corson

Oh Sam, why? Why did you betray me? I loved you. You promised we would be together, forever, but you broke my heart and disappointed our Master. I wish you could look upon me now, no longer the scrawny half-wit you once saw! Oh no! Thanks to the serum, your serum, I am strong, handsome and can have my pick of any woman in the room. But why, why must I compare them all to you?

The cold mountain air blanketed Corson's underdressed body, but he felt no chill. He felt more alive than ever and ready to take vengeance on another human soul.

It's her fault—that disgusting excuse for a woman—the one who calls herself God's messenger. She led me here to this mountaintop. Months I've searched. She sent me on a wild goose chase around the world only bring me to that disgusting, damp, green hell. I hate that town and those ridiculous people in it who follow the woman's misguided ways. I don't know how, but I will destroy her and everyone she controls!

Crouched low against the rocky precipice overlooking the lonely meadow, he waited patiently for his prey. Before the change, Corson's legs would surely cramp maintaining that position, but now he was strong, muscular, seemingly impervious to pain. A low growl rumbled in Corson's chest, but it was not his own. His Master growled, sensing the vile one's approach. The serum resurrected Corson's body, but his supernatural power came from his Master who now lived inside. Corson could feel his Master's strength as his own.

A herd of elk grazing below shifted uneasily. Corson knew his victims approached. It wouldn't be long now. This time his own snarl tore from his throat. Corson's heart accelerated in anticipation of the kill.

That revolting woman is so close to me now I can smell her. The man she's with can't protect her. He's just as worthless as he was in the lab, despite his miraculous resurrection. Yes, Master promised if I did this one thing he would bring you back to me — make you love me. My sweet Sam, you will return to me. We will be together forever.

His Master's growl deep within confirmed the promise.

Corson watched his enemies travel hand-in-hand down the deserted road.

This is almost too easy. I have a clear shot. Once she is dead I will incinerate her body, just as those vile priests destroyed you, beautiful Sam. I will revel in watching her burn! Then, you will return to me. You will love me! He promised to release you from your fiery prison! Master promises that not even God's inferno will keep us apart. Oh Sam, I love you. I need you. Now I will prove myself worthy. I have a clear shot.

Raising the rifle's scope to his eye, he took steady aim.

I will kill the man first. I will watch as the woman cries out in fear and anguish. Yes! Oh, that will be a beautiful thing. Better yet, maybe I should just wound him...

A shiver of excitement pulsed through his body.

Then I can make her watch while I burn him alive. Ahhh...how I long to watch her suffer. She may not fear death, but I will make her fear dying!

Something moved into Corson's line of sight, blocking his shot. A man. Where had he come from?

Lowering the rifle, another growl erupted, this one louder than the others. Corson felt his Master pull away...the great power no longer inside. The stranger on the road looked up. Corson watched in horror as the man's body transformed into a bright, burning light. Corson's blood boiled beneath his skin. Falling to the ground, he thrashed against the flame that seared his skin. Flailing he tried to put out the fire. Horrifying screams echoed around the mountainside...several seconds passed before Corson recognized them as his own.

"Master!" he howled. "Master save me!"

There was no escape. The pain blinded. In his mind it lasted an eternity.

"Master!" Corson cried again.

Corson woke crumpled on the ground...weak, but not dead. Much to his surprise, his skin was intact, he wasn't burned. Confused, he sat up and looked toward the road, but the man, woman and strange being of light were gone.

Corson felt his Master return. Once inside, Corson's power returned, his senses heightened. Corson picked up the rifle and started down the rocky cliff. He didn't know how long he'd been out, but he knew the woman couldn't be far.

"I will finish this," he said aloud.

"Wait," his Master whispered from within. "Not now. Wait. Our time is coming, but you must have patience. *He* protects them. They can't be harmed, but we, we will find other ways...there are so many other ways."

"No," Corson snarled. "I *need* this. They are mine!"

"Defiant one!" his Master howled, stopping Corson in his tracks. "*I* brought you back to life! *I* give you power! You do not make decisions, *you* serve *me*! The time has come for me to take over."

Corson tried to fight, but he could not move.

"Do not fight me! You will not win. Save your energy. You will have your Samantha, and we will have our revenge, but for now, you must wait. Our time is coming...not yet, but soon."

Turning Corson's body against his will, they fled back into the mountains.

"Soon," his Master repeated. "Very soon."

16028884R00208

Made in the USA
Charleston, SC
01 December 2012